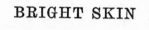

BRIGHT SKIN

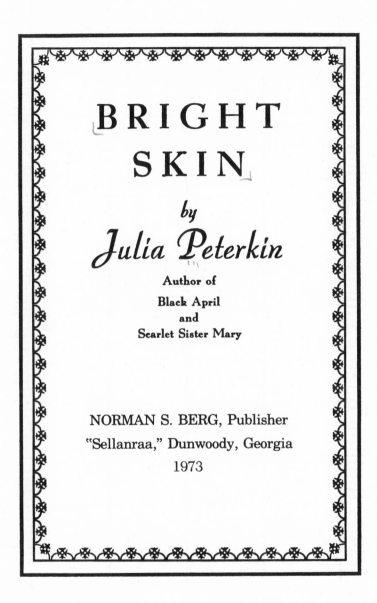

BRIGHT SKIN

by

Julia Peterkin

Author of

Black April
and
Scarlet Sister Mary

NORMAN S. BERG, Publisher

"Sellanraa," Dunwoody, Georgia

1973

Printed in the United States of America

by arrangement with
THE BOBBS-MERRILL COMPANY

ISBN 0-910220-37-9

For
DORIS

BRIGHT SKIN

BRIGHT SKIN

CHAPTER I

BLUE was roused from sound sleep before dawn that morning. His father's voice called him, his father's hand shook his shoulder.

"Blue, wake up, son, an' put on you clothes. Me an' you is gwine* off. Dis house ain' no decent place for we to stay in. I'm gwine to take you to you Gramma's to live, so get up and let's go."

Blue opened his eyes and looked around him trying to take in what his father meant. Day was not yet clean. The only light in the room where he and his small brothers slept shone through the open door, from the fireplace in his mother's room. Although it was early, a bright fire of pine knots blazed and popped live coals on to the floor.

Something was wrong. Blue's mother sat on a low chair at one side of the hearth. Her head bent down until her face rested in her hands.

His father called him again, "Make haste, Blue. We got a long journey. I want to catch dis fallin tide to help me paddle de boat down de river."

Blue hopped up, but instead of dressing he ran to his mother and whispered:

"Is you gwine too?"

She shook her head without raising it at all. Then she lifted her apron and wiped the water out of her eyes.

———
*Gwine means going.

11

"Whe' is me an' Pa gwine?"

She burst into a storm of weeping.

Blue put his arms around her, begged her not to cry, patted her cheeks, her bowed head, tried his best to soothe her as he often soothed his baby sister when she was hurt. It did no good. His mother cried on and on.

Blue wondered what had happened. He had seen his father vexed many a time but now he was worse than vexed. He stood by the mantel-shelf leaning a shoulder against it. His bloodshot eyes stared at the fire, lifted and stared at the mother. Strangest of all, he had on his Sunday clothes.

"Cryin don' change nothin," he muttered. "What you done, you done. You better thank God I ain' done worse than beat you. If I killed you I'd be inside my rights. I just ain' got de heart to do it. I'm takin Blue to my Mammy. You can have dem other chillen. Put on your coat, Blue. Get you hat. We got to hurry to catch dis tide."

Blue loved his mother. How could he leave her like this?

"What must I do, Ma?" he asked her, hoping wildly she would say to stay with her. He threw both arms around her and held her close. His breath almost cut off when she whispered:

"Go on wid em, Blue. You Gramma can do more for you dan I can. My brother Wes will be good to you, too."

His throat ached, his heart was ready to burst.

He pressed his face against her wet cheek and
sobbed.

"I'll be back soon, Ma——"

"I won' be here," she whispered back. "I'm
gwine off my own self. Act nice as you can, son;
make friends wid you Gramma an' you Uncle
Wes."

"Come on, Blue," his father's voice called, and
Blue took up his hat. His mother gave him a
cloth-tied bundle, and he started down the path
to the river where the boat stayed chained to a log.
His heart leaped up when his mother called him
back. She had a hoe in her hand and was going to
the chimney corner. She dug down in the earth
until the hoe struck the tin can that held her
buried money. She took out a few coins and tied
them in the corner of a pocket handkerchief.

"Blue, son, I got a lil niece yonder whe' you
gwine. E* is a motherless an' a bright skin. His†
Mammy was my sister what died."

His father called, and Blue could not wait to
hear more. He hurried away without finding
out what a bright skin was.

He crawled into the narrow dugout and put the
clean sugar sack holding his clothes under the
seat beside the quart bottle of drinking water and
the greasy paper package of bread and meat.

The early morning was gray, chilly. Willows on
the river bank made dull greenish clouds, the black

---

*E is used for *he, she, it, they.*
†*His* is often used for *her.*

water breathed up fog. The paddle in his father's
hands dipped on one side of the boat, then on the
other. Not a word was spoken. Blue wanted to
ask questions and dared not for fear the answers
would be troubling. Small birds flitted about,
twittering over their plans for the day. Now and
then a wild duck flapped up. Two cranes, one
blue, one white, stood knee-deep in water, making
harsh croaks with their long, greedy fishing bills.
Clouds of hungry mosquitoes followed the boat.
Blue crushed them on his cheeks, his neck, his
forehead. His skin stung, his heart was heavy,
his eyes sleepy.

"Mind how you nod, son," his father warned.
"If you fall out de boat dat 'gator would swallow
you down befo you hit de water."

"Whe' de 'gator is?" Blue pulled himself up
and looked all around. Cooters sat on logs waiting for the sun to rise, and three dark ugly bumps
showed in the water ahead. They were the alligator's eyes and nose.

He shivered miserably and wiped tears out of
his sleepy eyes.

"Fix you bundle of clothes for a pillow, son.
Ease you'self down on de floor an' go to sleep."

The paddle halted its dipping while his father
spread a coat over him to keep off some of the
chill. Blue covered up his head for the alligator
was ugly and fearsome, the mosquitoes greedy.
Sleep was good.

When he woke the whole world had changed. A

bright noon sun shone overhead and the warm
fresh air was full of spring. The river had
doubled in width and changed from clear black to
yellow brown. Small scrawny trees, green with
tender buds, marked its banks in the midst of
wide wet spaces filled with marsh grass. Flocks
of wood ducks whistled by, their bright colors
marked by the glare. A spotted green snake with
his head held high swam slowly along with proudful curves. When he reached midstream he halted
fearlessly, looked at the boat, then glided on. A
kingfisher dived with a splash and rose with a fish
in his claws. As he shook water from his feathers,
a bald eagle's wings sliced through the sky's hard
blue. The fish dropped but the bald eagle caught
it and sailed away.

"Whe' we is, Pa?" Blue asked.

"Is you wake, son? You had a good long sleep.
We ain' got so far to go now. See dem big oaks
over yonder next to de hill? Dat's whe' I was
born and raised. It's God's own country, son."

The drinking water in the bottle was warm, the
bread cold, but Blue swallowed them greedily
for his mouth was dry and his sides empty. His
legs were stiff and numb, one foot was asleep.
He thought sadly of a song his mother sometimes
sang, "Po' boy, long ways from home . . ."

The river was vexed and yellow waves beaten
up by a stiff wind reared sunny edges above
shadowy troughs. Water slapped the boat-sides
and spray flew up as the bow cut through the

ridges head on. Blue sighed with relief when at
last the boat turned aside into a quiet creek.

"Blue." The paddles slackened, the boat drifted
slowly with the current.

"Yes-suh."

"I got to talk some close talk wid you, son. You
must listen good."

Blue pricked up his ears to hear, for the marshes
were noisy with water birds' chatter and squawk-
ing.

His father said Blue's Grampa and Gramma
were fine folks. His Gramma was named Fancy,
his Grampa Al-fred. People called them Cun*
Fred and Aun Fan for short. Aun Fan was a mid-
wife, and caught chillen when they came in the
world. Cun Fred was foreman of the finest plantation on this whole neck of land. These old
marshes used to be rice-fields that made the best
rice ever was. The best sea-island cotton still
grew on the high lands.

"Do the plantation belong to my Grampa?"

His father gave a short laugh. "Great God,
no."

He explained that black people never owned
land. White people always owned it, black
people just lived on it. The white people who
used to own this plantation were proudful and
vast-rich but one by one they died. The man who
owned it now had gone to live in a far country.

---

* Cousin.

Everybody was glad when he left for he was sinful.
He counted black people no more than the mules
that plowed his fields. Thank God he was gone.

The plantation came slowly nearer and nearer,
his father talked faster and more earnestly. Blue
must remember to be mannersable, to mind what
he was told. He must not tell lies or take what was
not his. He was ten years old, big enough to look
after himself and be useful to Aun Fan and Cun
Fred.

Sunshine blazed through willows and evergreen
shrubs, dappled the water rushes with yellow spots
of light. Willow bugs swam in quick circles and
scattered hurriedly when a fish splashed up among
them.

"Great God, Pa, looka dat fish," Blue cried.

"Quit lookin at fish an' listen to me, Blue."
His voice was mournful as he went on: "I ain'
gwine be wid you much longer. You Uncle Wes is
you Ma's brother, but e is a fine man. E ain' to
blame for how his sisters act. You Ma's sister
acted bad too, only worser. It makes me have
shame when I think on how dem two women done.
You got dat same heathen blood, son. You got to
be careful or it'll git you in trouble, too." His
father gave him a sorrowful look.

"What's a bright skin, Pa?"

"Whe' you hear bout bright skin, Blue?"

"Ma said I got a bright-skin kinnery."

"A bright skin is a bad thing, son. You
Mammy's sister birthed one an' died."

"Is e a white trash?"

"No, son. E ain' white trash. E ain' white, neither black. A bright skin is yellow as dis river water."

Bruised water weeds smelled bitter as the boat brushed through them. A bull alligator groaned and sobbed in the distance, and Blue thought of his brothers and sisters. Sometimes for fun his father called them alligator bait. Now they were far away and he was in this stranger country.

Small, thin-legged waders with long keen bills folded their brown wings and settled to catch minnows where water flowed smoothly between level marshes. Closer and closer the moss-draped trees came, taller and taller they towered. Blue thought they must be the biggest trees in the world. The boat bow slid up on the bank near their black twisted roots, the paddle was dropped. Blue's father gave a long stretch and sighed.

"We's here, son. We made good time, too. Get you bundle an' get out."

As Blue stepped on the warm damp earth his heart trembled. What lay behind those trees? Who lived beyond them?

"Pa," he quavered, "when is we gwine back home?"

"We ain' never gwine back, son. Not never whilst we live. But don' fret bout dat. Dis is God's country. You have luck to get here. We done left trouble behind, thank God."

CHAPTER II

A PATH led up the shallow bank, ran alongside the edge through tender spring grass. Blue soon saw a low whitewashed house squatting under great moss-hung oaks. Smoke curled sleepily out of its low rock chimney but the door and windows were closed.

On the narrow front porch an old man sat in a big armchair, sound asleep. His white whiskered chin rested comfortably on his breast. His outstretched legs were crossed, his arms folded. Hoop earrings shone in his ears, but his feet were bare and no sign of a hat covered the white wool on his head.

Hens dusting themselves in a pile of ashes ceased fluttering to stare when Blue's father whispered:

"Yonder is Big Pa, son. E's you Mammy's Grampa, but e's de nicest old man ever was."

Tiptoeing behind the chair, Blue's father laid both hands over the old man's closed eyelids.

"Eh, eh," Big Pa roused quickly. "Who dat?"

Blue's father made no answer nor move.

Big Pa grunted.

"You ain' no chillen. You hard hands says you's a workin man. But seems like I smell boychillen."

The white hairs in his broad nostrils quivered as he sniffed the air.

"Guess who I is, Big Pa."

"I can' tell to save life, but you better get back to plowin. You ain' got no business playin chillen games when grass is in de cotton."

Blue's father lifted his hands and Big Pa's eyes blinked at Blue; his loose old lips spread in a smile that showed a solid row of sharp-pointed teeth.

"Now who is dis new somebody?" His knotted fingers shook as they took Blue by the arm and drew him closer. "Who is dis nice lil boy-child?" he asked gently.

His face was lined, his voice cracked, but kindness shone in his dim old eyes and warmed every word his trembly lips spoke.

"I know every boy-child round here but I never seen you befo. Tell Big Pa you name."

Puzzlement drew his fuzzy white brows together.

"I name' Blue, suh." Blue pulled his foot and made a mannersable bow.

"Blue? Great God, what Blue is dis?"

Blue's father stepped forward and Big Pa stared at him in bewilderment.

"What might be you name, suh?" he asked stiffly.

"Is you forgot me, Big Pa? Now you hurt me to my heart."

With a joyful cry Big Pa dropped Blue's hand.

"Jim—Jim—whe' you come from, son?" His old hands reached for the strong ones which grasped and held them fast.

"I'm past by glad to see you, Jim. I never thought to see you no more in dis world."

"Why, Big Pa, you look young as a boy."

"I might look young, but I feel like old people, Jim."

"Why, you back is straight as a shingle, suh."

The old man wiped his wet eyes and sighed. He said his time was mighty nigh out, but he was ready to go whenever the Master saw fit to call him home.

"E ain' gwine call you no time soon. Not spry as you is. De plantation wouldn' seem right widout you. Who would fix de charms an' cunjures if you was gone?"

"Hester can make em now. I learnt em how. Big trees is due to give room for de saplin's, Jim. Plenty o' young people is here to take de old ones' places."

"No, Big Pa. De big trees must shelter de saplin's. I fetched dis lil saplin to-day for his kinnery to shelter. Whe's Aun Fan?"

"Fancy's washin clothes at de spring. I come to fetch him a charm to help his short wind, an' I must be went to sleep." He glanced at the long shadows. "De sun is droppin. Fancy'll be here soon. Get a chair out de house an' set down, Jim. Tell me de news bout you'self. How's you lady?"

"I better go fetch Aun Fan, den we can all set down an' talk together."

Big Pa chuckled. "You made a joke on me, Jim. Let's make a lil joke on Fancy. Let dis

boy go tell Fancy a gentleman what looks like
a preacher is here. Dat'll fetch em a-runnin.
Fancy ever was pure raven bout preachers.''

His father was all for it, but Blue hung back.
He was shy before strangers and he had never
seen his grandmother. His father joined Big Pa
in urging him to go. He could not get lost. He
need only give that short message and hurry back.

"Make haste an' you'll catch up wid Cricket.
E will show you de way. Cricket ain' so long
gone.''

"Who's Cricket?''

"Dat's de little bright-skin gal, Jim.''

"You mean dat lil motherless?''

Big Pa nodded yes and smiled.

"Cricket's you kinnery, Blue. You an' Cricket
is two sisters' chillen. Cricket's de sweetest lil
gal ever was. Take de path, son, an' you'll see em
if you make haste.''

Blue's heart was divided. He was curious to
see Cricket yet he dreaded to meet a stranger.
He walked slowly past myrtle thickets, dogwood
trees, banks of jessamine in full bloom. Where the
path made a sharp elbow around a steep shelv-
ing bank he heard somebody singing. Looking below he saw a little girl on her knees picking
white violets beside a clear stream. He stared
down at her in amazement. All the women and
girls he knew were black and had short kinky hair
carefully wrapped into tight cords with ball
thread. This child's skin was the color of a ripe

gourd and her hair hung in a tousled black mass
clear to her shoulders.

She must have felt his gaze for she turned her
head and looked up at him with big startled eyes.
Instead of saying "Good evenin," as he knew
quite well how to do, he stood tongue-tied, awkward, rooted to the ground.

"Who is you?" she asked sharply.

When Blue made no answer, dimples twinkled
in her cheeks and her teeth shone white as rice
grains.

"Is you deef or is you dumb?"   Laughter
sparkled in her soft black eyes.

"Dis is me, Blue," he answered huskily, for
blood beat hard in his throat.

"Whe' did you come from?" One narrow black
eyebrow quirked up.

"I come from home."

Leaves stirred and sighed as a breath of air
fell from the sky and fluttered her strange long
hair. One small hand full of violets pushed a
black lock off her forehead.

"Is you lost?" A mischievous smile played
over her mouth.

"I don' know. I'm tryin to find my Gramma."

He did his best to talk stout but a dry mouth
made his words stumble.

"You Gramma? Who you Gramma is?"

"His name is Aun Fan." Blue felt shamed
by his stammering, but her face brightened with
sudden interest.

"You don' mean Cun Al-fred's lady?" She stood up to examine him better.

When Blue nodded yes, her whole expression changed.

"Cun Al-fred is us foreman," she said solemnly, as if she spoke of God himself.

This made Blue feel better, somehow. She had been making sport of him but now her eyes measured him quietly and gave him a friendly smile.

"Whe' does you live?"

"I live in a far country, way up de river."

She must have sensed the homesickness that flooded his heart for she said gently:

"Wait a minute, an' I'll take you to Aun Fan. E is at de spring washin clothes."

She gathered up her violets and climbed the steep bank like a squirrel, catching to bushes to help pull herself up. They walked in silence along the narrow path. The dropping sun flamed through the trees and bound leaves and branches together with glowing light. It shone on her bright skin and tousled hair, marked her features clearly. Her nose was too high and narrow, her full-lipped mouth too wide, and a tinge of red blood showed in her yellow cheeks.

Once Blue's hand brushed against her bunch of violets and for some reason he got all a-tremble. He dropped behind, but she went on without noticing.

She was a thin little thing. Her fingers, curled around her bunch of violets, were small as a baby's. Blue had never seen anybody like her before. In spite of her queer looks she held her little head high and walked like a proudful somebody. Suddenly she turned and pointed through an opening in the trees.

"See dat fat lady wid de blue dress on? Dat's Aun Fan."

Blue saw many women, full clothes-lines, garments spread on the grass to dry. His heart thumped, his throat quivered. He could not bear to face that crowd.

"Please—you go tell em for me."

"Tell em what?" Her dimples twinkled again.

"Please go tell em my Daddy is come."

"Who's you Daddy?"

"E's name Jim."

"How-come you is so shamefaced?"

Blue dropped his eyes before her gaze.

"I dunno," he murmured, and he spoke the truth for he had never felt like this before.

"I had aimed to go on home, but I reckon I'll go tell Aun Fan for you. Good-by," she laughed over her shoulder as she sped away.

"Good-by." Blue answered with a breath of relief and turned back to Aun Fan's house. His heart was unsteady and confused thoughts whirled around in his head. How could this bright-skin child be his cousin, his own blood-kin cousin?

He found his father and Big Pa sitting side by side, talking close talk. They both looked so down-

in-the-heart that Blue knew they talked about his
mother.

"Did you find Aun Fan, Blue?" his father asked
sternly.

"Yes-suh."

"How-come you didn' wait an' walk back wid
em?"

"E said e would be here toreckly," Blue lied
and then sighed with relief, for he heard her voice
hurrying ahead, calling on God and Jesus just
like somebody was dead. Blue's father ran to
meet her and they held to each other, laughing and
crying.

Her eyes caught sight of Blue and she stopped
short in her tracks.

"Who dat lil boy-child is?" she asked.

"Dat is you gran-boy, Aun Fan. Make you
manners, Blue."

Blue pulled his foot and bowed low. She burst
into a funny clucking laugh and ran to gather him
into her short fat arms.

"You ain' got a meat on you bones, but you sho
is got nice manners."

She held him close to the solid bosom that filled
the whole front of her dress, and pressed her fat
wet cheek against his face.

"Dis boy ain' had enough to eat, Jim." She
held Blue off for her keen little eyes to examine
him better.

"Blue eats much as a man, Aun Fan."

"I hope e ain' no runt." Narrow lines came in her forehead.

She took one of Blue's hands, looked at the palm, turned it over and sighed.

"My people ain' got small hands like dis, Jim. De boy favors his Ma's people. De same big solemn eyes, de same tar-black skin. Is e got blue gums? Open you mouth, son. Lemme see."

Her strong finger lifted Blue's lip.

"Same like indigo. Big Pa's breed all has em. Dey bite is pizen as a rattlesnake."

"Blue's got you nose, Aun Fan, an' you mouth, too."

"I believe e has," she agreed with a pleased laugh.

Blue felt his nose to see if it could be flat and broad like hers and wondered if such wide thick lips could get on his face.

"Big Pa, how you like de looks of you great-gran?" she called. The old man's pointed teeth flashed against the sun.

"E stands like a nice lil boy, to me. How you like em, Fancy?"

"I wish e wasn' so small an' dry."

Big Pa smiled good-naturedly. "I'll fix a charm to make de boy grow, Fancy. E will fatten like a pig in a pen."

"For God's sake don' miss an' give em de grow-fast, Big Pa. Grow-fast is a dangerous ailment," Aun Fan warned. "You mixtures work backwards sometimes. You give Jule dat tea to stop em from breedin' so fast an' Jule had twins befo de year was out."

Aun Fan told how Big Pa gave a boy named Man Jay a charm to make him grow. Man Jay took the grow-fast. His bones got so long the meat on them shrunk. Man Jay had never acted right since.

"I never seen Man Jay act wrong, Fancy," Big Pa objected, but she said Man Jay was too bold, too impudent, to be a common field-hand boy.

"Man Jay is got sense, Fancy. Man Jay knows e is good as de best."

"Man Jay is a bastard woods-colt."

"Shut you mouth, Fancy. God made Man Jay same like e made you."

Aun Fan gave a scornful laugh.

"God! You know good as me, Satan made Man Jay, same like Satan made Cricket."

Big Pa gave her a hard look but made no answer.

CHAPTER III

A GAY kerchief tied up Aun Fan's head but two
bits of sooty black wool stuck out above her small
ears. Her fat body bulged above and below apron
strings tied around her middle, but her thick hands
were quick and for all her weight she was as light
on her feet as a girl.

"Who does you other chillen favor, Jim?" She
took her cane stem pipe from behind her ear and
filled it with tobacco from her apron pocket.

"God knows."

"Is dey boys or gals?"

"Dey is all-two, Aun Fan, but dey can go to
Hell wid dey Mammy for all I care bout em."

Big Pa straightened up.

"A man ain' to cuss his lawful lady, Jim."

"I got to cuss em, Big Pa, when I think on how e
fooled me. I give dat 'oman every God's cent I
made. De whole time e been throwin sand in my
eyes."

"Don't talk so rash, Jim."

"I ain' talkin rash. I give em a good knockin
befo I left em. I ought to had killed em. I would
'a' killed de man if I could 'a' caught em."

"Who de man was?" Aun Fan whispered.

"Don' make me talk bout dat slue-foot devil.
Just to think on em makes me have sin. I'm
leavin de country, Aun Fan. Dat's how-come I
fetched Blue to you."

Tears sprang into Aun Fan's eyes and she covered her face with her apron.

"Who will cook and wash for you when you get in dem far-off places?" she sobbed.

Big Pa got up and patted her shoulder.

"Don' fret, Fancy. Jim'll have wife again. Plenty o' gals is left to choose from."

"No more wife for me, Big Pa. I done lost my taste for womens."

"You ought to had let me pick you wife first time," Aun Fan sobbed. "I would 'a' got you a gal you could rule."

"All womens is a case, Fancy," Big Pa said gently. "Mens ain' to expect too much of em."

Aun Fan's head thrust forward, her voice rose with anger. "You ain' got no cause to down-talk womens because all you breed goes wrong. Jim's wife ain' de first shameless one. Cricket's Mammy done a heap worse. In de face of de whole plantation, too."

Big Pa's folded hands quietly settled themselves in his lap, his lips closed tight together.

"What color is you other chillen, Jim?" Aun Fan sniffled.

"Dey ain' my own, Aun Fan. I examined em all befo I left home. Blue is de only one favors me."

"What color dem chillen is, Jim?" she persisted.

"Dey black as de back of de chimney."

She drew such a deep breath the step squeaked under her weight.

"Thank God, Jim, you wife stuck to his race. Dat's better'n his brazen sister done."

"Don' down-talk de dead, Fancy," Big Pa chided.

"I ain' down-talkin nobody. Right is right. Color is color. I would hang my head wid shame if one of Jim's chillen had bright skin."

Big Pa stirred in his chair. "Bright skin or not, Cricket's de smartest, prettiest lil gal on dis whole plantation."

Aun Fan groaned. "Big Pa thinks Cricket is made out of gold. Wes spiles de gal until e is rotten. Cricket don' do a hand's turn. Wes won' even let em hoe cotton."

"How old Cricket is?" Blue's father asked.

Aun Fan reflected.

"Let me think. Cricket was born de week of de big April storm seven or either eight years ago. Lord, I'll never forget how rain filled up his Mammy's grave fast as de mens bailed it out. Dat was one pitiful buryin in dis world. Not a preacher to pray, not a soul to ask God to have mercy. Just de rain beatin down on de box."

"De gal's Daddy was a preacher. How-come e didn' pray?"

Aun Fan sighed, her round body rocked from side to side.

"When e found out what de gal done, e lost his religion, Jim. E tried to kill somebody." She gave a warning wink.

"Just to look at Cricket makes my eyes feel rich," Big Pa said gently. "Cricket ain' to blame for what somebody else done."

"Some of dese days you'll see what's in Cricket's blood. Dat gal don' come from mild people."

"Why, Fancy, Cricket is mild as any new-born lamb. E is a smart gal, too. E helped to hoe my cotton an' e jerked his hoe good as a grown somebody."

"It ain' no use to lie, Big Pa. Cricket don' know a God's thing bout field work," Aun Fan disagreed.

"Cricket ain' due to do field work. You must be forgot Cricket is a high-bredded gal."

Blue listened eagerly, for he knew Cricket was the child he had seen. Aun Fan saw his interest and said:

"It ain' good to talk dis talk befo chillen."

"You de one talkin, Fancy. It ain' me." Pa stood up and took Blue by the hand.

"Son, you Ma is my gran, same like Cricket's Mammy was. I think a lot of my kinnery, no matter if dey is right or wrong. You is small and dry, for-true, but blood is what counts in dis world, not looks." A pleased smile tangled the wrinkles around his eyes as he added:

"My smallest game rooster whips all dem big dung hills in de Quarters. I'll give you a clutch o' game eggs for seed. Fancy can set em under one o' his hens."

"I'll make sweeten bread wid em. I ain' gwine raise dis boy to have sin, Big Pa."

Big Pa smiled and patted her shoulder.

"I wish to God I had a piece o' sweeten bread right now. Jesus couldn' cook no better'n you, gal."

Her face softened and she led the way into the house.

Opposite the door was a wide rock chimney whose opening stood above Blue's head. The pot rack fastened to its sooty back held iron pots over a charred back log as long as a man. Empty skillets, gridirons, trivets filled the hearth, but dead coals covered the lid of an iron oven sitting on a pile of ashes.

Blue's father looked at a white-faced box on the mantel-shelf. "How-come you got a clock?"

"We had so much cloudy days de sun couldn' tell time. Al-fred went all de way to town for dat clock. It's got sense, too. De man what sold em told Al-fred every time e speaks somebody dies."

An ember snapped, sparks shot out. *Click-clock, click-clock*, the box spoke slowly, steadily.

"I wouldn' have em in my house," Big Pa grumbled. "People dies too fast like it is."

Click-clock, click-clock. The box did not halt at all. Aun Fan brushed dead coals off the iron oven and lifted out a big, brown sweeten bread. Blue's mouth leaked when she broke off a hunk and handed it to him.

"Go see de creeters in de barnyard, son. We got pigs, calves, pigeons, lambs."

Blue held fast to his father's breeches.

"You must mind Aun Fan, Blue. Go look at de barnyard."

Blue's eyes swam in tears but he walked humbly away, munching his bread.

Between the house and a high whitewashed fence a white cow with long crumpled horns lay chewing her cud. The bell on her neck gave a dangerous clang and Blue made haste to climb the fence. Inside the barnyard, a spotted white calf looked at him and bleated hungrily. Bright-eyed pigeons strutted over the roof of a small house on tall legs, puffed out their breasts and cooed, "Looka de coon, looka de coon." A crow flew across the sky and they all rose quickly, circled around him, their wings rustling and glistening in the sunshine. A huge, black boar hog with long tusks wallowed in a mud-hole made by water pouring steadily from a long iron trough, but he faced the open barn door where a rat gnawed greedily on a pile of corn in the shuck. In a long stable fat pigs rooted in straw and dung close to the heels of a sleek sorrel mare. A horse's neigh rang out and the mare pricked up her ears, whinnied and trotted toward the fence where an elderly black man held a fiery bay stallion by a halter. The brute's voice redoubled its strength and his hoofs stamped the ground with short patience, but the man held him back and shouted to somebody Blue could not see.

"Don' come here now, Cricket. Dis ain' no place for you. Plat-eyes'll catch you, an' de boar hog'll eat you. Go on home, honey."

The stallion's nostrils flared red, his neck arched, his smooth hoofs shone, as he reared and leaped until the gate opened and let him inside.

Blue climbed up on the fence to watch in safety, but the boar hog got up and slouched lazily toward him. The fence was high but the ugly beast was big as a barrel. His rough black hide was smeared with mud and his tusks were mean and yellow.

As Blue hopped down he caught a glimpse of a vanishing pink frock. He knew it was Cricket. He wished he dared call or whistle to her, but before he could make up his mind, she was gone.

CHAPTER IV

A STRANGER-MAN was in the yard with Aun Fan and Big Pa, but Blue's father was nowhere in sight.

"Whe' is Pa?" Blue tried to hold back his tears, for Aun Fan's eyes were keen as two knives.

"You Pa's gone an' left you," she said flatly.

His breath tore through his gullet in a scream, and she clapped a thick hand over his mouth. "Hush you racket!" she ordered. "Is you gwine holler again if I let you catch air?"

Blue shook his head and the hand fell away, let him breathe. Tears blurred his sight but a man's voice beside him asked kindly, "How you do, son?" and a warm hand took his and held it.

"You can' blame de boy for cryin, Fancy," the voice went on, "I'm you Cun Fred, son. I'm gwine be you Pa from now on."

A short black mustache half hid his big mouth, and his words jerked like his tongue did not fit. The wad of tobacco lodged in his cheek may have been to blame for it kept him busy spitting.

"I'm glad to see you, Blue," he stammered. "No longer'n to-day I was wishin I had a boy-child to wait on me."

"Do hush, Al-fred," Aun Fan growled. "You ___ ___ ___rybody waitin on you from mornin till

Cun Fred spat.

"You would work me to death if I stayed round home. I have to go to de field to rest."

"Whe' is Pa?" Blue quavered above the choking in his throat.

Cun Fred put a hand on his shoulder. "Son, you Pa's gone. E thought best to leave you wid me."

Blue burst out crying. Nothing Aun Fan or Cun Fred said made any difference.

"Let me talk wid em, Al-fred." Big Pa knelt down and two long bony arms held Blue close against a warm breast. "I know how you feel. I wasn' much bigger'n you when I come to live mongst strangers." He pulled out a big red pocket handkerchief and blew his nose with a loud snort. "Cryin don' do no good, son. I tried it plenty o' times. You got to face trouble brave as you can."

Spent and sad, Blue leaned against Big Pa's breast, until Cun Fred said, "Come on, let's go in de house, Big Pa. De dew is fallin an' you ain' got on no hat."

Big Pa sat in a big chair on the piazza and took Blue in his lap.

"You is too big to set in Big Pa's lap, Blue," Cun Fred objected, but Big Pa held fast to him.

"My old legs enjoys de boy's weight, Al-fred. It makes my mind go back to long time ago. My own lil boy-child used to set like dis in my lap after his Mammy died. Me an' him would cry together.

E was named Blue, too, same like dis lil boy. God knows whe' he is to-day.''

"Lord, how time do fly.'' Cun Fred sighed. "Just de other day I was a boy myself.''

"Book-readin ruined my Blue.'' Big Pa shook his head sadly from side to side.

"Blue used to be a fine preacher, Big Pa.''

"Book-readin put wrong notions in his head, Al-fred. Book-readin is bad for black people.''

"Wes'll jump Juba when e sees dis boy,'' Cun Fred spoke up cheerfully.

"Wes'll hang his head wid shame when e hears how Blue's Mammy acted,'' Aun Fan called above a clatter of pots and pans.

"Wes don' hang his head bout nothin. Not proudful as Wes is.'' Cun Fred spat far into the yard.

Aun Fan came to the door, her hands covered with dough.

"If Missie wasn' a Christian e would 'a' left Wes long time ago.''

"Left em for what?''

"My God, Al-fred, for de way Wes acted wid Bina.''

"Dat's crazy talk. Bina had a fine boy-child for Wes. It's more'n Missie ever done. Exceptin for Bina, Wes wouldn' have a seed to his name.''

"Missie ain' to blame. E tried every charm, every root Big Pa had to make em breed.''

"Missie is too stingy to breed,'' Cun Fred laughed.

"Missie has to be stingy, bad as V
Aun Fan came back, but Cun Fred
Wes had a right to play skin if it p
Wes made fine crops; he hauled log
mill; he had money buried all und
The boys tried to win it in skin ga
never lost, and he never cheated, even when luck
went against him.

"Cards an' dice is like all in life; dey ever
falls well for bold players," Big Pa said.

"Wes'll get his due if e don' quit gamblin an'
sinnin," Aun Fan declared.

Cun Fred said Wes would outlive Missie. She
looked like an ageable woman but Wes was young
and supple as a boy.

"It will be a sad day for Cricket if Missie was
to die. Missie done everything for Cricket but
birth em," Aun Fan snapped.

Big Pa agreed that Missie had been good to
Cricket, but Wes was Cricket's heart-string. Aun
Fan argued that Wes treated Cricket like a tender
wax doll, but Missie did her duty. Missie was
a good provider, too. She ever had chickens and
eggs to sell. Her cow was never dry, her pig-pen
never empty. She knew every trout drop in the
old rice-field creeks and would paddle her boat
across the river without batting an eyelash, no
matter how rough the water was.

Cun Fred argued that Missie was no smarter
than Bina. Bina earned good money sewing
dresses for the women, shrouds for the dead,

baptizing robes for church candidates. When
Bina dressed for church on Sundays, in her
pretty red frock and black hat bobbing with
flowers, Bina sure looked like an angel from
Heaven.

"Shut you mouth, Al-fred. Bina looks like de
devil e is. Bina's too lazy to cook. E feeds Man
Jay on dat white store-bought bread until his consecution is nigh ruint." Aun Fan sounded so cross
the men said no more.

Crickets chirped sleepily, a katydid answered.
The white-faced box on the mantel spoke steadily,
click-clock, click-clock. Bing-bang, bing-bang,
something answered from the woods and through
the stillness echoed sharp beats of iron against
iron.

"Dat old ram sho is faithful. It wouldn' stop
runnin until Judgment Day if a leaf or a crawfish didn' get in his insides."

Blue wondered at the strangeness of the creature as Cun Fred went on.

"When I was a boy, my Daddy used to tell me
de ram said, 'Work hard, work hard!' Fancy
thinks de ram says, 'Be saved, be saved!' "

Big Pa groaned when Aun Fan snapped back:
"You better start thinkin on bein saved. People dies mighty fast dese days."

"Do de ram butt people?" Blue ventured.

Aun Fan burst into sudden loud laughter, but
Cun Fred explained that this ram was an engine.
Day and night, year in, year out, it pumped water

to the barnyard trough, same like it used to pump
water to the Big House for white people.

"Po' lil ign'ant boy," Aun Fan sighed. "Come
on an' eat, son. Supper is on de table."

Blue sat down with the two men, while Aun Fan
walked around the table piling food on their plates.
He ate hominy and honey-cooked meat until his
clothes were tight and his eyes so sleepy he could
not hold them open. Aun Fan took him to another
room, unbuttoned his clothes and helped him into
bed. As he sank deep in the soft feather mattress
he thought of his mother, but he held back his tears
until Aun Fan left the room.

Sleep had just ended his sorrow when she called,
"Blue, did you say prayers?"

"No, ma'am."

"You can' sleep in my house befo you pray.
Git up an' kneel down."

"Ma lets me pray in de bed when I'm weary."

"Well, I ain' you Ma. I can' stand slack ways."

Blue crawled from under the quilts and knelt
on the cold hard floor.

"God bless Ma——" he began.

"For God's sake!" Aun Fan cut him off.
"Dat ain' no way to pray. Say 'Our Father who
are in Heaven——' "

Blue looked at her, bewildered and speechless.

"You don' know 'Our Father'?" she cried.

"No, ma'am."

"Well, suh! You Ma sho is a case. Git back
in bed. I'll learn you 'Our Father' to-morrow."

CHAPTER V

DAWN was announced by crowing of cocks, chatter of guineas, geese, ducks, steady *beat-beating* of the iron ram. Cun Fred's feet hit the floor with a thud. Almost at once the big farm bell fastened to a gallows at the back porch corner began ringing briskly. Before one peal was done another followed, until the whole world filled with the bell's voice. Blue hopped up and put on his clothes for he wanted to see everything in this new exciting world. Bare feet tramped toward the barnyard, trace chains tinkled, man voices laughed, wagon wheels creaked, mule hoofs tapped the ground.

Breakfast was ready on the table, but Blue was eager to follow the men and mules, see where they went, what they did. Aun Fan set his panful of food on the hearth to keep warm until he got back.

The black earth was dark, shadowy; dew dripped from tree branches and long beards of moss. Blue followed the road straight toward sunrise side until he reached a field whose end lay hidden in misty distance.

The plowmen sang as they walked side by side up and down long rows of young cotton. Blue had heard his mother sing that same tune and those words.

"Oh, you better mind whe' you walk,
Oh, you better mind what you walkin about,

42

You got to give account on de Judgment day.
Oh, sinner, you better mind.''

These men and mules looked taller, bigger than
any Blue had ever seen. Even crows flying over
his head were blacker and cawed louder than
crows at home.

Trees flashed green as the sun climbed the sky
and woke the world up, newly turned furrows
smelled earthy and rich. Grass quivered, leaves
danced as the morning haze melted. A snail
walked leftward along the narrow road edging the
field, toward a sizable house with a whitewashed
front. Farther on a mass of plumy treetops rose
above a cluster of dark houses. Smoke poured out
of chimneys, people moved in and out of door-
ways. Cocks crowed, guineas potracked, calves
and goats bleated. A strain of music sang out
above the confusion of sounds, and Blue saw a
boy not much larger than himself shuffling down
the road to a tune he played on a mouth-organ.

A tin bucket was perched on his head and one
hand swung a glass bottle by a string on its neck
to keep time with his capering feet. Shyness
tempted Blue to run home, but lonesomeness made
him tarry. The music came closer and closer.
The boy suddenly halted and stared with wide
curious eyes.

"Good mornin," he said with a bold white grin.

"Good mornin," Blue answered huskily.

"What might be you name?"

"I name' Blue."

"Who you belongst to?"

"To Cun Fred."

The boy's grin widened. "Is Cun Fred got a boy small as you? Who's you Mammy?"

"Cun Fred ain' my Pa. E's my Grampa."

"Aw, dat's different." His grin faded into a smile as he asked, "When you come?"

"Yestiddy."

"How long you gwine stay?"

"All de time."

"Wid Cun Fred?"

Blue nodded.

"Aun Fan will work you breeches clean off."

"What you mean, 'Work my breeches off'?" Blue asked stiffly.

"Aw, don' get vexed so quick. I was just makin a joke."

"What you name?" Blue tried to sound bold.

"Man Jay's my name. I'm a mans of monkeys too."

"Whe' you stay?"

Man Jay looked toward the grove of trees.

"Mostly I stay yonder to de street wid Ma. Sometimes I stay wid Uncle Wes, in dat wash-white house."

"Uncle Wes is my kinnery," Blue boasted.

Man Jay's whole manner changed. "Well, I declare," he said cordially, "Uncle Wes is my kinnery, too."

Man Jay's shirt was patched, his old flopping breeches were a grown man's cut off. He was

barefooted, his hands were greasy, his thick hair
lay in knots on his bare head. His words were
quick and free, although as he talked he chewed
chinquapins which he took one by one out of his
dirty breeches pockets. He told Blue the name of
every plowman, every mule. Hattie, the small
black mule, kicked if the line got under her tail—
George, the spotted mule, had sense like a man.
But Uncle Wes's two white oxen had all the
mules beated. Uncle Wes bought this mouth-
organ; Uncle Wes dug his boat, a trust-me-God,
out of a cypress log; Uncle Wes made his sling-
shot from a dogwood prong and it shot as straight
as a gun.

Blue admitted sadly he had no mouth-organ, no
sling-shot, no dugout.

"Can you plow?"

Blue could not even plow.

"Every boy high as de plow-handles has to plow
on Sat'day mornins. Cun Fred pays em too.
Fifteen cents in trade at de store. Plowin is
fun when you know how. I can plow all day an'
not weary," Man Jay bragged.

"You don' never play?"

"Sho I plays. I goes to school endurin de week
but on Sundays I bats ball. Dem two gals comin
down de road yonder can bat ball good as boys.
De fat one is Toosio, de dry one is Cooch."

"I don' play wid gals," Blue said loftily.

A chinquapin cracked sharply as Man Jay bit
it in two.

"I rules de gals I play wid. I knocks de devil out em."

"You would knock a gal?"

"Quick as I'd knock a boy," Man Jay answered promptly. "Last night Cooch said I smell like a ram goat an' my head looked lousy, an' my hands was filthy as possum paws. I knocked em good," Man Jay grinned and added that when Cooch got vexed she kicked like a mule and scratched like a wildcat. She tied strings to June-bugs' legs to see them zoom around her head until the legs broke off. She pulled heads off June-bugs and let them go spinning blind away up in the sky. She made sport of frogs smashed in wheel tracks and laughed when baby birds fell out of nests. She even bit a worm in two.

"Good mornin," Man Jay called as the two girls passed.

"You needn' think I care if you don' speak," he called with a jeering laugh when neither answered him.

They looked at Blue, mumbled to each other and trudged on with a few backward glances.

Man Jay said Cooch had no respect for old people. She mocked Cun Hester shouting at meeting, and squinted up her face like Brer Dee when he read the Bible at meeting, funny enough to make a dog laugh. Cooch knew all about grown people, all about where babies come from and everything. She told things that made Man Jay feel blush. When the weather got cross and thunder rolled,

Toosio got in bed and put the pillow over her head, but Cooch stood in the door and sang reel songs right in the lightning's face. If God ever heard her he would strike her dead, but Cooch was not scared of anything. Cooch was a heavy case in this world. Aun Missie would not let Cricket play with her.

"How come Cricket ain' black?" Blue asked.

Man Jay gave him a hard look.

"Me an' Cricket is two sisters' chillen," Blue explained, but Man Jay looked doubtful.

"If you don' believe me, ask Cun Fred."

"I ain' got time to ask em dis mornin. I want to git back to de landin befo de *Comanche* comes. Lord, boy, dat's a boat. Some o' dese days I'm gwine ride em clean to de end of de world."

He put the mouth-organ to his lips.

"Come to see me, Man Jay. Let's shoot pigeons wid you sling-shot."

"Aun Fan's pigeons?" Man Jay grinned. "Now I know you is fool in de head."

CHAPTER VI

AUN FAN and Cun Fred did their best to keep Blue from being down-in-the-heart. Cun Fred gave him a bull yearling and said Big Pa could fix a charm to make the beast gentle and easy to break. Blue could drive the George mule and new wagon when Aun Fan went to church next fourth Sunday. Blue should have a Sunday shirt and cap from the crossroads store this very afternoon.

Blue tried to talk but when he mentioned that Man Jay asked him to bat ball at the Quarters on Sunday, Aun Fan's lips tightened.

"Sunday ain' no day to bat ball an' dat Quarters ain' no place for you. De foreman's gran-boy ain' to run wid every common somebody."

Cun Fred spat far back into the chimney corner, rolled his wad of tobacco against his cheek.

"Eat you breakfast, Blue," he said kindly. "Dat's chicken gravy on you hominy."

"I ain' hongry," Blue faltered.

Cun Fred cleared his throat. "Blue ain' to scorn his blood kin, Fancy."

Aun Fan sniffed.

"Man Jay is a woods colt. Cricket is a no-nation. Blue may as well know de truth."

"Man Jay comes from mighty good stock, Fancy, an' Cricket's blood can' be beated nowhere in dis world."

Aun Fan fell to sweeping the hearth with brisk strokes.

"I wish to God you'd quit chewin tobacco, or learn to aim better when you spit. I reddened dis hearth wid clay last Sat'day. Look at em now."

Cun Fred got up so suddenly his chair fell backward.

Aun Fan's eyelids snapped. "You needn' get vexed wid me, Al-fred. You ought to be glad I hold myself above sinners."

"Come on, Blue," Cun Fred answered, "let's walk out an' look at de crops."

Blue was glad to get out of the house where cooking smells and fire heat made the air hard to breathe.

Out-of-doors the day was cool and fresh, the sun burned bright in a clear blue sky. As Cun Fred strode along the road, birds sang lustily, soft green shadows and spots of sunshine danced over the road, yellow jessamine on the pasture's rail fence nodded pretty blossom bells.

"Yonder's de lady what leads de shoutin at meetin," he said.

A little distance ahead a short square woman stood bawling abuse at a brindle cow bent on eating in a patch of tender grass.

"Whyn' you let you cow eat, Jule?" Cun Fred called.

She dropped the rope and wiped her face on her skirt. "I'm pure outdone with dis crazy cow. E

bawled all night till I couldn' sleep. Now when
I'm takin em to de bull e won' think on a God's
thing but grass."

"You is too short patience, Jule. De bull is
in de barnyard. E will soon git de cow straight."

He went closer, whispered something and she
gave a boisterous laugh.

"Do shut you mouth, Cun Fred. You ain' to
talk such a talk to a married lady."

She fixed her beady eyes on Blue, but the cow
raised her head, gave a hoarse low and galloped
toward the barnyard, jerking Jule along by the
rope at a full run behind her.

The gin house was near by, a large weather-
stained building, shut up to rest until fall. Behind
it a low blacksmith shop squatted in the midst
of broken log carts, rusty harrows, old plow stocks.
Clouds of dingy smoke poured through the open
door, leaked through cracks in the shingled roof.
Foot bellows creaked, the forge roared wildly,
iron clanged against iron. The big blacksmith
looked up above a shower of sparks, nodded good
morning and hammered on.

Cun Fred said a young moon would shine to-
night and Andrew's dead father, the old blacksmith, might come back. When Andrew's work
failed to please him the old dead man beat on the
anvil until nobody could sleep.

When they reached the field Cun Fred halted
to feast his eyes on the long clean rows of young
cotton.

"My old Daddy was de foreman, but if e comes back to-night e won't see a sprig of grass in dat field, thank God."

The blue air shimmered over a dim white spot against the distant trees. Cun Fred said it was Heaven's Gate Church where all the dead lay buried. Big Pa's son, Blue, used to preach there every fourth Sunday before he left the country.

"Me an' Wes works too hard all de week to set on a hard bench on Sunday. Fancy drives de George mule to de wagon, an' takes Missie to church, Missie an' Cricket."

He straightened his hat, smoothed his shirt down in his breeches, and faced the whitewashed house beside the road.

"Yonder whe' Missie lives. We'll stop an' get Cricket to go wid us to see Big Pa."

As they walked toward the house Cun Fred told about the white overseers who lived there during slavery times. It was big enough for three families but Wes farmed three shares of land so he and Missie and Cricket could have it to themselves. Wes came from house-servant stock and he would not live in the Quarters among field-hands.

Fig trees clustered around the vegetable garden which was fenced in with new hand-split clap-boards. The front yard was bright with blossoms and tin cans on the piazza shelf held geraniums and wandering-jew. The door and window facings were painted blue to keep lightning out.

Nobody was home, but Cun Fred opened the door and walked inside.

Gay colored pictures were pasted over broken places in the plastered wall. A bright patchwork quilt covered the wide bed, a glass lamp stood on a table. Two big split-bottom armchairs were in front of the hearth and a small rocker with a white cowhide seat stood between them. A string of eggshells hung on a nail beside the fireplace to make the hens lay, a square looking-glass and two red vases were on the mantel-shelf.

"Dat glass is a bad-luck thing. It made Cricket teeth awful hard. Wes keeps it because it belonged to Cricket's Mammy."

The glass mocked every move Cun Fred made but his frown changed quickly to a smile when Cricket came running in with an old hound following at her heels. Her wild hair was in two short plaits tied together with a cloth string that matched her short pink frock. Her bright skin was moist and her cheeks flushed with a soft red glow.

"Hey, Cun Fred, whe'd you git dat boy?"

Blue's eyes dropped before her laughing gaze.

"I found em in de briar patch."

"What you gwine do wid em?"

"I'll give em to you. You need somebody to wait on you, lazy as you is." Cun Fred's playful tone denied his words, but her eyes flashed.

"I picked dese boll-evils off Uncle Wes's cotton since sunrise."

"Better keep you hay, gal, you might marry a mule. How come you ain' hoein cotton?" he asked gruffly.

"I got to mind de chillen for Ma."

Her head disappeared and tinkles of laughter poured through the window.

"Cooch plays wid hop-toads. Warts was all over his hands until Cun Hester took em off," Cricket disapproved.

Cun Fred spat to one side. "Cooch'll do well if e don' play wid nothin worse'n hop-toads. Cooch don' come from decent people."

The last house had new steps and its roof was patched with new shingles. Rusty hinges creaked as a window blind swung open and a woman's black smiling face appeared.

"Good mornin, Bina. You sho looks like a flowers garden," Cun Fred greeted her.

"Do hush you sweet talk!" The long string of red glass beads around her neck clicked merrily against the sill. "My old rooster been crowin at de door to tell me somebody was comin. Now it's you wid you sweet-talkin mouth."

"A dumb man would sweet talk you, Bina. I sho missed you whilst you was gone."

She smiled and patted her chest. "I fetched you a present, Cun Fred. A preacher yonder in town is so holy, his picture will cure any ailment." She took a folded paper out of the front of her dress and opened it up.

"Look at em good. See if you know em."

Cun Fred studied the black man's picture on the paper.

"Dis is de spittin image of old Blue."

"Dat's ezactly who it is." Her laugh rippled out.

"Is e back in dis country? I thought he went to Africa."

"E did went to Africa. E calls hisself Reverend Africa now. I swear to God every time e walks inside de church, de spirit comes wid em so strong, people falls down and rolls on de floor. Dey had to wrap quilts around de posts in de church to keep em from brokin dey arms and legs. I ain' hardly slept dis whole week, I got so much religion. You ought to go hear em preach. You might get sanctified, too, Al-fred."

"Sanctified? Is you crazy, Bina?"

"No, I ain' crazy. Reverend Africa told me e prays for you every day, same like e prays for Big Pa an' Wes."

"I'd like to see em, but it's a po' time for you to get religion. Cotton is ready to chop, gal."

Bina gave a short laugh. "Cotton-choppin ain' in de back part of my head. I ain' no field-hand. I'm a seamster."

Cun Fred smiled. "You ever was big-doins, Bina."

A hollow cough made her lean out of the window and spit.

"If Reverend Africa's picture don' cure my cold, I gwine jine de Bury League next week."

"No need to do dat. Me or either Wes'll cure you. Which one you choose?"

"I might choose you if you'd polish you hair. I don' crave no old-lookin gentleman."

Cun Fred took off his hat and stroked his graying hair. "Fancy wanted to put soot and lard on em de last time e polished his own, but I ruther my head be white dan filthy."

"Put Reverend Africa's picture inside you hat. It might turn you hair black," Bina suggested.

Cun Fred looked at the picture again.

"Just to think, Blue left here befo Cricket was born. E would 'a' shot somebody if it hadn' been for me. People wid blue gums is dangerous, Bina. Dey gets crazy when dey gets vexed."

"I'm glad I ain' got em," Cricket said solemnly.

Bina laughed. "You ain' due to have em. You blood is too weakened down. But Reverend Africa asked me all bout you, how big you was and everything. E wants to see you but e said e wouldn' set foot on dis place again. E sent some money to Big Pa. E wants you an' Big Pa to come live wid em."

"I wouldn' leave Uncle Wes for nobody," Cricket said quickly.

"Maybe you is right. Reverend Africa sho ain' got no use for white folks. E says all of em is gwine to Hell."

"Come on, let's go, Blue," Cricket whispered as Cun Fred started up Bina's steps.

She walked so fast the Quarters was soon far

behind them and Big Pa's log cabin on a hill above
the river in sight. It had a strange lonely look
under the moss-hung oaks. Behind it a small clearing held patches of cotton and corn, clumps of fig
trees, a grape-vine on a wide flat arbor.

Big Pa was not home, but Cricket knew where
he dug roots. They found him rubbing his knee,
scolding it soundly.

"What de matter ail you knee? You can'
stand up straight dis mornin?" When he saw
the children, he grunted, "Better thank God you
is young. Dis east wind is bad on old people."

Blue offered to take his tow-sack full of roots,
but Big Pa said the roots were too powerful to be
trusted with somebody who could not rule them.

A small red stain on the side of the sack grew
slowly larger as juice bled from a root inside.
The spade looked tricky, too. Its edge glittered
sharp although its worn handle was dark with
swamp mud. Blue took it gingerly but Big Pa
told him not to be fearsome; that spade had
sense like people. Yet when Blue carried it inside the house, he cried, "Great God, boy. Dat
spade will fetch bad luck in my house," and slung
it out in the yard.

"Blue ain' got much learnin, Big Pa. Don'
talk hard at em," Cricket said kindly.

The water in the bucket was stale and she went
to fetch some that was fresh so Big Pa could make
an ash-cake. Blue followed her to the clump of
trees where a little spring bubbled into a barrel

sunk in the sand. Mosquitoes swarmed over it, a spring puppy clung to the barrel side. A small green snake wriggled out of the way when Cricket dipped the bucket down. Blue grabbed a stick but Cricket held his hand.

"Dat snake makes de water cool an' sweet, Blue. Don' kill Big Pa's friend."

Big Pa mixed fresh water and meal into stiff dough, wrapped it in shucks from a pile behind the door and laid it in a pile of hot ashes.

"Now fill my pipe an' light it for me, Cricket. Let me set down an' thank God for life." He gave a heavy sigh. "If it wasn' for leavin you, honey, I would pray to die to-day. Seems like de grave would feel sweet."

"You ought to button up you breeches, Big Pa. You catch too much air wid em open," Cricket reproved him.

"A man needs to catch air. It ain' healthy to shut breeches up tight."

"Aun Missie says when a man don' button up his breeches, dat's a sign e's gettin old."

"It ain' so!" Big Pa shouted angrily. "Missie is a fool. E wants me to join dat Bury League what puts de dead in store-bought boxes an' lays em away in broad daylight." Big Pa's breast heaved as he said the sun must set in a grave to make it pleasant for the last long sleep. He could never rest in a store-bought box. All store-bought things are bad. One taste of store-bought victuals gave him bellyache.

Cricket made no answer but peeled the shucks off the ash-cake, washed it carefully and broke it in three pieces. Blue started to take a bite but Big Pa held his hand.

"Wait, son. Victuals won' do you no good lessen you ask God to bless em."

"Uncle Wes don' pray when e eats."

Big Pa groaned. "Don' pattern after Wes, honey. E is a good man but e's a terrible sinner. Wes ain' broke his knees to pray since you Mammy died."

Big Pa changed the subject quickly by saying Blue talked like his palate needed lifting. He pulled up Blue's forelock and tied it so tight with a string his eyelids could hardly wink. As for that sassy bull yearling, Blue must catch some red ants, burn them crisp an' mix them with meal for the beast.

"Looks like ants would make him meaner," Cricket disapproved.

"No, honey. Ants is wise. Only fools is mean. If Blue will mix a roasted blue-tailed lizard wid dem ants, dat will make de yearlin swift."

A long low whistle boomed, and Cricket ran to the door to look out.

"Let's take Blue to de landin to see de *Comanche!*" she cried, but Big Pa shook his head. The *Comanche* made him sorrowful. It took live people off and brought dead ones back.

Cricket's coaxing made Big Pa come along anyhow, and Blue's heart leapt in his breast when the big white boat with its stern-wheel churning the water eased up against the rotten brown pilings. Aun Bina was with a crowd of women switching around and talking to the mouthy roustabouts. Sacks of fertilizer, barrels of flour and sugar, boxes of cloth, were taken ashore. A bell rang. The gangplank was withdrawn. The half-clothed crew waved good-by and the *Comanche* eased away. One of them bawled, "Hey, boy! How come you roostin in dat tree?"

Aun Bina looked up. "Git out dat tree, Man Jay! I got a good mind to make you drop you pants an' lick you right here befo everybody."

"You keep away from dis landin, Man Jay. Watchin de *Comanche*'ll make you feet itch to leave home," Big Pa rebuked him.

"Dey is done itchin to ride de *Comanche*," Man Jay grinned.

"My own is too," Cricket echoed. "I'm raven to go to town an' see Reverend Africa. Uncle Wes says e's us Grampa."

"I'll drench all two o' you wid a tea to make you stay home. People what rides de *Comanche* comes home in a box," Big Pa grumbled.

Aun Bina called him aside and talked some close talk in his ear. He got so upset he had to sit down on a log.

"I'm too old to leave home, Bina, but I'm glad my Blue is livin an' preachin to sinners. God bless em for sendin me money." Big tears streamed down wrinkles in his cheeks.

CHAPTER VII

THE days went swiftly, for Blue had tasks to fill each one. He hunted eggs, cut wood, swept yards, went on errands. Cun Fred paid five cents for every hundred boll-weevils he put in a bottle of kerosene, so he always had money to spend on Saturday afternoons when he rode his bull yearling to fetch the week's rations from the crossroads store. On Sundays he and Cricket and Man Jay slid down a steep pine-straw covered hill on barrel staves, waded in the spring branch, caught crawfish, made mud pies and cakes which Cricket called "Dirty mammy."

One Saturday afternoon Uncle Wes took him to the river to teach him to swim. The day was warm but Blue shivered when he stood stripped beside the stream. Uncle Wes undressed slowly. "Jump in, son," he said, but Blue was paralyzed with fear of the deep dark water. Uncle Wes gave him a hard look and frowned up his bony forehead.

"Cricket swims like a fish, Blue. Man Jay can cross de river. You'd be shame' not to learn how, wouldn' you, son?"

When Blue made no answer, Uncle Wes took his hand and led him to the bank.

"Cricket was scared to jump in deep water at first, just like you, son. I had to drop em in. De only way to swim is just to swim. De only way to do anything is to go on and do em no matter how

you feel. A boy-child is got to act brave. You'd
be better off to drown to-day dan to grow up a
coward-hearted man.''

Blue felt keenly the hint of scorn in Uncle Wes's
deep-set eyes, although his words sounded kind.
He knew Uncle Wes was surprised, distressed to
discover his cowardice, and shame made him
cringe.

''I got pain in de belly,'' he quavered, but
Uncle Wes smiled and without a word picked him
up and dropped him into the river.

Down, down he went, up, up he came, blind,
strangled, all but dead. Uncle Wes did not lift
a finger to keep him from drowning but stood
watching him flounder and splash. Not until Blue
gave up to die did Uncle Wes jump in and swim
with him to the bank. Blue lay limp on the
ground, gasping for breath while Uncle Wes
praised him.

''You done well, son. To-morrow you come
back an' jump in again. Jump in every day till
you know how to swim. Don' mind de alligators,
neither de moccasins. You'll meet alligators an'
moccasins long as you live. If dey see you is
scared, dey'll run you down; but if dey know
you ain' got em to study bout, dey wouldn' bother
you.''

Uncle Wes dived in and swam off with long
bold strokes. Blue cried out with horror when he
disappeared and a circle of waves closed over the
spot where he went down. He came up a short

distance away, snorted spurts of water from his
nostrils, then laughed and rolled over and over.

It was a relief to see him swimming toward the
bank, then to have him safe on solid ground. Blue
looked at his long lean legs and arms, the broad
shoulders and back where sinews and muscles
bulged into knots. A man like that could not
know how it felt to be small and weak.

"You sho dressed in a haste. I'm glad you's a
quick-motioned boy. Man Jay is powerful slow.
E always keeps me a-waitin," Uncle Wes praised
and Blue's bare feet made happy pads on the path
as he trotted home through the dusk and in spite
of the terrors that pestered him he went with
Uncle Wes every Saturday afternoon and jumped
into the river. At last he could swim as far and
dive as deep as Cricket.

He learned too to bridle and ride Hattie, the
buckingest mule in the barnyard, although every
time he went near the beast's head he feared she
would paw him to death. He learned to fight fairly
well, even when he knew he would be licked. He
could face with some show of steadiness the teasing and jibing of children in the Quarters. He
did most of these things because he craved Uncle
Wes's approval, not because he had gained any
faith in his own strength and bravery. Cun Fred
was a fine man and kind, but Uncle Wes was a
grand somebody, a man to pattern after. No
wonder Cricket loved him, prized him above everybody else.

Life was happy enough until Aun Fan said Blue must start to school. He pleaded not to go but she shamed him for wishing to grow up in ignorance. The foreman's grandboy was due to set a pattern for other children.

Some day the plantation would need a new foreman. Would Blue be willing for Man Jay to be foreman and he taking Man Jay's orders? If he failed to outdo Man Jay she would hang her head in shame.

"Cricket don' go to school," Blue argued.

"You ain' no bright skin, Blue. Thank God, you is black as de back of de chimney."

Aun Fan never lost a chance to down-talk Cricket, who was a queer little girl. Full of life, full of fun, grown up in some ways, a pure baby in others. Blue never could quite make her out. She-She, her old dog, was her only playmate except Man Jay, for Aun Missie would not let her play with Quarters children. She and Man Jay were curiously alike for all their difference in color and size. Both could climb like squirrels and swim like fish. Both loved to make music on Man Jay's mouth-organ and, lord, how they could dance! They were quick to get vexed but neither held their mad long. They had the same soft black eyes, bubbling laugh, and they understood each other in a way that made Blue feel left out. Man Jay taught Cricket how to walk on her hands and turn a backward somersault. Blue tried and tried to outdo her, but she was like a cat on her feet.

Her play-house was under a big oak by the
spring back of Aun Missie's house. A myrtle
thicket made one wall, cedars and hollies made another. Her tiny flower yard was lined with green
ground moss, edged with pebbles. Wild blossom
stems stuck in the moss made flower-beds, sweet
myrtle sprigs made hedges. These faded every
day but blue flags and violets grew along the
stream and the woods were full of wild blossoms.

Big oak roots marked off the rooms and Man
Jay had whittled some funny toys to live in them.
A dog, a pig, a deer and a cow. Cricket prized
these foolish things even more than the white-
faced doll Santy Claus brought her Christmas, although the doll had hair like people.

Blue was jealous of Man Jay. He tried to think
of something to make Cricket. His knife was
sharp but his hands had no magic. One day Cun
Fred helped him make a bird trap and Blue
hurried to set it near the play-house. It never
caught anything but it gave him an excuse to sit on
the tree roots with Man Jay and Cricket and listen
to their talk after school.

Man Jay talked mostly of what he would do
when he grew up. How he would go away to a far
country and get vast-rich. Then he would send
for Cricket to come live with him and be a grand
lady. Blue tried to boast how he'd act when he
was foreman but he never could think up exciting
things like Man Jay.

Cricket craved to go to school, even though Blue

told her school was no fun and Man Jay said Aun Missie was right to keep her at home.

She always listened with interest when Blue told about his mother, his little sister, his brothers, the white-trash boy who lived near his home, but Man Jay's primer was Cricket's chief joy. Man Jay had read his lessons for her until she knew every one by heart. She never wearied of the first lesson about Baby Ray. She would gaze at the picture with shining eyes, and repeat, "Baby Ray loves Mama; Mama loves Baby Ray." Her Christmas doll's name was Sophy. She changed it to Sophy Ray. She said when she grew up she would have a baby like Baby Ray.

"Baby Ray's mama is a white lady," Blue told her, one day.

"I ain' black like you," she answered scornfully.

The schoolhouse was a broken down log cabin near Heaven's Gate Church. Its warped clapboard door swung on wooden hinges. Its sagging clapboard roof was held down by heavy logs. Two small square windows left it so dark inside, fire in the chimney had to help give light. Every rain washed holes in the chimney which had to be plastered up with mud.

The rough board benches with peg legs could not hold half the children. The first class said lessons while the second stayed outside, where nobody dared to laugh or make racket because the stylish black lady teacher had short patience. Her

hickory whip had been roasted in the fire so it
never wore out although it kept busy cutting out-
held palms, whizzing on backsides, leaving raw red
marks on legs.

The only thing that made school bearable for
Blue was that sometimes Cricket walked a piece
of the way with him in the morning or met him
when he came home. Whenever he was kept in
Cricket made sport of him, asked him why he
could not read like Man Jay. The first time he was
whipped he hated to tell her, but when she saw
his blistered palm her eyes blazed and a warm tear
fell on his wrist as she pressed her soft lips on
the hurt.

"I ain' no baby for you to kiss."

Blue wiped the kiss off on his breeches, for Man
Jay laughed. She wiped her wet cheek on Blue's
shoulder and looked straight in his eyes.

"If you ain' no baby how-come you can' learn
nothin? I ain' never been to school but I can read
better outside de book dan you can read inside
em."

It was true. Cricket could glance at any picture
in the primer and repeat its lesson without a mistake yet she did not know one letter from another.

She made him find the next day's lesson and
read it, but Man Jay corrected his mistakes with
such a superior air Blue got vexed and went home.
It was already late and Aun Fan looked cross.

That same night she told Cun Fred Blue killed
too much time between the schoolhouse and home.

"Where does you go, Blue?" Cun Fred looked very stern.

"Not nowhere."

Aun Fan sniffed.

"If you don' come straight home after dis, I'm gwine give you a lickin you won' never forget, not long as you live."

"Don' talk so rough, Fancy. Heaven's Gate is a far piece an' Blue's legs is lame from de teacher's whip."

Blue promised to do better and he meant to, but the next day Cricket met him with exciting news. Uncle Wes was putting up gourds for martin birds. Blue forgot all about his promise to Aun Fan, and went with her to see them.

Uncle Wes had trimmed a slim tree into a long pole and was nailing narrow board arms across its small end. A pile of big round gourds lay on the ground.

"Looka de nice lil doors, Blue." Cricket pointed to small square openings in the gourd sides.

"What's de doors for?"

Uncle Wes's quick laugh made him wince, but Cricket quickly explained that martin birds would nest in the gourds and fight off crows and hawks that stole Aun Missie's chickens.

"You ought not to laugh at Blue, Uncle Wes."

"You can' tell a martin bird from a swallow, you'self, Cricket." Uncle Wes's eyes twinkled.

"I can, too," Cricket answered hotly. "Dey's black and dey bills is sharp as needles. You told

me so you'self. You told me too, Man Jay ought
not to make sport of Blue.''

''Martin bills ain' sharp as you tongue, honey.''

She dropped her eyes and her soft throat gulped
like a baby's, but Uncle Wes said quickly: ''Dat's
all right, honey. Come tie on de gourds. I didn'
aim to hurt you feelins.''

Blue marveled at the strength of Uncle Wes's
lean arms and back when he lifted up the heavy
pole and put its blunt foot in a deep hole. The
gourds tied to the ends of each arm were hoisted
in the air and the pole stood firm when the hole
was packed with dirt, but the sun had rolled down
and first dark crept out from the woods. Blue
ran home and before he could speak Aun Fan shook
him until his eyes saw stars, then boxed his jaw
until his nose bled.

Next morning one eye was closed and he could
not go to school, which made him joyful until
Cricket came that afternoon to invite him to her
birthday party. She would be eight years old,
and Uncle Wes wanted all the children to come
and play games with her.

Hot cloths had melted some of the swelling but
Aun Fan told her Blue had toothache unless it was
mumps. Cricket looked very sorry.

''I wish we could put off de party until Blue's
well, but Uncle Wes bought lemons for lemonade,
an' Aun Missie made a cake for de chillen to eat.''

''Blue ain' got money to buy cake an' lemonade,
Cricket.''

"It's a free party, Aun Fan."

"Free? You must be think you is a white some-body."

The warmth and light in Cricket's eyes faded. "Aun Missie wanted to sell, but Uncle Wes don' want chillen's money."

"Missie could make a lot on a birth-night sup-per, sellin fish and rice to grown people. Andrew could beat de drum for de Christians to march an' Wes could squeeze his 'cordion for de sinners to dance." Aun Fan looked sour. "Wes ever did act like a ram sheep, buttin round, puttin on proud-ful airs. Wes can' change you from what you is, Cricket."

"Uncle Wes don' want to change me. E likes me how I is. Cun Fred does, too. I don' care bout nobody else."

Cricket's eyes held sharp points of angry light and Aun Fan's mouth clamped shut. Such bold talk pure took her breath.

CHAPTER VIII

Aun Fan had gone to catch a child for somebody and Blue had to dress by himself for the party. When his face and hands were carefully washed and his Sunday clothes on, every single button buttoned clear up to the neck of his shirt, Cun Fred laughed.

"Great God, de gals' mouths will water when dey see you, son. I bet dey will pure jump Juba." He added more seriously, "I want you to pleasure you'self to de highest, but don' forget you manners; don' forget who you is."

Blue promised to remember and hurried away.

"Don' play too rough wid de gals!" Cun Fred shouted after him.

"No, suh," Blue answered, and sped ahead.

A crowd of children were playing in the road, for the front yard was full of jonquils, butter-and-eggs, red fire-bush. If one blossom stem got broken no telling what Aun Missie would say, cross as she was about everything.

Man Jay looked like a new boy. His hair was clipped short, his face greased and shiny, his new suit well fitting. Now and then he took off his new hat, looked at it and cocked it back on one side.

"Hey, Blue? How you do?" Cricket asked, but Cooch turned and whispered something to Toosio who looked at Blue and giggled.

"Whe' did you get dat ugly cap, Blue?" Cooch asked.

Blue's heart fell; his mouth got so dry he slipped inside the house for a drink of water. He forgot his thirst and Man Jay's hat when he saw Cricket's birthday cake on the table, white with icing, topped with eight pink sugar-plums which told that Cricket was eight years old. The water bucket was brimful of lemonade. Yellow skins floated thick on the top and made his mouth leak. He hankered to dip the water gourd down among them for one little taste, but the looking-glass was watching, so he only pinched a bit of icing off the cake's far side and ran out-of-doors again.

The afternoon passed quickly; cocks crowed for sundown; the west blazed bright through the trees.

"De sun is droppin, Cricket; play fast, gal," Aun Missie called from the wood-pile where she picked up chips in her apron.

"Dat's what we's doin," Cricket answered happily from the center of a great ring made by the children holding hands around her. They had played hide the switch, taint-no-bears-out-to-night, Jump, Jim-Crow. The game was Shoo-Ducky-Shoo now and Cricket was Ducky. She was like a blossom in her little full-skirted white dress. Her hair was plaited and a streak of late sunshine beamed through the trees on her red hair ribbon. The other children kicked up their heels, strutted around, squealing, shouting boisterously as they circled in the ring around her.

"Is Aunt Katy dead?" their voices chimed.

"Yes, ma'am!" Cricket sang happily.

"Is you been to de buryin?"

"Yes, ma'am!"

"Did you get some cake?"

"Yes, ma'am!"

"Did you get some coffee?"

"Yes, ma'am!"

The joyful questions came faster and faster, feet in the ring pranced and stamped the gay measure of the song, then everybody scampered away with the merry shout, "Den, Shoo, Ducky, Shoo."

Cricket had to catch somebody to be Ducky in her place, and old She-She ran with her barking excitedly, as she made a quick dash for Cooch who sped out of reach crying:

"You can' catch me!"

"Me, neither." Fat Toosio shook with a giggle.

Cricket's eager hands reached out wildly for one child after another, but everybody dodged and outran her.

She did her utmost best, but Blue saw she could catch nobody. She looked so helpless he could not bear it so he hopped behind the garden fence, gave a low whistle to make her look, and waited until she had her hand on his arm. Cooch peeped around the fence corner and he dropped on his knees, groaning like he sprained his foot.

Cooch came toward him crying angrily, "Dat ain' fair, Blue, you just let Cricket catch you."

"You is crazy, Cooch. A root caught my toe and likened to pulled em off." Blue limped painfully to prove it.

"You can' fool me. You know good and well you is lyin." Cooch's voice was husky with vexation.

The other children flocked to see what had happened.

"How could Blue help it if a root tripped em, Cooch?" Toosio asked.

"I ain' gwine play," Cooch declared.

"If you don' want to play, den quit playin, nobody cares," Man Jay scolded.

"You ain' my Daddy, neither my Mammy. You can' rule me," Cooch snapped so fiercely that Man Jay pushed back his new hat and scratched helplessly in the wool on his head.

"Aw, let's play something else," Toosio suggested. "My wind is done short from so much runnin."

"Man Jay, play us a tune, so we could sing," Cricket said.

"Play *Sallie Ann,* Man Jay. I too love dat song." Toosio slapped her fat sides and hummed the tune as Man Jay reached into his limp breeches pocket, pulled out his mouth-organ and shook it to rid its holes of dust and trash. He breathed out the chords, and Toosio led the children in the lusty song.

> "Sallie Ann, oh, Sallie Ann—
> I'm dreamin bout my Sallie Ann."

Even Old She-She yelped and tried to sing. Cooch took Blue by the hand and whispered:

"Let's me and you dance em, Blue?"

Blue got suddenly shy. "I can' dance, Cooch."

"Aw, come on." She tried to pull Blue forward to face her, but his feet felt paralyzed and would not move. Cooch stuck out her pointed red tongue and turned her back on him.

"Can't you dance, Blue?" Cricket asked.

"I never tried to dance wid no gal."

"Oh, it's easy. You just do like dis."

Her little feet marked the time slowly at first, bare yellow heel, bare yellow toe, forward, backward, faster and faster until her short white skirt spun round and round. Her rigid arms pointed this way and that, her slight body writhed, twisted. Man Jay's breath had to labor to keep his music abreast of her steps for she could dance far better than she could run. Light and swift she whirled gaily toward Blue, then away. The ribbon on her hair began bobbing up and down, up and down, and when her full skirt flared up with a last quick leap, the children squealed out with pleasure. Old She-She sat on her haunches, patting the ground with her long stringy tail, her dim eyes watching every step Cricket took.

"Lord, Cricket, you's one dancin gal in dis world." Man Jay was well-nigh out of breath but the children shouted: "Dance em again, Cricket! Dance em again!"

Cooch laughed an ugly scornful laugh.

"What you mean by dat, Cooch?" Man Jay growled.

"I'll show you how Cricket dances." She swaggered forward and made such funny mocking steps the children screamed with laughter. Man Jay jerked her by the arm.

"Stop dat, Cooch," he said hoarsely.

Cooch shrugged her thin shoulders and sucked her teeth.

"If I danced like Cricket I wouldn' have de face to be showin off."

"I wasn' showin off," Cricket faltered.

"You danced nice," Blue said.

"What you know bout dancin, Blue?" Cooch snapped. "You better go wash you rusty knees." With a quick turn about she slapped her narrow hands sharply together. "Let me see Cricket do dis." With a toss of her head she stuck out her thin hips, wriggled her body and sang,

"Oh, de hog-eye gal am de hell of a gal,
Now what de debbil ail em?
E drinked a pint o' buttermilk
Den say his belly hot em."

"Aun Jule told you not to sing that song," Man Jay bawled.

Cooch's loose heels and toes patted up dust from the ground.

"Roly, boly, sholy, hog-eye—
Roly boly, sholy, hog-e-y-e!"

She danced up in front of Man Jay and with a touch of the devil shining in her eyes, she changed her song.

"Cricket's Mammy ain' nuttin
His Daddy ain nuttin
An' nuttin from nuttin leave nuttin."

Man Jay bared his teeth and made a quick reach for her, but she slipped from under his hand and landed right on She-She's tail. She-She yelped with pain and ran to Cricket who took the hurt tail between her hands and rubbed it gently, while she crooned comforting words as if She-She were a child.

"She-She is Cricket's sister. All two is yellow just alike," Cooch jeered.

Cricket's eyes blazed.

"I don' care what you say bout me, Cooch, but I got a good mind to kill you for mashin She-She's tail."

The hair on She-She's back bristled, and a long snarl showed her worn-out fangs.

"You think I'm scared of you mangy old dog?" Cooch's thin hands became threatening claws.

"If I'd turn She-She loose e would tear de frock off you back." Cricket's brows made a black knot, and her teeth shone sharp between quivering lips. Blue had a frightened, sinking feeling. He had seen Cooch fight and she made it an ugly business. If she put her hands on Cricket he would beat her even if she killed him.

Aun Missie called pleasantly from the doorway, "Yunnuh chillen come get you cake an' lemonade."

"I got a good mind to tell Aun Missie you said Cricket's Mammy ain' nuttin," Man Jay threatened.

"Aun Missie ain' Cricket's Mammy," Cooch sneered.

"E is," Cricket declared angrily.

Aun Missie called again. The children must come and eat for it was getting late.

All the fun had died and a strange uneasiness took its place.

"What de matter ail you, Cricket? Whyn' you come on?" Aun Missie called sharply.

Cricket led the children slowly up the steps, into the house. Everybody was silent, troubled.

The day's light had grown thinner. First dark was creeping up out of the earth, hovering in sheltered places. Smoke streamed out of the chimney, settled in a blue cloud over the roof, among the treetops. Frogs croaked out sad evening songs, little birds chirped down-hearted words.

Aun Missie gave Cricket the first slice of cake, but instead of eating, Cricket broke it, and let crumbs fall over the floor. One taste of sweet lemonade made her shiver as if a rabbit ran over her grave.

"What de matter ail you, Cricket? Why don' you eat you cake an' drink you lemonade?" Aun Missie asked anxiously.

Cricket dropped her eyes.

"Cooch hurt his feelins," Man Jay explained.

"Who? Me?" Cooch asked, innocent as a lamb.

A cold silence fell over the room, for two deep lines came between Aun Missie's brows.

"I hope you ain' acted ugly, Cricket. How-come you hangin you head?"

Cooch answered in a cool sweet voice, "Cricket got vexed because I laughed when Blue couldn' dance."

"Whe's you manners, Cricket? Would you make Cooch feel bad at you party?"

"Cooch said you wasn' my Mammy," Cricket answered in a low voice.

"What?" Aun Missie's thin lips quivered, her deep-set eyes glittered. "How-come you said dat, Cooch?"

"Ma told me so." Cooch gave a pert grin.

"Well, Jule is a no-manners woman. An' you is a no-manners gal. After dis, you keep way from my house."

"Yes'm," Cooch answered, but her voice was not a bit humble.

She-She moved back and forth among the children, whining for bites of cake. Blue tossed her a piece and she snapped it up before it touched the floor.

"Stop messin up de floor an' wastin good cake on She-She, Blue."

Aun Missie looked vexed to the heart. Blue cast

his eyes down abashed. The cake was so good, except that She-She was Cricket's dog he never would have given her a bite.

"You chillen is a no-manners lot to quarrel here at Cricket's party. Not a soul fetched a birthday present, not even a bunch of blossoms."

"We got plenty of blossoms in de yard," Cricket said quietly.

"Don' back-talk me, Cricket. I know what I'm sayin."

The air in the room felt tight. Blue's legs felt so strengthless he leaned against the chimney-side, but Cooch stuffed her mouth with cake and drank lemonade so fast it spilled on her Sunday clothes.

She finished eating first of all, and wiped her mouth on her sleeve.

"I got to go now, Aun Missie," she said politely, and sidled toward the door.

Toosio followed her, giggling. "I got to go too."

Aun Missie said it was time for everybody to go. She began gathering up empty lemonade cups, and putting them in a big dish-pan. She hardly answered when the children told her good-by. When all were gone but Man Jay and Blue, Cricket stood shivering by the fire whose flames were weak and pale. Blue picked up a piece of wood, but before he could lay it on, Aun Missie grabbed it out of his hand.

"What you doin, Blue? It's too hot to build up de fire. You better go home before dark catches you."

"Good night, Cricket," Blue said gently. He could think of no other words.

"Good night, Blue," Cricket answered in a small far-off voice.

Aun Missie's eyes were full of impatience at his tarrying.

"You sho is one slow-motion boy in dis world, Blue. You won' never get nowhere if you can' move no faster'n dat." Her restless hands gathered up the broom and swept at crumbs which were scattered about.

"I'm gwine right now, ma'am," Blue said quickly, and without another word hurried through the door.

CHAPTER IX

WHEN Blue woke the next morning Cun Fred was gone and Aun Fan not yet come. He dressed quickly, fixed a cup of molasses sweetened water to wash down his bread and sat on the steps to eat. Yellow sunshine filled out-of-doors, making the day shiny and beautiful. Sallie, the game pullet Big Pa gave him for seed, was with the other fowls, scratching among leaves, hunting bugs and worms. When she lifted her beak and sang happily two cocks strutted quickly toward her, then halted to cast such jealous-hearted looks at each other Blue could not help laughing.

Big Pa had promised Sallie to Cricket, but Aun Fan made sweetened bread with the game eggs he gave Blue, and Cricket said Blue must have Sallie in their place. Sallie was the prettiest hen on the yard. Her eyes were yellow beads, her comb a red blossom. She was so happy she had to sing. Poor little Cricket was down-in-the-heart. Maybe—maybe if he took her Sallie, that would cheer her up. The day was too fine to waste inside the ugly old schoolhouse. He would take Sallie to Cricket now.

"Chick-chick-chick," he called and dropped a few crumbs on the ground.

Soon Sallie was under his arm and he was on the way to Aun Missie's house.

"How-come you ain' gone to school, Blue?"

83

Aun Missie was tying up a pile of dirty quilts to be washed.

"I come to fetch Cricket a birthday present."

Aun Missie felt Sallie's breast bone to see how fat she was, fingered her hip-bones to see how soon she would lay, and smiled.

"Cricket ain' wake, Blue. His party didn' agree wid em. Hags rode em so bad in de night I had to lay Wes's gun across de head of de bed. Go put de pullet in a coop."

When Blue came back Aun Missie was shaking Cricket, calling her a lazy no-'count gal.

When Cricket gave a sleepy yawn and reached her arms out from under the covers in a long weary stretch, Aun Missie's patience shortened.

"Sleep on, den, Blue can take his present back home."

Cricket sat up and rubbed her sleepy eyes.

"Whe' is Blue?"

"Here's me."

"You brought me a present?" Cricket smiled, and hopped out of bed.

Fringed newspapers on the mantel-shelf fluttered briskly, the black kettle spouted steam and clattered its lid as Aun Missie scolded, "You's too big to go widout clothes before Blue," and made Cricket go into the shed-room.

She dressed in a hurry and came dancing back. "Whe's my present, Blue?" she cried.

"You can' see em until you eat breakfast."

Aun Missie got a pan, dished some hominy out

of a pot and poured a cup of milk over it. Cricket took it and made haste to swallow it down.

Aun Missie looked at her and grunted. "I declare to God, Cricket, you head looks like a mare's nest an' I combed it no longer'n yesterday. Get de comb, let me untangle some o' dem knots before you eat."

With the first jerk of the comb's broken teeth through her hair tears leaped into Cricket's eyes, but she said nothing while Aun Missie fought and abused the tangles.

"Get one o' my head-rags, Cricket. Let me tie up you head. I can' be combin' hair every day."

"Please tie em wid my ribbon, Aun Missie."

"Don' be a fool. Dat ribbon's for Sunday." She knotted the head-kerchief over the hair.

"Get de soap an' lather you face an' hands good. I can' stand a dirty skin."

"My skin ain' dirty, Aun Missie."

"Drinkin goat milk is what makes you so hate water. Pour dat out an' put meat grease on you hominy."

"I don' hate water, but de lye soap burns my eyes an' stings my skin."

"Better to sting dan be filthy. You is bad as Big Pa bout washin."

"Big Pa ain' filthy," Cricket answered slowly for her lips quivered.

"Hush you mouth an' eat you breakfast. Man Jay an' Big Pa all two goes pure filthy when Bina ain' home to make em wash."

Cricket sat in her little chair looking at the pan of hominy and meat grease on her lap.

"I ain' hongry, Aun Missie."

"Eat anyhow. A full belly makes strong arms an' a willin heart. You'll need all two to-day."

Cricket swallowed all but a white pat of hominy she hid under her spoon. Aun Missie's keen eyes saw it.

"Eat every speck of dat victuals, Cricket. You got to do a big work before sundown."

Cricket gulped down the last white morsel, washed the pan and put it in the cupboard.

"Now, can I see my present?" she asked, and Aun Missie nodded yes. She hurried with Blue to the coop, and joy filled her eyes as she stroked Sallie's feathers.

Aun Missie's old cock strutted up to look and the guineas potracked excitedly.

"What'll Big Pa say bout you givin Sallie to me?" she whispered.

"Big Pa'll be glad. E loves you more'n me, Cricket."

Aun Missie walked up with the bundle of quilts on her head and a coat of Uncle Wes's in her hand.

"Don' make me wear dat coat, Aun Missie. I ain' cold," Cricket begged.

Aun Missie said the morning was airish; if she heard another word Cricket would have to put on Uncle Wes's breeches too. Cricket frowned and held out a slim leg.

"It ain' long enough to hold up breeches."

"A few more years an' it'll be long as my own."
Aun Missie sighed as if long legs were sorrow and
rolled up the long sleeves so Cricket's hands were
free.

"Shut de back door an' latch em, Cricket. Get
de ax off de wood-pile an' fetch em," Aun Missie
said.

It took all Cricket's strength to drag the heavy
door shut, all her height to reach the padlock; her
arms could hardly lift the ax from the wood-pile,
but Aun Missie would not let Blue help. She said
Cricket must learn to work.

"Let me go wid you, Aun Missie. I'll help to
fetch water an' cut wood," Blue offered.

"You better go to school," Cricket said. "Man
Jay's way ahead of you. E is readin bout Rover
de dog."

"A lot o' good it does him," Aun Missie
snapped. "I don' know B from bull-foot, but I
got more sense dan dat teacher."

CHAPTER X

THE road was full of recent tracks for mules, wagons, people had been over it this morning.

The long heavy coat hindered Cricket's walking, but Aun Missie stepped briskly past cows and goats tied to graze on green ditch banks, but she paused to look at a heavy black sow, gathering honeysuckle vines by great mouthfuls and making a bed in the shallow ditch.

"Jule's sow is gettin ready to birth his family. From his looks it'll be a big-sized family, too. My Jane didn' had but five pigs an' I was countin on ten."

She heaved a sigh and said it was funny how luck followed a common field-hand like Jule. All those Quarters people were common. They quarreled over pigs and chickens, stole from one another, scandalized everybody. Rain or shine they had to do whatever Cun Fred said from raking pine straw for the stables to scattering stable manure in the fields.

"You rake straw, Aun Missie," Cricket answered thoughtfully.

"But I get paid for it, Cricket."

"You scatters manure too."

"I just does dat to break up my head colds. Scatterin manure is de best medicine ever was."

"Does Cun Jule know e is common?"

Aun Missie chuckled. "One funny thing bout

88

people is they never know the truth bout themselves.''

''Is Big Pa common?''

''I wouldn' say e is common, Cricket, but his
people is heathens what don' wear no clothes.''

Between gullies on the broken hillside behind the
Quarters, bluebonnets made a soft cloud above
crimson sour-grass heads. Yellow butterflies
danced over the path which picked its way carefully around gullies and thickets of crab-apple.
When a rabbit scampered across it Aun Missie
halted with a groan, but Cricket said cheerfully,
''De rabbit ran leftward, Aun Missie. Dat's a sign
of good luck.''

''Good luck, nothin! Turn you cap hind part
befo, Blue. Maybe dat'll shed de rabbit's evil.''

''Mind, Cricket,'' she warned presently. ''Don'
step on dat pizen oak. You skin is awful tender.''

Wisps of blue smoke curled up through the trees
and marked the clearing above the spring. The
path dropped swiftly into shadows, became soft
and brown with pine-needles, then darted into
clear sunshine.

''Good mornin, gals,'' Aun Missie called cheerily
from under the great bundle of quilts on her head.

''Good mornin,'' a chorus of answers came.

Cun Jule's narrow black snake eyes peeped sidewise as she bent and rose over her washboard with
short quick jerks, but her fat lips pursed up tight
and dumb.

Long-handled gourds dipped up water from the

spring to fill buckets; big black iron wash pots squatted over fires, breathing up steam. Soapsuds foamed up over black arms, cutting sweat, melting dirt out of garments.

Aun Bina laid a pair of ragged breeches stained with dirt on a block and frailed it with a hickory stick.

"You'll break all dem buttons off, Bina," Cun Jule warned.

"Big Pa don' button his breeches nohow," Aun Bina laughed, but Cun Jule stayed glum.

"How-come you is so lated, Missie?" Bina asked. Aun Missie pulled a long face.

"I ain' hardly slept none, hags rode Cricket so bad."

"All de unrestless dead people walks when de moon is young," Aun Bina said pleasantly, but old Cun Hester shook her head.

"Hags ain' dead people, Missie. Dey is livin' people what wishes you harm. Next time one rides Cricket, make em open his eyes quick. E will see who it is. If e calls de right name, dat somebody will dry up an' dead. I know by I done it two or three times."

Cricket's eyes looked troubled.

"I was dreamin bout Uncle Wes. I thought e was hurted——"

"Shut you mouth, Cricket. Does you want to kill Wes?" Aun Missie cried.

Cricket clapped her mouth shut and walked slowly away to the spring with her empty bucket.

"Cricket ever talks too fast," Aun Missie growled as she borrowed a piece of fire and a fat light-wood splinter from Cun Hester to start a blaze under her wash pot. The blaze flickered, faded, did not thrive.

"Try a piece of my fire, Missie. It's stronger'n Cun Hester's," Aun Bina suggested.

"Cun Hester's fire is good enough for me, Bina."

Aun Bina shot her a hard look, but Aun Missie's eyes were on Cricket who had halted beside a mass of yellow jessamine.

"For God's sake, Cricket," she bawled impatiently, "you know jessamine is pizen. Smellin em will give you de worst headache ever was."

Cricket quickly filled her bucket and walked bravely along with it balanced on her head.

"Cricket sho walks proudful in dat old worn-out coat," Aun Bina laughed.

"Cricket would strut if e was stark naked," Cun Jule agreed.

Cricket dropped her eyes, but Cun Hester told her she was right to strut. People must wear clothes and not let clothes wear them. She patted her own shabby man's coat and pulled her skirt aside to show a man's worn shoes much too large for her feet. Her kind old face beamed with pride.

"Dese shoes an' dis coat belonged to my Daddy. Dey is more'n forty years old, but I ruther be warm dan stylish. I got a misery in my knee right now because I can' buy no red flannen. White

long-boys is de coldest thing in dis world even if
dey is de style."

"Stop grinnin like a chessy cat, Blue. Pour
de water in de pot," Aun Missie scolded. "Don'
you hear dat jay bird singin, 'Laziness will kill
you, kill you, kill you?' "

"I wonder what Cricket's Mammy would say if
e saw em totin water on his head for you pot,
Missie."

"Keep you mouth off Cricket's Mammy, Bina,"
Aun Missie snapped.

"I ain' sayin nothin wrongful. Everybody
knows how Cricket's Mammy was. E toted hot
water in a silver pitcher for white gentlemen to
shave in but e wouldn' tote water on his head from
de spring for nobody."

Cun Jule gave an oily laugh. "Maybe if e had
jerked a hoe in de field e might 'a' been livin to-
day instead of dead an' hoppin in Hell."

"Shut you mouth, Jule," Aun Missie cried
angrily. "You Quarters women dogged and dom-
inized Cricket's Mammy until his first breast milk
pure turned to pizen."

Cun Jule's fat body bulged with scorn. "Nobody couldn' dominize dat gal. E was big doins
up to de last breath e drawed. E didn' have no
shame."

Cun Hester put up a hand. "You gals stop dis
talk before you have hard feelins. What Cricket's
Mammy done is between him and his God."

Aun Missie glared at Cun Jule. "You birthed

a whole litter of chillen widout a piece o' husband. You ain' got no reason to down-talk Cricket's Mammy.''

Cun Jule's fat hips swelled. ''Husband or no husband de Bible tells people to stick to dey race.''

''It sho do,'' Aun Bina agreed warmly.

Aun Missie almost choked.

''Does de Bible say take another woman's husband an' keep em off from home three long years?''

''For God's sake, shut you mouth, Missie!'' Aun Bina's tied-up skirt flounced around her thin knees.

''If I wasn' a Christian I wouldn' speak to you or either let Man Jay come in my house.''

Aun Missie was vexed to the heart, but Cun Hester said gently:

''Better let all dat rest, Missie. Bina's repented an' gone back in de church. If de deacons forgive em you ought to forgive em too.''

''Oh, I done forgive em, Cun Hester; but a day don' pass over my head widout thinkin how Bina done me.''

''You better be thankful Wes is got a fine boy-child like Man Jay,'' Cun Jule grumbled.

''Thankful? Well, I ain' thankful, Man Jay ain' in de same class wid me or either Wes!''

''How bout Cricket?''

''Cricket's blood is good as any in dis world.''

''How you know so, Missie? White trash used to live in you house.'' Cun Jule gave a loud laugh, and Aun Missie all but foamed at the mouth.

"You know good an' well Cricket didn' spring from white trash. You ought to be shame' to talk such a talk, good as Cricket's Mammy was to you when Cooch was teethin an' you didn' have a God's husband to do a hand's turn."

"For Christ's sake, don' holler so loud, Missie, I ain' deef." Cun Jules's eyes flamed.

Cun Hester shook her head sorrowfully. "God ain' deef neither, Jule. E hears every word yunnah say. E will hold you to account for em too. In his sight one skin is same as another. De back o' my neck where a mustard plaster took off de skin is white as any white somebody."

Cun Hester bared the scar, but Jule declared:

"Dat don' prove a thing. A bright skin ain' got no place in dis world. Black people don' want em an' white people won' own em. Dey ain' nothin but no-nation bastards."

Cricket stood rooted to the ground. Water spilled from the full bucket on her head all over her shoulders as her trembling fingers twisted the thin white cord around her neck.

"Take you hand off you charm-string, honey. You'll be ruint if it brokes, but long as it's solid nobody can' harm you," Cun Hester warned kindly.

"Jule is jealous-hearted. Jule knows Cooch ain' fittin to sociate wid Cricket," Aun Missie declared as she took off Cricket's wet coat. "All dis talk ain' decent for chillen to hear. Take de ax, honey, an' go cut me some solid wood. You go wid em, Blue.''

Cricket walked slowly away like somebody asleep. Her feet stumbled, a tree limb plucked at her head-rag, a briar scratched her cheek and left a red mark but she paid no attention at all.

''Don' be down-in-de-heart, Cricket,'' Blue ventured when they were out of the women's hearing.

''You'd be down-in-de-heart too if you was a bright skin,'' Cricket answered sadly.

The air was chill where no sunlight fell through the shadows. Blue knew these woods were pure full of spirits.

''Come on, let's run, Cricket,'' he urged, but she lagged along like somebody paralyzed.

A bee-bird kept swooping and pecking at something on the ground. Blue loaded his sling-shot with a little stone rock, took careful aim, and the bird dropped right beside a coiled snake whose eyes were picked out.

He picked up the limp bunch of gray feathers as death sent a quiver through them. The white tail feathers fluttered, the small eyes dimmed and closed.

''Poor lil bird. E was fightin de snake off his nest——'' A sob cut Cricket's breath.

Blue told her the bee-bird was wicked, and spread the tiny feathers of the red-tipped top-knot to show her how this bird made its head like a blossom to fool bees so it could catch them. Like as not its craw was full of bees now.

"Life was sweet to em, Blue——" She could
hardly talk for crying.

"Please don' grieve so hard, Cricket. I'll bury
de bird in a nice lil grave."

He dug a grave and lined it with leaves, laid
the bird in, covered it up.

When he finished Cricket was quiet except for
the shadow of a sob that shook her now and then.

"I can kill plenty o' birds if you want a lil
graveyard by you play-house," he suggested.

Her face started to break up again.

"Please, Cricket. If you won' cry no more, I
promise I won' kill another bird long as I live."

"You swear to God?"

Blue hated to swear it but he could not endure
her tears. "I swear to God," he repeated, and
she wiped her eyes.

"We better go cut de wood for Aun Missie,"
she sniffed.

The hillside was covered with blown down trees.
Great roots wrenched out of the ground clutched
the earth with dead twisted fingers. Blue's ax
chops filled the woods with queer echoes. A dry
rustle sounded, leaves quivered sharply when
Cricket took off her head-rag and began tying the
cut sticks into a bundle. Blue thought of Cricket's
mother. Suppose her spirit came walking out.

"Let me tote de wood, Cricket," he quavered.

"No, Blue. I want dem ladies to see I ain'
lazy."

He took off his coat and tied his sticks together with the sleeves. They stayed in balance on his head without trouble, but Cricket's head-rag was too weak to hold her load of sticks tight together. When she stumbled or stepped on thorny vines, they tried to leap to the ground. When she crossed the foot log over the branch, they wabbled so she almost fell in.

"Leave de wood, Cricket. I'll come back and get em," Blue pleaded. She did not crack her teeth but walked straight on.

The clothes-lines were strung with clean garments. Legs and arms of white long-boys filled with wind, kicked and grabbed at puffed-out nightgowns. Cricket's bundle of sticks got contrary, gave a sudden tilt.

"Take you time, Cricket. Don' drop em now. De ladies is lookin," Blue whispered.

"Well, I declare," Cun Hester called. "Cricket sho is a smart gal to tote all dat wood."

"Walk slow, Cricket, don' let you foot stumble," Blue warned.

Her wood did its best to fall, but Cricket ruled it until she dropped it beside Aun Missie's wash pot.

The fire leaped out and seized it with a glad bright blaze; the rich tar fired and smoke made a black cloud over Cricket's head.

"Look how dat smoke seeks Cricket," Cun Hester cried. "When smoke seeks people dey'll be rich. It's a sign what don' hardly fail."

"De smoke can' help seekin Cricket when de wind it blows em so," Cun Jule objected.

"De wind an' smoke all two knows Cricket'll be rich some of dese days," Cun Hester declared with a knowing nod of her head.

Cun Jule sucked her teeth. "Cricket's white kin wouldn' spit on em, much less give em money."

Cun Hester smiled. "I ain' talkin bout no white somebody, Jule. Old Blue is Cricket's Grandaddy, an' e's got plenty o' money. I been to town to hear em preach, an' I told em not to turn his back on Cricket, no matter what de gal's Mammy done."

"What e said to dat, Cun Hester?"

"E ain' said much. Old Blue's heart is hard. But God will soften em. You'll see. God promised long time ago to be a Father to de fatherless."

"Cricket ain' fatherless."

"Cricket is worse off dan a fatherless, Jule. Heap worse."

CHAPTER XI

AT SUNDOWN when Blue helped fetch the clean clothes home, Uncle Wes sat on the front steps with a full pan of victuals on his lap. His lean long face was sweaty, his clothes were covered with mud, but he smiled and called, "How you chillen do?"

"Like a lamp a-jumpin," Blue answered, but Cricket said sadly:

"I feel betwixt de sap and de bark."

Uncle Wes reached out a hand and drew her up to him.

"You been workin too hard, honey. You got black rings all round you eyes."

Aun Missie swallowed hard. "Weary as I is from washin you filthy clothes, you don' crack you teeth to me."

"Yes, I does, Missie, but I wish you'd cook me decent victuals. Whyn' you put some hog jowl in de greens? A workin man needs meat-kind."

"I don' waste my good hog jowl on no man what spends his money buyin Bina gold ear-bobs." Aun Missie's words fell hard and stiff from tight lips.

"Ear-bobs? What I know bout ear-bobs?" Uncle Wes dropped his pan with a clatter. "Let me tell you dis, Missie——"

"Please don' fuss, Uncle Wes." Cricket reached up and patted his bristly cheek.

"I don' aim to fuss, honey, but Missie excuses
me wrong. Missie knows I can' swallow dry
greens. I ain' used to field-hand victuals. I don'
like dat head-rag on you head neither." He jerked
the head-rag off Cricket's head and threw it aside.
"Cricket's eyes look mighty hollow, Missie. His
lil hands ain' made to wash clothes. His lil slim
back would be easy to strain."

"For God's sake quit babyin Cricket, Wes.
You ought to thank God I'm learnin em to work."

"Cricket don' need to work not long as I live."
His big hand stroked Cricket's hair gently.

"You is mighty quick to sweet-talk Cricket now,
but I can remember when you didn' want em in
you house. E was a po' lil new-born baby too."

Uncle Wes stirred uncomfortably.

"I'd take de shirt off my back for Cricket any
day in de year, Missie."

"E would too," Cricket spoke up. "An' I'd
take my-own off for him."

Aun Missie gave her a dark look, then leaned
to whisper something in Uncle Wes's ear. He
jerked himself up with his big mouth agape as if
he did not grasp her meaning.

"When?" he asked.

"To-day at de spring."

His strength melted all of a sudden.

His big shoulders drooped, his elbows sought
his unsteady knees.

Aun Missie lighted her pipe, sucked in mouthfuls of smoke and let them trickle slowly through

her thin lips. "De truth will out," she said dryly.

Uncle Wes raised his head and spat furiously in a bed of blossoms near the steps.

"I'd like to kill Jule," he said bitterly.

"I don' want to be no bright skin, Uncle Wes." Cricket laid her head down on his knee and sobbed until her whole body shook.

"Honey," Uncle Wes cleared his throat. "Honey, you listen to me. I ain' never lied to you yet. I wouldn' lie to you now. I wish you was black same as de rest of we, but I'd love you if you skin was white as cotton stead of yellow an' pretty like it is. Jule ain' half as nice as you. You Mammy was my sister, an' I know. I'm talkin what God loves: de truth, de naked truth."

"My Mammy is hoppin in Hell, Uncle Wes."

He drew her up close to his breast.

"No, honey. God wouldn' have de heart to put you Mammy in Hell. God ain' mean as dem church-members says. I wouldn' have surprise if you Mammy is an angel in Heaven lookin down on you right now."

Little birds in the apple tree twittered and scattered pink petals over the ground, as Cricket's wet eyes lifted to the soft blue sky which had come so low its pale light lay over the world.

"You reckon people up in Heaven can see we?" she asked with a catch in her voice.

"Sho dey can," Uncle Wes answered promptly. "Heaven ain' so awful high up. I bet you Mammy is wearin white wings an' silver slippers, a-walkin

on gold streets an' playin a gold harp. E could
squeeze a 'cordion grand.''

"Whe' is Hell, Uncle Wes?''

"I don' know nothin bout Hell.''

"You will know. If you don' stop gamblin and
runnin round at night, you will go straight to Hell
as a martin to his gourd.'' A puff of smoke fled
from Aun Missie's mouth.

"I'd as soon be in Hell as home, Missie, de way
you quarrel an' fuss.''

"I wish Uncle Wes an' me could go off to some
far country,'' Cricket said between quivering lips.

Aun Missie's mouth flew wide open. "Great
God, you talk like dat after I took such pains wid
you, Cricket?''

Uncle Wes sat dumb before her flood of angry
words until she said, "I'm gwine wash Cricket's
mouth out wid lye soap. Dat'll learn em to treat
me mannersable.'' Then he caught her skirt, and
roared:

"No, you won't neither. You won' touch
Cricket's mouth.''

"Stop bawlin at me like a bull cow, Wes. If I
did my duty I'd tie Cricket up in a sack an' cut de
blood out his hide. Dat's how my Mammy done
me.'' Aun Missie's voice rose high and shrill.
"Dat's how-come I'm a church-member an' a child
o' God to-day.''

"I don' care if you got wings sproutin, you won'
wash Cricket's mouth wid soap neither lick em.''

Uncle Wes strightened up and gave a queer hard

laugh. "You is a case in dis world, Missie. I come home feelin good. I had aimed to squeeze my 'cordion an' sing a new song what de singin machine played at de store last night."

"Don' say singin machine, Wes," Aun Missie corrected. "Victoria is his name. You is bad as dat store man what calls swimps shrimps."

Uncle Wes seemed not to hear Aun Missie. He smiled at Cricket and said, "If dis crop turns out good, I'll buy you a singin machine to make music when I ain' here home."

"You better buy em a sewin machine. A Victoria don' play nothin but sinful reel tunes."

Uncle Wes was outdone. Strong and able as he was, Aun Missie could rule him with her tongue. He got to his feet and gave such a long stretch, his bony head almost touched the ceiling, his lean arms went almost from wall to wall.

"Whe' you gwine?" Aun Missie asked when he put on his hat.

"I'm gwine whe' I'm gwine, dat's whe' I'm gwine," he growled.

Cricket held to his hand as he walked down the path; then stood at the road watching while he strode toward the Quarters. Once he looked back and called something but the evening breeze scattered his words.

"I declare to God," Aun Missie croaked, "I hate to cunjure my lawful gentleman, but I'm gwine to get a charm from Big Pa to keep Wes home."

CHAPTER XII

THE Sunday dinner was eaten and Cun Fred flung himself across the bed for a nap while Blue helped Aun Fan wash the pots and pans. No sooner had Cun Fred begun to snore than a rooster came to the door, flapped his wings three times and crowed.

"Wake up, Al-fred. Somebody's comin," Aun Fan called him.

His snores halted a few breaths and started again.

"Sweep de floor, Blue. Get dem crumbs out de door before company comes."

The dish-rag fell from Blue's hand with a sudden greasy splatter and Aun Fan gave it a dark frown. "Dat ain' no good sign, Blue. Somebody's comin heavy-hearted."

"Dis wart on my finger made me drop de dish-rag," Blue explained, but Aun Fan insisted that the dish-rag foretold sorrowful company.

Before Blue could scour the grease off the floor, Uncle Wes and Cricket were in sight.

"For God's sake, get up, Al-fred. Wes mustn' catch you on de bed wid shoes on." Aun Fan hurried to put on a clean apron.

Cun Fred groaned and stretched, yawned and got up to meet the company.

Cricket had on her white Sunday dress and her hair was tied back with a shiny red ribbon. Uncle

Wes was all dressed up in a new blue suit. His
new tan shoes squeaked cheerfully, a shiny stick
pin glittered in his red cravat, but his big shoulders
sagged and his eyes had a sparkle Blue had never
seen before. Blue thought of Aun Missie's threat
and wondered if Uncle Wes was conjured.

"You look like de cards run against you, Wes,"
Aun Fan greeted him.

"Not me, Aun Fan. My name was ever high,
low, jack an' de game. Cards ain' de thing what
troubles me." Heavy lines lay around his mouth
and his voice was dull, his words husky.

"What de matter ail you, Wes? I ain' never
seen you look so down-in-de-heart."

"I is all whipped down, Al-fred. I feel weak as
a drop o' water."

"Whyn' you take sulphur and molasses?"

"Dat's too slow for me. I bought a set of
medicine from a travelin gentleman. De strongest
bottle is for mens, de next is for ladies, de weakest
for chillen. I drank all de men's bottle dis mornin,
but it ain' done me no good."

"Maybe you is cunjured."

Uncle Wes's startled eyes jumped from Aun
Fan to Cun Fred who said quickly:

"Shut you mouth, Fancy. It's dis spring
weather makes Wes feel so logy. I'm logy myself."

Uncle Wes slumped low in his chair and heaved
a sigh deep as a groan. "Sometimes I feel like
I may as well be dead. Livin don' pleasure me no

more. I got plenty insurance in de Bury League
to take care of dem I leave behind."

"You work too hard, Wes. You don' sleep
enough."

"Work don' hurt nobody when dey mind is
peaceful. It's worryation got me all flatten
down."

"You ain' got cause for worryation, Wes.
You ought to jump up and crack you heels wid
joy every day God sends."

"I ain' come here to talk about me, Al-fred. I
come to talk bout Cricket gwine to school. Cricket
ought to be educate' even if de chillen at school
ain' in his class."

Cun Fred nodded and Uncle Wes went on:

"Cricket might learn how to be a teacher.
Book-readin comes natural to em. E can read Man
Jay's primer good as Man Jay."

"Dat sounds like sensible talk to me, Wes,"
Cun Fred answered. "But Big Pa will be powerful upset. E thinks book-readin was what ruint
de onliest boy-child e had."

Cricket's eyes flashed Cun Fred a bright smile,
but Aun Fan shook her head and said:

"When de dish-rag fell out Blue's hand, I
knew somebody was comin troub-led."

"Dis wart on my finger make me drop things
all de time," Blue excused himself.

"Cun Hester's got wart beans," Cricket suggested. "Let's go get one, Blue."

"De moon is young, Cricket. Spirits'll be

walkin round dat Big House befo sundown. Dey
is white spirits."

"Stop scarin de gal, Fancy."

"I ain' scarin em, Al-fred. I'm talkin what God
loves, de blessed truth. Every time I go to Cun
Hester's when the moon is young, I spends half
my time bowin to spirits on de avenue tellin em,
'Good evenin, suh! Good evenin, ma'am.' Same
like I speaks to people."

Blue was horror-stricken but Cricket asked
hopefully:

"Did you ever see a spirit, Cun Fred?"

"No, Cricket. I can hear em but I don' ever
see em."

"Al-fred ain' got second sight like me," Aun
Fan boasted.

"I thank God I ain' got it," he answered. "I
don' crave seein dead people."

"I'm glad I see em so I can shun em. You
would walk spang into em if I didn' pull you out
de way."

"How does dem white spirits look, Aun Fan?"
Cricket's interest in the fearsome things made
blood glow in her cheeks.

"Well, Cricket, de one I sees morest is a high-
standin white gentleman. E wears a long-tail coat
wid brass buttons all down de front. Sometimes a
slim lady in a flowery white dress walks wid em.
When I say 'Good evenin,' dey bows back nice
as can be."

Cun Fred wiped the sweat off his forehead with

a red pocket handkerchief. "For God's sake, Fancy, let dem dead people rest."

"I don' keep em from restin. It's de way dey died."

"How dey died?" Cricket asked breathlessly.

"Big Pa used to belong to em. E will tell you. Yonder e is comin now."

Big Pa came hopping in with a painful knee. He said he felt low in the mind, but before he got breath Cricket had him telling about the Big House spirits.

The gentleman in the long-tail coat got killed enduring the war when he tried to make white trash be soldiers. He put them in a camp at the avenue gate, and gave them a pass word to keep Yankees away from the Big House. When he found them asleep they woke up so scared they shot him in the head with a bomb shell and busted his skull.

Big Pa was there and saw it all with his own eyes. He helped to tote the dead man home all the way down the avenue.

Uncle Wes groaned. "White trash is a case. Dey never did have no sense. Dey ain' got no sense to dis day."

"Dat's de God's truth," Cun Fred agreed. "Dem what owns land now acts awful big. But what's in de blood stays in de blood to de bitter end."

The clock struck for middle afternoon and all the roosters crowed. Cricket got up.

"Come on, Blue. Let's go get de wart bean. Maybe we will see dem spirits."

"Jesus, no." Blue flinched, but Aun Fan shot a look at the leather strap hanging on the wall and he went to get his cap.

"Spirits ain' nothin but wind, Blue." Cricket's eyes smiled, bright as two stars.

"Wind don' wear no long-tail coat, neither a flowery dress," Aun Fan flung back.

"I'd like to see em anyhow," Cricket said boldly, and Uncle Wes told her if she saw a spirit to face it for she had as much right to walk up that avenue as any living somebody.

Big Pa looked worried. "You watch out for snakes, honey. Dey is awful bad in dat avenue."

"Snakes? Why, Big Pa, you is de very one told me not to fear snakes."

Aun Fan wrapped some cakes in a cloth for Cun Hester, and Cricket took off her shoes.

"Now I can run better if dem spirits look vexed."

Uncle Wes frowned and said if they looked vexed she must suck her teeth in their faces.

The iron gate at the entrance to the avenue was locked, but Cricket climbed over and Blue followed her. Huge oaks draped with moss made the long straight road dark with shade. Thick black twisted roots coiled over the ground and their new spring leaves hissed noisily overhead as the swarms of mosquitoes that sang in Blue's ears and stung his face and legs. Cun Hester's

flock of geese stopped to gaze, and a big white
gander stretched his neck out wickedly. Cricket
picked up a stick and faced him so boldly he fell
to eating grass again.

The Big House came nearer and nearer. Red
chimneys and white columns loomed up behind
cedars and magnolias. Blue felt uneasy for a
dropping sun reddened the west.

"Let's go through de flowers yard, Blue. De
rose-blossoms is pure beautiful now."

"No, Cricket. Let's go round de back way. Dis
is a white people's house."

Cricket gave him a pitying smile, lifted the gate
latch and stepped inside the low iron fence.

"Don' be scared, Blue. I been in here plenty
of times. I just ain' told nobody."

So many paths were confusing. Each was
bordered alike with a dark green hedge that
fenced in masses of blossoms tangled with weeds.
Cricket chose one that curved around a gray stone
lady with a broken hand. She said the lady's name
was Fountain.

A flock of pigeons walked back and forth on the
high shingled roof cooing, "Looka de coon," just
like those at Aun Fan's.

The air was green, scary shadows danced on the
tall white columns which shed their paint in scales.
Two long green boards on frames were against the
wall on each side of the door.

"Come on, let's ride de joggling boards,
Blue."

As Cricket ran up the crumbling brick steps and mounted one board, a lizard sped across the floor and a key rattled noisily in the front-door lock. The door cracked open and a loud voice asked, "Who dat?"

Blue's blood froze, but Cricket laughed. "Dis is me, Cricket, Cun Hester."

"My God, gal. I thought sho you was a sperit. What you doin at dis front door?"

"We was gwine to you house. I just stopped by to see de roses."

"Whyn' you go de back way? Whe's you manners?"

Cricket smiled. "Don' be vexed, Cun Hester. I ain' harmed nothin. I just smelled de blossoms wid de tip end o' my nose."

Cun Hester frowned but said gently, "You ain' to be so brazen when de moon is young. God knows what would happen if de white people's spirits was to catch you at dis front door."

"Uncle Wes said if I saw one I must face em an' suck my teeth at em."

Cun Hester all but jumped out of her old wrinkled skin. "Wes is fool in de head to talk such a talk to you, Cricket. You keep away from dis Big House, gal, befo something bad happens to you."

To Blue's surprise, Cricket's dimples twinkled.

"Uncle Wes says I got much right as anybody to walk straight up de avenue." Her voice rippled with a nervous sort of bragging.

"Dat ain' so. An' you may as well know it too."

"Is you vexed wid me, Cun Hester?" The corners of Cricket's mouth twitched.

"No, I ain' vexed," Cun Hester said warmly. "I love you too much to put fool notions in you head. You come wid me while I lock up de house. Dis ain' no safe place for you to wander."

CHAPTER XIII

A QUEER feeling seized Blue as he crossed the Big House threshold. The high white ceilings and smooth dark floors looked unfriendly. The air smelled moldy although andirons in the big hall fireplace shone bright as sunshine. His heart began a dull pounding when a white man's picture over one mantel stared down at him with stern black eyes.

"How you like dat lookin'-glass, Blue?" Cricket slid her arm in his and drew him toward a great mirror in a gold frame which covered half of one wall. Its dim face made Blue a dull shadow, but Cricket's red ribbon and white dress showed clear.

She moved sidewise, and turned all around to see herself.

"Stop you doins, Cricket," Cun Hester said. "Lookin at you'self in dat glass so proudful will make you have sin."

"I was lookin at my clothes. I wasn' lookin at myself."

"Clothes ain' to be trusted. Dey is deceitful as Satan. Wear you clothes, gal, don' let em wear you."

"I made my petticoat." Cricket lifted her dress to show the small even stitches, but Cun Hester's eyes fastened on the bright red brand stamped on the front.

"Dat flour sack made a nice petticoat for-true. What kind of flour come in it?"

Cricket had forgotten.

"Read de name, Blue," Cun Hester ordered.

Blue spelled slowly T-O-W-N-T-A-L-K, but could not make out the words. "I ain' had no lesson bout flour not yet," he excused himself.

"De room is too dark. If dem candles was lit Blue could see to read em." Cricket looked up at a shiny frame hanging from the ceiling with hundreds of glass sticks that sparkled like stars.

"Book-readin will strain what little brains Blue's got. If I had forty chillen, I wouldn' let one of em learn to book-read again."

"Uncle Wes wants me to learn."

"Wes is wrong. I birthed nine head o' chillen, honey. God was good an' took all of em back exceptin two; but dem two couldn' stand still, not after dey learned book-readin. God knows where dey is to-day."

She looked gloomily at the books filling shelves against the wall. "Books is contraptions of Satan, Cricket. You better leave em alone."

"Didn' white people used to read em?"

"Lord, yes, but you ain' white, Cricket."

"De lady in dat picture could sew writin wid needle and thread. E sewed dat sample in de frame on de wall." Cricket held her ground.

The lady in the picture had soft dark eyes and small white hands. Her lovely red mouth smiled gently.

"See if you can read de sample, Blue," Cricket said, and Blue did his best to make out each letter. "G-o-d God; B-l-e-s-s," he paused.

"Anybody wid two eyes knows dat sample says, 'God bless our home.' " Cun Hester turned away in disgust.

Blue tried not to show he was uneasy as he followed her past deer heads whose pitiful scared eyes faced a rack of guns and a glass case of long bladed knives.

"Who killed all dem deers, Cun Hester?"

"De white gentleman, Blue. Dey minds runs on shootin an' killin. No wonder God cut em all down."

"De white ladies wasn' mean like de gentlemen, was dey, Cun Hester?"

"No, Cricket, dey was sweet as a rose. But dey is lyin yonder in de graveyard most of em wid babies in dey arms." Cun Hester sighed. "Birthin killed some. Trouble killed de rest."

The high back porch overlooked green marshes and the wide yellow river. Creeks winding through old rice-fields were shining ribbons. Distant trees were misty blue. The outside world looked beautiful, but the Big House smelled moldy, musty, as if everything in it were dead.

Across the shady back yard was the low white-washed kitchen. Cricket opened the door to show Blue the brick ovens on each side of the chimney where his own grandmother used to cook bread for the white folks. She was Cricket's grandmother too, and the finest cook ever lived. A short distance away Cun Hester's cabin squatted beside an orchard where crooked old peach trees were pink, pear trees white, knotted fig trees green with tender leaves. A vine full of small pink roses sprawled over her tiny front porch and a brown wren chirruped under the eaves as she fumbled with the stubborn chain and padlock holding her front door shut.

"Everything goes crazy when de moon is young," she said as the door fell open.

"Come in, chillen, an' I'll give you some tea to drink whilst we eat Fancy's bread."

Blue flames muttered over the blackened logs in the fireplace as she took three flowered china cups and saucers out of the cupboard and put them on the small table.

"I don' let everybody drink out dese cups. I keeps em for particular company."

She handed Cricket one full of sassafras tea and said, "Dis is de best medicine ever was to cool a gal's blood in de spring." But to Blue she said sharply, "Mind, boy, don' break dis cup. It used to belong to de white folks."

She filled her own cup with life-everlasting tea, and sighed. "My blood is too thin for sassafras. Life elastic is better for old people."

"Me an' Man Jay smokes em. We calls em rabbit tobacco," Cricket laughed.

"No matter how you use em, God made life elastic to keep life in old people."

Tree shadows fell through the open window and danced over the floor as Cricket sipped her tea slowly.

"Hurry up and drink you tea, chillen," Cun Hester said. "De sun is low. I got to say my evenin prayers."

The tea was hot, but Blue gulped it down while Cun Hester moved the table and chairs back against the wall.

"You chillen go walk round in de yard whilst I pray."

"Let we stay an' hear you pray, Cun Hester," Cricket coaxed.

Cun Hester hesitated, looked thoughtful before she said, "You is a child of God. You ain' come to de age of sponsibility, not yet. Blue is so runty, I can' tell if e is old enough to have sin, but I reckon e won' hinder my prayin." She turned to the window, faced the sunset and stretched her long arms up high.

Bright clouds flamed through the trees. Yellow bands of light poured through the branches on her head and hands.

"Oh, Master Sun, you day's work is done," she prayed solemnly. "You plowed you shinin furrow cross de sky. Now you is gwine down to rest." Her eyes pressed forward as her voice strengthened. "If all I done to-day be pleasin in dy sight—if you got a good report of me to give to de Great I-Am, give me a sign!"

A flock of crows cawed brazenly on their way

to roost. A bird flitted past with a sleepy *tweet
tweet*. Cun Hester drew a long deep breath and
prayed louder.

"I know I'm a poor weakly creeter, but I tries
to keep shet of sin. I been talkin wid Jesus since
day was clean, a-pleadin wid em to keep Satan an'
sinners from comin here to-night."

She watched and waited, then dropped her arms
and turned from the window. With her head
bowed she knelt on the hearth and warmed her
hands. Her lips moved without sound until the
fire spat out a tiny shower of sparks. She slapped
at them, then leaped to her feet with a cry and
began circling the room in a strange slow dance.
Blue could not make out the words she crooned to
a beating tune. Her eyes were glassy, her forehead
shone with sweat drops, her body bent and swayed
until she halted in front of the window.

"Hear me, Sun," she cried with her rigid arms
held high. "You's a shinin light up in Heaven!
I'm a poor black creeter on dis earth! But I
follow my Jesus! Some o' dese days I'll walk
wid you on dem golden streets."

Cricket stood against the wall as still as the
lady named Fountain in the Big House flower
yard.

A little sunset breeze rose through the trees,
sang out bravely, fluttered the leaves and died
away.

"E's shoutin, Cun Hester. I see de sun
shoutin," Cricket cried.

Cun Hester made a low bow and deep curtsy to the blazing west. "I see you shoutin and givin me answer. Praise be to you blessed name!" Her two long teeth shone as her old face wrinkled up in a happy smile.

"Did you see de sun shout?" Cricket asked Blue excitedly. "Didn' you see em jumpin Juba? Givin Cun Hester de sign?"

Blue had seen nothing but fluttering leaves, yet Cun Hester kept saying, "Thank God. Thank God. I can sleep in peace dis night."

All of a sudden, thin high voices, like marsh hens' cackle, floated through the window. Cun Hester looked troubled. "Hear dem white ladies laughin in de graveyard? Sometimes dey laughs so pitiful, I have to beg em to hush."

"How do spirits laugh, Cun Hester?"

"Dem ladies ain' no common spirits, Cricket," Cun Hester said.

"Looks like dey would stay up in Heaven."

"Dey ain' went to Heaven. Satan fooled em. Poor creeters. Dey used to own all dis land. A narrow grave is all dey got now, an' dey have to share dat wid tree roots. No wonder dey laughs at dey-self."

"Why didn' dey pray?"

"Dey was too rich. Dey thought fine damask curtains an' tester beds could hinder death from layin his hand on dey hearts. Lord, how dey hated to die. Fast as dey went, dey spirits came back to de Big House. Even de trees is haunted. When

de wind comes in from de sea, dat old gray moss
pure weeps, de tree limbs pure moan and groan.''
"You ain' scared of em, Cun Hester?'' Blue
shivered.

"Not me, son. Jesus is my captain, de sun is
my shield. I been through many deep waters, but
I face spirits same like people.''

"Give me a charm for my wart, please, Cun
Hester. It's gettin dark. We got to go home.''
Blue felt goose-flesh all down his back.

Cun Hester took a bag from a nail on the wall
and got out a small black bean.

"Take dis bean, Cricket. Rub em hard on Blue's
wart, den plant em in a secret place. When de
bean sprouts de wart will go.''

When Blue pulled his foot and bowed his
thanks, Cun Hester said kindly, "Come back to
see me, son. I raise you Mammy, I thought
a heap of em too. I'm sorry e had sin. I hate
sin, but I don' hate de sinners.''

"My Mammy had sin too, Cun Hester,'' Cricket
said sadly.

"You ain' to blame for dat, honey. Try not to
fret bout you Mammy. What e done, e done.
We can' change it now.''

The twilight was filled with weird noises. Frogs
and katydids chattered. A fox barked, a whippoorwill called. Horror of spirits was on Blue's
mind, but not until a screech owl shivered was
Cricket willing to run and then she ran so fast
Blue could hardly keep up with her.

CHAPTER XIV

SATURDAY nights and Sundays were always fine, but Monday mornings were cheerless times.

Shouting and praising God so long and hard on Sunday nights made Aun Fan's muscles sore and her spirit weary. She always groaned when she got out of her soft warm bed Monday morning. While she dressed she grumbled at the way the plow-hands and hoe-hands came late to work. Cun Fred tried to defend them. He said the nights were too short and sunrise too soon. Some of the sinner men had lost a week's earnings playing skin. Others were so fretted by fickle sweethearts and unfaithful wives they could not do decent work.

On the Monday morning after his visit to the Big House with Cricket, breakfast was gloomy, but Blue whistled as he got his book and slate. The day was clean and bright and Cun Fred had persuaded Big Pa and Aun Missie to let Cricket go to school.

She met him at the road, all dressed up in her best clothes. Aun Missie was with her, telling her she must keep her dress clean, and not play with the Quarters children, especially Cooch and Toosio. Cricket promised and started off skipping, but Aun Missie yelled out she must stop kicking dust before she dirtied her clothes and wore out her shoes.

121

A cool wind had the trees' heads bowing. Dust puffed up in clouds and hung over the oat-fields where tender green blades ran in long shivering waves.

Redbirds twittered in hedgerows, thrashers hopped about, song sparrows with brown-leaf patterns on their breasts trilled gay tunes. Cricket halted when the schoolhouse came in sight. Old cedars above its roof shone blue in the sun, but restless ugly scraps of white paper fluttered around the sagging steps with no resting-place among last year's brown leaves.

Blue lifted the latch, opened the creaky door. A chilly damp musty smell flowed out. Cricket peeped in the dark room and shuddered.

A long string of children straggled up. Short, narrow girl skirts fluttered in the wind, hats were blown off heads. Shrill voices laughed and shouted as quick hands snatched up clods of earth and shot them at sparrows and field larks.

Cooch and Toosio looked surprised to see Cricket. They stared at her shoes and clean frock. Blue thought they did not seem glad. Cricket hardly spoke she was so filled with amazement.

Cooch and Toosio got straw brooms from the chimney corner and swept the littered floor. Papers, trash, bits of mud hurried toward the door under their strong drive, gray dust hid the naked rafters and streamed through the small square window. Man Jay knelt on the sunken hearth, making a fire in the broken chimney. He nursed

the small blaze carefully, added sticks of wood
until the flames grew tall and melted the chill.
Children crowded around Cricket, asked how-come
she was here and giggled at her confusion. They
gave long grudging glances at her hair and her
shoes for everybody else was barefoot.

A sudden silence told the teacher had come.
Blue took Cricket's hand and pulled her through
the crowd to the front bench.

"Set still as you can," he whispered. "De
teacher will lick you if you talk." He held tight
to her hand to stop its trembling.

The teacher took her place in front of the table
with the long keen whip in her hand. Blue watched
the plump arm fitting snugly in her dark blue
sleeve for it could deal a stunning blow.

"Go cut some wood, Man Jay," she ordered,
and fastened her eyes on Cricket.

"Who are you?"

Cricket sat speechless.

"Dis is Cricket." Blue stood up to answer.

"Let her talk for herself, Blue. How old are
you?"

Blue waited for Cricket to speak, then said
timidly, "Cricket is eight, gwine on nine."

"Is she dumb?"

"No, ma'am. E is scared."

"Scared of what?"

Blue did not dare to say.

"Come here, Cricket."

Cricket's trembling legs lifted her weight,

carried her forward in reach of the hateful whip.

"Is Cricket you name?"

"Yes, ma'am."

"Is it a nickname?"

"I don' know, ma'am."

"What is your surname?" The teacher's blue skirt rustled impatiently.

"I don' know, ma'am."

"Ask your mother what your surname is."

"E's dead."

"Where do you live?"

"Wid Uncle Wes."

"Is he your father?"

"No, ma'am."

"Your surname is the same as your father's. Find out what it is."

"I ain' got no father"—Cricket's voice shook—"lessen it's God."

"Everybody has a father, Cricket."

"No, ma'am. I ain' got none."

"You may not know your father, but you have one." The teacher's eyes narrowed curiously.

"Tell your Uncle to write your father's name on a piece of paper, Cricket. Bring it to-morrow."

"Uncle Wes can' write," Cricket faltered.

The teacher frowned. "Get him to tell you your father's name."

"Yes'm."

"Have you a book?"

"No'm."

"Cricket can read in my-own," Man Jay offered.

"Learn the first page, Cricket."

"I already know em. 'Baby Ray loves Mama, Mama loves Baby Ray,'" Cricket repeated glibly.

"Have you been to school before?"

"No, ma'am."

"Cricket can read all my lessons widout lookin at de book," Man Jay explained. "E knows up to de cow what eats de green grass."

"You must learn to read when you look at the book, Cricket."

"Yes'm."

The teacher rang the old cow-bell and more children crowded the room. They filled the benches, packed against the wall, jammed the broken-down porch and sagging steps; some had to stand outside in the yard. Cricket sat between Man Jay and Blue, holding tight to both their hands. Her bright skin and white dress shone among dark faces and clothes. Rows and rows of eyes were on her. Heads with close-clipped hair, hair wrapped into cords with ball thread craned necks to see her until the teacher said, "Let us stand and sing, 'My Country 'tis of thee, sweet land of Libertee.'" She led the tune and the children chimed in, with such a clear beating that Blue's ears tingled. When the song was done the teacher took a Bible from the table and turned the leaves.

"The Lord is my Shepherd, I shall not want." She read on and on, her words falling like a song.

Cricket's hold on Blue's hand slowly loosened, her soft lips parted as she listened eagerly.

Cracks in the roof showed the naked blue sky, narrow streaks of light came through the broken walls. A spot of sunshine fell on Cricket's bowed head as she followed. "Our Father Who art in Heaven."

"Amen," was said, and restless feet shuffled. Whispers hissed, teeth flashed, but the whip made a threatening wave and the children became a silent, many-eyed thing.

"Second class, go outside. Walk quietly. Don't push. First class, take your seats. Read the lesson in concert."

Book pages fluttered all over the room until the lesson picture showed.

The teacher read crisply, clearly about the hen and little biddies around a pan of water. Cricket listened greedily and her finger tried to follow the words.

> "Kippy, Kippy, what a pleasure.
> Kippy, Kippy, what a treasure.
> Here's a lake of water clear.
> Little Polly put it here."

The bench was too crowded. Man Jay sat back, Blue sat forward so Cricket would not be mashed. The rough bench's splinters came through Blue's breeches and pricked his skin. Chilly wind rose through the floor cracks in restless gushes. The window was small, the fire gave poor light. The words mixed up on the page so Blue could not tell one from another.

"Look at your book, Blue." The whip shook a little.

Cricket shivered as the teacher read on.

> "See the water has a sky.
> Like the one that shines so high."

The lesson was read to the end, and the class led by Man Jay repeated it in concert three times.

Spelling came next.

"Blue," the teacher called.

Blue jumped to his feet.

"Spell *bat*."

Blue could not remember the first letter. His eyes rolled about, his fingers twisted his breeches leg. "F-a-t," he risked, then cried, "No," for the teacher's face told he was wrong.

"M-a-t—No! S-a-t—No! R-a-t—No!"

He broke out in cold sweat when Toosio giggled out loud right behind him. The teacher's eyes lifted to search for the offender, and Cricket plucked at Blue's sleeve. Her lips formed a clear *b*.

"B-a-t, bat," he spelled promptly.

"Who told you, Blue?"

"Not nobody, ma'am."

"Spell ball, Blue."

A dry cough seized him. "I can' spell em," he quavered.

"Come forward."

The whip lifted high halted. He braced himself for the cut, but the whip did not move. The teacher told him he was not only stupid, but a liar. She would give him two cuts now for the words he missed. At recess she would thrash him for lying. When the lick whizzed down on his outstretched palm, Blue's breath sucked in but he did not let himself flinch. When he went back to his place tears were in Cricket's eyes. Poor little Cricket. She had not known school was like this.

After recess the teacher told about the school-breaking to be held at Heaven's Gate Church four weeks from Sunday. People would pay ten cents to hear the children speak and a prize would be given to the best speaker. Everybody must wear shoes and stockings. The prize would be a Testament.

Cricket's eyes got bigger and bigger, as the speeches were given out.

Man Jay's told about a boy on a burning boat, Blue's about a twinkling star. Cooch's began, "Needles and pins, needles and pins, when you get married then trouble begins." Toosio's told about a watermelon seed which struggled to make roots and become a big vine full of fruit.

At last time to go home had come. Cricket had no speech, but she walked up to the teacher's table and stood there.

"What de matter ail you, Cricket?" Cooch laughed. "School is done out."

"What do you want?" The teacher looked up.

"I wish I had a speech to say."

"You are too small to speak."

Cooch snickered but Cricket answered bravely, "Please, ma'am, let me try."

The teacher thought and thought. "You might try, 'Kippy, Kippy,' the lesson you had to-day."

"Please, ma'am, let me speak what you read out de Bible about 'De Lord is my shepherd.' "

"You couldn't learn that, Cricket."

"Man Jay would help me."

"He can't read it."

"I'll learn to read em," Man Jay declared, and the teacher gave in wearily.

Children filled the yard. Knots of boys and girls talked excitedly about the speeches as they ate scraps of lunch left over from recess.

"I'm sho gwine get dat prize," Cooch boasted.

"Not if I live." Man Jay's mouth was full of bread and crumbs fell out with his words.

"For God's sake, Man Jay, you couldn' stop eatin long enough to speak. You must be half chicken. You eats all de time an' you craw don' never get full," Cooch sneered.

"Man Jay looks more like a dirt dauber dan a chicken," Toosio giggled.

"You look like you swallowed dat watermelon in you speech," Man Jay came back good-naturedly.

"What's a Testament?" Blue asked.

Nobody knew but Cricket thought it was a little

small Bible like one Cun Hester showed her in
the Big House.

"You wouldn' catch me inside dat Big House,
neither wid Cun Hester," Cooch laughed. "Cun
Hester's a witch."

"Cun Hester ain' no witch. E's a Christian
lady," Cricket blazed back.

"Don' pay Cooch any mind, Cricket," Man Jay
said. "Come on, let's go home."

Half-way home, a drizzling rain pattered down.
Cricket's red ribbon grew limp, her white dress
was soaked, mud stuck to her shoes, but she
was happy as a bird until Cooch said:

"I'm sho glad I know my Daddy's name."

Toosio giggled: "Me too."

"Uncle Ben ain' nothin to be proud of." Blue
longed to slap both of their faces.

"Uncle Ben ain' my Daddy. Not dat pop-eyed
old man." Cooch laughed.

"E is married to you Mammy."

"Ma didn' married until year befo last."

"Who you Daddy is, Cooch?" Cricket asked.

"My God, Cricket. You been livin here all dis
time an' don' know my Daddy? It's Old Man
Kelly Wright."

"I'd be ashamed to tell it," Man Jay said.
"Old Man Kelly killed his wife."

"I don' blame em for killen dat oman. E was
de ugliest somebody in dis country."

"You can' kill people for bein ugly."

"E didn' kill em for bein ugly. E shot his heart

out for scourin de floor one Sat'day evenin when e
wanted to sleep."

"Dat was a sin."

"Sin, you foot! It was his wife. E had a right
to kill em if e wanted to."

"I'm glad Old Man Kelly ain' my Daddy."

"I ain' got no complaint of em," Cooch answered cheerfully. "E owns me before people,
so I owns him. Most every time I see em e gives
me a nickel. Last week e asked me to clean up his
house. I done it good for em too."

Toosio giggled. "Cun Jule licked you for doin
it."

"I don' care if e did. I'll clean up my Daddy's
house any time e axes me."

Aun Missie came to meet Cricket all wrapped in
a quilt.

"I'm gwine to speak at de school-breakin, Aun
Missie," Cricket shouted joyfully.

"You gwine get you death o' cold in dis rain.
I told Wes not to let you go to school."

"I'm gwine say a beautiful speech bout de Lord
is my shepherd."

Aun Missie looked cross. "Dat ain' no speech.
Dat's de Bible."

"Cricket don' know his last name, Aun Missie."
Cooch grinned pertly.

"Why, Cricket! You last name is Pine-sett
same like dem pretty red flowers what blooms in de
Christmas."

"De teacher says Cricket must learn his Daddy's name befo to-morrow."

"Cricket ain' got no Daddy, Cooch."

"De teacher says everybody's got a Daddy."

Aun Missie's eyes glittered angrily.

"If dat fool teacher asks who you Daddy is, Cricket, you tell em it ain' nobody in particular."

CHAPTER XV

On Wednesday night Blue stayed with Cricket while Aun Fan and Aun Missie went to prayer-meeting. Big Pa and Man Jay were helping her practise her speech, and the first time she said it without halting Man Jay clapped his hands and Big Pa laughed with pleasure.

"You sho speak it elegant, honey," he praised. "If God had made you a boy-child you would be a fine preacher, same like you Grampa. Say de speech again, honey. I too love to hear bout de Lord is my shepherd."

"De Lord is my shepherd I shall not want," Cricket began glibly, then halted.

"E makes me lie down——" Man Jay prompted.

"Wait, Man Jay. I'm gwine sing em slow like de teacher dis time."

"Honey," Big Pa said when the speech was done, "you voice sounds same like my Mammy's." His eyes had a far-away unseeing look.

"Please don' get sorrowful, Big Pa. Sing us one o' you Mammy's songs. Man Jay will play de mouth-organ, I'll knock de bones."

Cricket got her two polished cow-ribs, but Big Pa shook his head.

"My heart is heavy to sing."

"Tell we bout de time you sat on a log an' it was a snake," Man Jay suggested.

"Oh, no. Tell we bout you Daddy, King Taki."

133

"What's a king?" Blue whispered, but Cricket did not say for Big Pa settled in his chair and looked in the fire as if he saw things there.

He said African people lived in tribes. A head man ruled them, same like snakes in this country have a king snake to keep them in order. If he had stayed in Africa, he would be a king himself for he was Taki's oldest son.

Taki had many wives, many children, plenty to eat. Taki's wives caught fish, raised guinea fowls, planted grain and goobers, ground grain between boulders and baked it into bread. Big Pa's mother was Taki's head wife. She took extra pains with Big Pa so he would grow up fit to be king.

She bored his ears to make his eyesight strong. She had his teeth filed so they'd never rot. She named him Kazoola which means son of a king.

Dahomi was king of the village next to Taki. He was lazy and mean. He and Taki had wars, and whoever won out sold his captives to white men who smuggled them across the ocean to be slaves.

Big Pa was only a youth when the great dry drought came. The crops were scanty and Dahomi sent a message to Taki asking for part of his harvest. Taki would not divide.

Every Jesus had his Judas. Taki's head man was his Judas. He got unruly with one of Taki's wives and Taki made him leave the tribe. To get vengeance, he went to Dahomi. He told Dahomi how Taki's village had three gates. That was enough. Tricky old Dahomi parted his fighting men into three armies. When night came they slipped through the darkness. One army blew long blasts on cow horns at the first gate and Taki's men hurried there to fight them. More horns blew at the two other gates. The women and children fought with what weapons they had but were no match for Dahomi's giants and flint guns.

Big Pa was taken prisoner. He wept, and prayed. He called his mother, his father, his sisters; nobody came. Dahomi marched him to the sea with other captives and shut him inside a high fence. White men with terrible eyes came. They put Big Pa and seventy others in small boats, took them to a great ship, made them climb rope ladders, shoved them down into the great ship's hold. The hold was dark and stenchful. When the ship moved off, everybody took the seasick. Some died. Some lived. Big Pa wept night and day. The ship landed in a place named Unity States. He was smuggled up the river where the black people were strange as white ones. Nobody talked his language. His heart was ready to break. From day-clean to first dark he caught fish to feed the plantation people. Spring and summer he fished in the river, fall and winter he fished in the sea.

One hot summer night he slipped off and paddled down the river. Morning caught him in sight of

the Big House and he came ashore to hide. He
was hungry, weary, down-in-the-heart until a girl
saw him and brought him something to eat. She
had a good heart and he took her for wife, but he
tarried in the swamp until she got her master to
buy him. She birthed him a boy-child the same
year war freed the slaves but she died before the
boy cut his second teeth. He missed her so bad,
he decided to go home to Africa. He took the boy
and tried to find the Unity States. Nobody knew
where it was. At last he came back to the plantation but everything here had changed.

Before the war, the white people were vast-rich.
They hunted, raced horses, fought chickens and
pleasured from Christmas to Christmas. When
they rode out, gold on the carriage and harness
blinded people's eyes like lightning. The horses
had eyes like coals of fire. Races sixteen miles
long did not fag them for their breath was pure
hot steam. When they came in sight, everybody
ran and hid, for they trampled people down in the
road like leaves. Lord, those were fine days. But
war killed the old master, snake holes and
crawfish ruined the trunks in the rice-fields, slime
and weeds fouled the ditches. Everything went to
ruin.

Big Pa stayed single although willing women
were plentiful. None was fit to raise his Blue. Blue
was a fine high-bredded boy. He learned to book-
read, learned how to preach, then he took the Big
House cook for wife. She was older than Blue

but she birthed him three children before she died. Wes was the oldest, Blue's mother was next, Cricket's mother was the last. Blue was a preacher, but he was proudful and short patienced.

He forgot he was black, and tried to kill a white somebody. He had to leave the plantation, so he went to Africa where people never heard about Jesus or God.

In Africa a big shining sun was the father of everything. It healed sickness and sweetened filth, made things live and grow. Everybody in Africa said prayers to the sun. They did not know a white God up in Heaven made that sun. They had no Bible or preachers to tell about God. God may be merciful, but he treated Jesus bad. Jesus was his only son, too. God made him leave home and come to this country to save white people. They hung him on a cross. Poor little Jesus. God did not lift a finger to help him. Jesus would have been in his grave until now but angels took him back to Heaven. When they flew with him up to the sky, Satan's lightning tried to strike him and scorched the angels' wings. That happened on a Thursday in May when the fields were green with grass. The angels named it Green Thursday. To this day if people stir the ground on Green Thursday lightning will strike their fields and houses.

His mother knew none of this. She ever prayed to the Sun.

Big Pa lifted his arms and raised his wet eyes.

"Oh, Landa, coco, ebee; ad yo-co, nippee-coo,"
he prayed.

Cricket answered softly, "Our Father Sun,
shine bright on us dis day."

"I love de sun better'n God," Cricket said.

"But de sun can' take you to Heaven. God don'
let nobody in Heaven what don' pray to him.
God's heart is hard as a rock in de sea. I hope
Blue found my Mammy and told em how to pray.
I hate for em to go to torment."

Big Pa covered his face with his hands, his
white-haired breast heaved, tears poured through
his fingers. "If I could find de way I'd go home
to-day old as I is," he sobbed. "I want to see
my Mammy so bad."

Floor boards at the meeting-house clapped with
the beat of shouting feet and the night wind
brought in words of the shouting song.

"When de saints go marchin home,
When de saints go marchin home,
I want to be one of de number,
When de saints go marchin home."

Big Pa's head went down to his knees and
Cricket put both arms around him.

"Don' cry, Big Pa," she said. "When I learn
to read de Bible, I'll go to Africa an' tell you
Mammy bout God an' Jesus."

"I'll go wid you," Man Jay promised.

"I want to see my Mammy so bad——" Big
Pa sobbed pitifully.

Blue got up and stood in the door to hide his own tears. Bright stars marched across the sky as the people at meeting sang joyfully:

"I had a lovin mother,
E's gone to Heaven, I know.
I promised I would meet em,
When de saints go marchin home."

Blue leaned against the wall and wept. He wanted his mother, too.

CHAPTER XVI

Aun Fan bought cloth to make Blue a new shirt and pants for the school-breaking. When he took it to Aun Bina to make, Cricket and Cooch were there to try on their new dresses. Cricket's made a thin blue cloud on the bed while Aun Bina sewed a seam on Cooch's pink one.

"I wish I had long enough hair to tie em wid ribbon like Cricket's," Cooch sighed.

Aun Bina's needle clicked against her steel thimble.

"Whyn' you make Jule buy you some hair straightener from de store?"

"Ma won' give me no dollar."

"Make Old Kelly give you one."

Cooch lifted her slim arms and stretched. A yawn bared her sharp white teeth.

"Pa ain' give me much as a dollar since Ma married to Uncle Ben."

Aun Bina bit off a length of thread. "I have hear-say kerosene would straighten hair."

Cooch sat up. "Lord, I wonder if it would take de kink out dis Jesus grass on my head."

"You gwine win de prize anyhow, Cooch. You better stay like God made you."

"God made me buck naked," Cooch laughed.

She came to school next day with her head drenched in kerosene. The teacher made an ugly face and asked Cooch if the kerosene was to kill lice. The children snickered when Cooch nodded a brazen yes.

On Saturday afternoon before the school-breaking the crossroads store was thronged with people. Cun Hester was telling about a Jack-ma-lantern which floated past her house the night before headed straight for the Quarters, rolling along, bobbing up and down. Trouble was ahead for somebody.

"I hope it ain' me." Cun Jule was buying a pink hair ribbon, and Cooch danced with joy as the silken length was measured off and rolled up in a clean white paper.

"Here's you ribbon, Cooch." Cun Jule handed it over. "If you mind had been on you speech hard as gettin de kink out you hair you would win dat prize to-morrow."

"I is gwine win em," Cooch flashed back, and everybody laughed.

Cun Fred bought Blue some tan laced-up shoes and Uncle Wes got a pair for Man Jay who boasted he could wear from sixes up.

"Come on, Cricket, let's drink a Coco-Cola," Man Jay said.

Cricket followed him to the crate of bottled drinks and he counted out six pennies for one bottle, opened it on a bent nail in the wall and handed it to her. "You drink first, an' I'll finish em up."

Cricket put her lips to the bottle's mouth, took one swallow and made a wry face.

"Aw, drink some more," he insisted.

"It's so awful strong, it cuts my wind."

"My Gawd, Cricket," Cooch sneered. "Let me show you how to drink em." She shut her eyes and drank so fast, Man Jay jerked the bottle from her and finished it himself.

Cricket peered at the beads which lay in a glittering pile inside the dusty showcase. Blue's pocket was empty but behind the store in the restaurant Cun Fred was treating Cun Jule to store-bought bread and fried fish. Blue went in and stood beside him.

"What you want, boy?"

"I want to treat a lady."

"Dat boy is a chip off de old block," Cun Jule laughed gaily as Cun Fred reached down in his pocket and took out some coins.

Blue held them tight in his hand as he wound through the crowd looking for Cricket.

Cooch took him by the arm. "See my hair ribbon, Blue."

Blue pulled away for he spied Cricket eating sweet cakes with Man Jay.

"Come pick out you beads, Cricket," Blue said mannishly. "Dem blue ones is just de color of you school-breakin dress."

As the store man lifted them out, light glittered through them making them lovelier than ever.

Blue proudly handed over the money, but Cricket's fingers shook so when she took the beads they almost dropped on the floor.

"Put em around you neck, dey'll break if you drop em," Blue told her.

"I'd ruther wait an' wear em to-morrow," she whispered. "Dey might give me luck."

"Go on home and cook supper, Blue." Aun Fan frowned at Cun Fred who stood talking back in a corner with Cun Jule.

"You go wid Blue, Cricket. Stay at Aun Fan's until I come." Aun Missie was watching Uncle Wes treat Aun Bina to parched pinders.

"You better go hotten some water, Cooch. Dat kerosene must be washed out you head to-night," Cun Jule called across the crowd.

The people laughed and twitted Cooch but she faced them with a grin.

"Laugh if you want to but I'll win dat prize."

As Cooch, Cricket, Toosio and Blue walked toward Aun Fan's a whippoorwill called mournfully.

"You better go home wid me, Cricket," Cooch said. "A whippoorwill is a bad-luck bird."

"Aun Missie would be vexed." Cricket looked worried in her mind.

"Aun Missie ain' home an' dat Jack-ma-lantern might run you to death."

Blue said Cooch was right and at last Cricket gave in.

Except for a small blaze sputtering in the fireplace, Aun Jule's house was as still as death.

"Build up de fire, Blue. I got to hotten some water to wash my head," Cooch said.

Blue piled on wood, but instead of blazing up the small flame died.

"Blow on em, Blue. I'll name de blows an' see if you sweetheart loves you." Cooch took her pink dress out of the trunk to see if the hair ribbon matched, while Blue blew until smoke puffed out and stung his eye yet no flame came.

"Cricket don' love you," Cooch laughed and laid the dress on a chair. "I'll show you how to make fire burn." She got her bottle of kerosene and poured some on the wood. "I'll name dis blow after you, Blue. I ever did wonder if you love me." She knelt on the hearth and puffed out a deep breath. A yellow flame answered, leaped from the wood to her head.

Blue turned to stone.

CHAPTER XVII

CRICKET screamed and dashed a full bucket of water on Cooch's flaming head. Her aim missed and the water fell with a splash over Cooch's new dress. Cricket grabbed it up, wrapped it around Cooch's head and Blue stood in the door shrieking for help.

"For God's sake get somebody, Blue," Cricket pleaded, but the Quarters was empty and silent.

Blue ran outside and strove to send his voice across the big field. Dull thuds of running feet answered at last and Cun Hester came running up the street.

"What dat smell? Who dat burn?" she asked breathlessly, and peered through the door at Cooch who lay shivering in Cricket's arms.

"What de matter ail Cooch?"

"Fire burnt his head," Cricket sobbed.

"Did e swallow de fire?"

Cricket did not know, neither did Blue. Toosio could do nothing but blubber, and Cooch made no sound, not even a moan.

"Po' lil gal," Cun Hester said gently. "If e swallowed fire, e's gwine dead for-true."

Toosio gave a long mournful howl.

"Shut you mouth, Toosio," Cun Hester snapped. "Nothin don' ail you but fatness."

Toosio's howls dwindled as she shrank back in a corner to face the wall while Cun Hester brushed

145

off the charred wool. Blue could hardly bear to
look yet could not turn his eyes away.

"Stop you gazin, Blue. Get me de lard bucket
an' de box o' cookin soda. Get a sheet out de
trunk, Cricket."

Horror weighted Blue's feet down. "For God's
sake, Blue, stop actin like a corpse," Cun Hester
screamed.

Cricket got the lard and soda and bed sheet.
The cloth was tough but her sharp teeth cut it and
the sheet gave a long snarl as she tore a band from
its side.

Cooch's naked skull was a pitiful sight. Long
hard shudders ran over her body as Cun Hester
smeared on the soda and lard.

"Don' fret, Cooch. I ain' gwine suffer you
long. You skull ain' burned so awful deep. You
hair might come out straight. God takes strange
ways to do his work."

A crowd of excited chattering people burst into
the room. Cun Jule jumped up and down and
beat her breast.

"Oh, Jesus! My Gawd! I can' stand dis!" she
squalled. When she saw Cooch's white bound
head she gave a long horrible yell, rolled back her
eyes and fell in a trance.

Willing hands shot out from all sides. Some
helped to lift her limp weight and lay it beside
Cooch on the bed. Others loosened her clothes and
fanned her face briskly with hats. The room was
jammed, yet more people squeezed in. Groans,

moans, questions mixed with the smell of burned hair and strong sweat.

Cun Hester stood up and clapped her hands. "You people shut you mouth befo you tarrify Cooch to death."

"Great God!" "Jesus have mercy!" Heavy groans rose and fell.

"Cranin you necks to see Cooch won' put his hair back," Cun Hester rebuked them.

A fresh outburst of questions was noisier than ever until Cun Hester cried above the confusion, "For God's sake get de people out dis house, Alfred. So much talk makes me fool in de head."

"You ever was dat," Aun Bina mumbled, but Cun Fred said:

"Come on, mens, let's go in de yard so de ladies can have more room."

Women crowded around the bed asking questions. Who would have thought this would happen to Cooch? She had such a fine speech, such a nice dress too. "Only this evening Old Man Kelly gave Jule fifteen cents to buy Cooch a hair ribbon."

"How did the fire catch Cooch's head?" they asked, and Toosio told over and over what happened, changing it every time.

Somebody said axle grease was better for burns than hog lard, even kerosene was more cooling.

Hester answered sharply, "For God's sake don' call kerosene's name, when kerosene done it."

"Kerosene from de store is half water. It puts fire out," Aun Bina declared.

Cun Jule came to and sat up, screaming at the top of her lungs, "Who done dis to Cooch? Who done it?"

"I got a notion, but I ain' sayin." Aun Bina sniffed and shot a meaningful glance at Cricket.

"If somebody set fire to Cooch's head I'll kill em." Cun Jule clenched her fat fists and tried to get up but Cun Hester held her.

"God runs dis world, Jule. E didn' aim for Cooch to speak to-morrow. It ain' no use to put de blame on nobody."

Aun Bina held up a blackened rag. Cooch's beautiful Children's Day dress was an ugly sight.

"Looka dat dress, Cun Hester. You think God done dat?" Cun Jule shrieked and fell back on the bed.

"I done it, Aun Bina, tryin to outen de fire."

Silence fell over the room. Cricket shivered under hard accusing looks, for every eye in the room was on her.

"How come you didn' get a quilt off de bed?" Aun Bina's words were heavy with blame.

"I forget bout de quilt, but I didn' aim to ruin Cooch's dress." Tears poured down Cricket's cheeks and she did not lift a hand to wipe them away.

Cun Jule's cries got so terrible, Cun Hester held a cloth wet with vinegar to her nose.

"I told you to go home, Cricket. You know I don' allow you in dis Quarter," Aun Missie bawled.

"Jule better thank God Cricket was here. Blue and Toosio ain' got no sense," Cun Hester bawled back.

"Who ain' got no sense? Whe' is Cricket?"

Uncle Wes made a tall black shadow in the door. He pushed past everybody to reach her, but when he touched her hands she jerked them away.

He staggered on his feet when he found out Cricket's hands were burned raw. Women crowded around her to see them and Aun Missie wailed:

"Po' lil Cricket—— E won' be able to speak to-morrow."

"Cricket don' speak wid his hands," Uncle Wes answered gruffly and took Cricket up in his arms.

"I lost my beads," Cricket moaned.

"Don' fret, honey. I'll find em an' fetch em," Blue promised as Uncle Wes carried her down the steps.

Everybody helped Blue look for the beads, but they had disappeared.

"De fire must be burnt em up," Toosio whimpered. Her eyes were red slits from crying.

CHAPTER XVIII

Aun Fan was astir before dawn, frying piles of chicken and fish to go in her basket with sweetened-bread and green-apple pies. Clouds of grease smoke hung over her smutty head-rag as she wiped her hands on the greasy apron tied around her bulging middle.

"Milk de cow, Blue, den go find out if Cooch is dead."

"Cooch ain' dead," Cun Fred spat. "Fire couldn' kill dat tough gal. Cricket is de one got me fretted.

"Take you foot in you hand, Blue, an' go see how Cricket is. If e's better, tell Wes dey can go in de wagon wid we."

"Tell em no such t'ing. I feel too high-string to be crowded up to-day. Let Wes drive dem old oxen," Aun Fan objected.

Cricket's hands were bound in white cloth and Uncle Wes was taking her clothes out of the trunk while Aun Missie fixed her own hair.

"Did you fetch de beads, Blue?" Cricket asked at once. Her hopeful smile faded when she heard they were burned up, but Uncle Wes said she did not need beads to outshine the crowd. Blue's heart pattered with joy when Uncle Wes wished Blue's mother was here and Cricket's too. They would be glad to know how brave Blue and Cricket acted when Cooch caught fire.

150

"Look what Uncle Wes bought from de store
to cover up e rags on my hands." Cricket held
up a pair of white cotton gloves.

"Put dem gloves down, Cricket. I'm gwine wear
em myself." Aun Missie sat facing the looking-
glass which was down on a chair. She had un-
wrapped her tight rolls of hair and it stood straight
out from her skull. With a comb she made loose
puffs around her face and divided the rest in
patches which she plaited and pinned down. She
smiled at herself in the glass. "How does I look,
Cricket?"

"My heart pure trembles to see you, Aun Missie.
Cun Fred will call you star-lily to-day."

"Al-fred knows better dan to sweet-talk me, gal.
I ain' no fool like dem other womens."

Blue hurried home and washed his feet, pulled
the long black stockings up over his knees and
tied them with strings. Aun Fan urged him
to make haste, for the George mule and wagon
stood at the back door. The basket of food was
put in, then a chair for Aun Fan. Blue's new
shoes hurt so bad he could hardly climb up to the
board seat beside Cun Fred, but he dared not men-
tion his misery.

The dusty road was full of wagons, carts, buggies. Many people walked with shoes in one hand
and baskets in the other. Across the big field
Heaven's Gate shone with whitewash. Its gray
hunched back looked no bigger than a goat. The
steeple made a tiny horn pointing to Heaven.

Reverend Duncan was just ahead, his huge body filling the whole buggy seat. Now and then his thin horse stopped to pant for breath, unable to keep up with the buggy in front that held Reverend's fat lady and a stranger-man.

"No wonder Reverend is fat. E's got nine hundred members an' every one pays em a chicken, a peck o' meal, an' a dollar, every year God sends," Cun Fred chuckled.

"I could get fat myself on dat much." Aun Fan sighed and said the dry drought was parching up all the corn.

"We got a Judas on dis place, Al-fred. God's promises is for dem what do his will. If a need pinches anybody in dis world it's because dey have sin."

"Dis dry drought suffers things what ain' people, Fancy. De birds is pantin for breath, de cotton's head is dropped down, de corn's hands is shut up tight."

"Everything is callin on his Maker, tellin em de need is great, Al-fred. You ought to bend you knees and bow you head too."

The wagon wheels creaked in crooked sandy ruts. The George mule foamed with sweat.

The churchyard was filled with buggies, wagons, carts, and the clean white hides of Uncle Wes's oxen stood out among the dark mules and horses. Bright dresses and hats enlivened shadows with gay colors. Groups of men stood together talking, looking anxiously at the blue sky.

People Blue knew well looked strange in Sunday clothes. Every man wore a coat, every woman a hat, older women had hats perched over head-rags. They talked, laughed, shook hands, made lively gestures, but Blue's heart made dull thumps. "Twinkle, twinkle," something in his head kept saying over and over. His toes burned like fire, as he limped forward and took his place beside Man Jay, who said Toosio's short red dress showed off her slue-feet and knock-knees, but Cricket was a blue morning-glory.

Reverend Duncan mounted the church steps, cocked his broad-brimmed hat on one side, pushed aside his long-tailed coat so one hand could rest in his breeches pocket. His broad sleek face dripped with sweat and he mopped it off with a white pocket handkerchief before he bellowed to the crowd of grown people:

"De chillen will march round de church whilst de congregation sings.

"Come all ye dat love de Lord,
And let you joys be known."

Strong voices burst forth and lifted the words to the sky.

"Join in de song wid sweet accord
While we surround de throne."

Man Jay's long tan shoes kept time, Blue's lame

feet hobbled along, Cricket and Toosio sang as
they led the procession of school children.

> "We're marchin to Zion!
> Beautiful, beautiful Zion.
> We're marchin upward to Zion,
> Dat beautiful city of God."

CHAPTER XIX

AROUND the church they went, past people, sweaty mules, haggard horses, lean dogs sniffing at food in baskets. Blue limped doggedly up the church steps, down the right aisle behind Reverend Duncan. The boys filled one amen corner, the girls followed the teacher through the left-hand door and filled the other. Brer Dee and Cun Andrew stood at the doors taking dimes from people who surged in to crowd the benches, stand against walls. The church was jammed and people stood in wagons drawn up to open windows.

Palm-leaf fans fluttered. Stylish red rubber sponges and pocket handkerchiefs wiped streaming faces. Reverend Duncan and a little wiry stranger-man sat behind the pulpit with the teacher who was dressed all in white.

A hush went over the congregation when the little man got up, put on gold spectacles and opened the big black Bible. He turned the leaves until he found the place, then said, "The children will now sing, 'My Country 'tis of thee.' "

Blue's feet hurt so he could hardly stand. When the ladies on the front bench began easing off their shoes he could have wept.

The song ended and Reverend Duncan's deep voice boomed out that many of these children over twelve had not come into the kingdom. They looked like angels. They sang like angels.

155

But God looks not on the outward appearance, he looks deep into hearts. A soul is no light breath of air but a solid body that lives through eternity in Heaven or in Hell where the fire is seven times hotter than fire on earth.

His fists beat fiercely on the pulpit and the congregation sat dumb, stunned for a heart-beat, then they answered with a storm of cries and groans. When it was spent, the wiry little man got up. He agreed that being saved is important but times had changed. The world moved forward. The ignorant were no longer respected. Those who opposed book-reading were fools.

He read from the Bible about a king named Pharaoh who made slaves of the children of Israel. He closed the Book with a bang and leaped to his toes as he cried that white people were like wicked Pharaoh. They made black people slaves, worked them like mules, sold them like cattle and hogs. God's patience was long but it gave out. He sent plagues on the white people. War killed some of them off, poverty sent the rest to far countries. Thank God, this beautiful Canaan land is the peaceful home of those born in slavery. They enjoy the fruits of fields and rivers and seas. They reap the harvest of their own labor. Only sin and ignorance could make slaves of them now.

The people went wild with joy. They shouted and laughed and cried until the rafters trembled and the little man shouted this was Children's Day. Grown people must be seen and not heard.

The teacher stood up and called Blue's name. He staggered up into the pulpit. His knees shook, his fingers plucked wretchedly at his breeches legs. Bright hats and dresses, black faces blurred into a quivering mass. His speech stuck in his throat, his heart beat louder than his words.

When Toosio's name was called she giggled nervously and bent over low.

"Come on, Toosio," the teacher said kindly, and Toosio ran forward, stumbled over the steps and fell sprawling. The shameless girl laughed and got up, walked into the pulpit with Cricket's blue beads on her neck.

"Needles and pins, needles and pins." She said Cooch's speech instead of her own, and said it so well, people smiled and nodded their heads.

Cricket's speech came last of all, and when her shiny little black shoes stepped lightly up the steps, into the pulpit, Cun Hester said loud enough for everybody to hear. "E pure looks like a angel from Heaven."

"E sho do. Ain' it de truth." Answers came from all over the church.

Fans ceased waving. Whispers hushed. People leaned forward to see Cricket better. Her little bound hands hid in the folds of her dress, but her eyes were two stars.

Uncle Wes waved his hat from where he stood by the wall. "Strut you stuff, honey," he called.

Cricket smiled and began.

"De Lord is my shepherd. I shall not want——"

As her voice rose firm and clear the congregation melted into a silent staring mass.

"When I walk through de valley of de shadow of death, dy rod an' dy staff shall comfort me."

A flood of answering voices rose.

"Praise de Lord!"

"Thank God!"

"Amen!" Reverend Duncan boomed.

Cricket lifted the words, rang them out like a bell.

"Surely His goodness an' mercy will follow me all de days of my life."

"Yes, honey, it will for-true!" Cun Hester shouted as she leaped up and wheeled round and round in the aisle. "I feel de spirit," she yelled, and her feet made sharp raps on the floor.

"Git right, soldiers! Let's follow dis angel to Zion." Her voice shaped a beating tune for the women who followed her shouting and singing.

But Cricket's head drooped and her body crumpled up on the floor.

"Yunnah git out my way," Uncle Wes thundered and headed for the pulpit, pushing women in the aisle right and left. Aun Missie howled horribly as she followed him through the back door with Cricket in his arms. Reverend Duncan bellowed above the confusion that Cricket had only fainted off. The fresh air would fetch her to.

The church emptied slowly, for people choked the doors. Blue went out the back door and sat in the graveyard to take off his shoes and rest.

Never had he felt so down-in-the-heart. Men's eyes slipped sidewise under lowered hat brims as ladies parted the thorny strands of barb-wire behind the graveyard and crawled between them to disappear in the bushes.

The baskets were unpacked, food spread out on long plank tables. Everybody ate in silence.

The sun was dropping when the small man mounted the church steps, praised the dinner highly and asked:

"Who will deliver dis prize to Cricket Pinesett?" He held up a small white package.

Wonder and respect showed in every face.

"You take em, Al-fred. You is de foreman," Reverend Duncan suggested, and Cun Fred stepped forward. The benediction was said and the crowd dispersed.

A little way down the road Aun Fan reached inside her clothes and unhooked her corset.

"I can' stand mashin," she sighed with relief and filled her pipe.

"Blue acted shamefaced as a suck-egg dog. I could 'a' spoke better myself."

"Don' talk hard, Fancy. Blue done well enough," Cun Fred answered.

"I had set my mind on Blue bein a preacher. I see I been wrong," she said sadly.

"I don' want no preacher in my family. I ruther Blue to work for his livin."

Instead of going home, they all went to see how Cricket was. She sat on the front piazza in

Uncle Wes's big armchair. Her skin was ashy, her eyes looked hollow and the prize lay unopened in her lap.

"Whyn' you look at em, Cricket?" Aun Fan asked.

"Cricket wants Cooch to have em," Uncle Wes answered.

"Cricket's de fooliest gal I ever seen," Aun Missie declared.

"If Cricket wants Cooch to have dis prize, Cooch can have em. You ain' to cross Cricket to-day, Missie."

Blue went with Man Jay to take it to Cooch. She lay in the bed with the top of a greased white stocking fitting snugly over her head and forehead. Her eyelids were swollen, her nose blistered, her pouting lips sad.

"Cricket sent you the prize, Cooch." Man Jay held out the little ribbon-tied package.

Cooch's mouth opened, her nostrils quivered.

"Is you deef, Cooch?" Cun Jule asked excitedly and grabbed the package, untied it in a hurry.

"Is it got any pictures?" Cooch asked.

Aun Jule could not find one among the small printed pages.

"See if you can read em, Cooch?" She held the first page before Cooch's eyes but Cooch turned her head away.

Poor little Cooch! She looked small and pitiful under the big patchwork quilt with her scarred cheeks and drooping eyelids. She was very different from the brazen girl who drank Coco-Cola yesterday.

"I'll read em for you." Man Jay took the book and began. "Now-in-de-days-of——" He squinted, balked, spelled out the letters: "H-e—he, r-o-d—rod, Herod, de king——"

"It's about a king, Cooch!" he encouraged.

Cun Jule sucked her teeth.

"No wonder Cricket give dat no-'count prize away."

"I ruther have dem blue beads," Cooch said.

"Toosio stole de beads," Blue told her.

"Toosio?"

"Toosio said you speech too."

"When I get well I'll kill Toosio," Cooch blazed out angrily.

"You won' get a chance, Cooch. I'm gwine kill em myself to-night," Man Jay declared.

CHAPTER XX

WHEN school was out field work began in earnest for every rain made a green beard of grass over the big field's face. Cun Fred followed the plowmen, warning them to be careful. Plowing is tight work when cotton laps in the rows. It takes watchful eyes and steady hands to throw dirt without hurting a root. Women and children were in the field before sunrise, catching boll-weevils or jerking hoes that crunched softly in mellow ground and clinked sharply when a stone-rock got in the way. Skirts were tied up high above the dew. Towels were hung over head-rags and hats were stuffed with leaves to keep the sun-hot from baking brains.

Old Brer Dee stayed with them trying to keep them from wasting time and slighting work. As day climbed the sky and the sun-hot strengthened, they lagged with more and more pauses for talk and frequent trips to the bushes. Then Brer Dee would get a stubby pencil and a scrap of paper out of his pocket and write down names of offenders.

"You won' git a cent when Sat'day comes," he declared, but everybody knew his bark was worse than his bite.

Blue and Man Jay were water-boys. From dawn until dusk they went back and forth from the spring behind Aun Missie's house fetching

water. Work makes sweat and sweat makes thirst.
Full buckets were drained quickly, and field-hands
urged the boys to hurry back. Blue's neck and
legs grew weary long before shadows shortened,
but Man Jay never lost heart. He beat drum
tunes on the bottom of his empty bucket and sang
reel songs all day long.

"Dance wid de gal wid a hole in his stockin
just above his knee," "Ham-bone, ham-bone, bite
off de end, Do, Mas John, don' do dat again," were
his favorites. Sometimes he made up words and
tunes like, "Kero-sene—E is mean—E will burn
you head off clean—Burn you head off clean," or
"Now in de days of He-rod de king—We will
sing——"

Cooch's burned head had healed. Before water-
melons ripened a big hat stuffed with leaves
shielded the new kinks that sprouted on her head.
Misfortune had not humbled her. She made sport
of Brer Dee when he scolded, back-talked Jule
who shamed her for laziness and said she was
getting trifling as Cricket. Cooch declared she
would scorn to be like that bright-skin hussy who
did nothing but eat, sleep, sit up in the shade keeping her hands soft, combing her long hair before
a looking-glass, acting like a grand lady when she
was nothing but a do-my-lord.

This made Aun Missie rave and rant that
Cricket was no beggarly field-hand. Cricket
churned butter, gathered elderberry blossoms for
wine, whipped the okra bushes to make them bear.

Cricket did not need to ruin her looks with heavy
work long as Wes lived.

Cun Jule said she felt sorry for the man who
took Cricket for wife, but Aun Missie answered
angrily that when Cricket got old enough to have
husband, Wes would take her to town and find a
man able to give her the best. Cricket was too
high-born and bredded to wash and cook for a
farm-hand.

One morning Aun Missie called Blue aside and
told him she wanted him to go to Big Pa's and get
a stronger charm to keep Wes home. The charm
she had made him ramble worse than ever. Blue
could not bear to take part in this thing.

"Whyn' you send Cricket?" he asked.

"I don' want Cricket to know bout me cunjurin
Wes. Take you foot in you hand, boy, an' run.
If Brer Dee quarrels I'll tell em you went to buy
me some tobacco."

Blue hurried away and gave her message to Big
Pa. The old man said Missie ought not to be so
tight on Wes, but if she was bent on keeping him
home he would fix a charm to hold Wes to her bed
the rest of his natural life.

Big Pa got a piece of cloth and made three tiny
bags which he filled with bits of ashes, pinches of
salt and something he took from a tin can. He
said if Aun Missie would put one of the bags under
Uncle Wes's pillow every night for three nights,
he would never sleep in a strange bed again. If
Blue cracked his teeth to anybody, the charm

would jump on him and maybe kill him dead.

Before noon the next day Uncle Ben came to the field at a run. It was plain that he brought distressful news. Blue thought of the three little bags and Uncle Wes. He felt relief when Uncle Ben said the hogs had cholera.

Everybody dropped hoes and plow-handles with moans and groans. Some suggested remedies to save the sick beasts, but Uncle Ben said nobody this side of Jesus could stop cholera once it started.

He wanted the dead hogs buried before sundown, or buzzards could scatter cholera all over the country. Cun Fred answered sharply that he had no time to dig graves for hogs.

"If dem hogs ain' buried not a piece of meat won' grow in de land long as we live," Uncle Ben insisted.

"My God, Ben!" Cun Jule stuck out her mouth like a toad fish. "You would bury dem fine, fat hogs scarce as meat is to-day? If de mens will butcher em we can eat some an' put de rest in brine."

Cun Fred's face brightened. "You got sense like a man, Jule. Knock off plowin, men. Let's go butcher dem hogs. We can scald an' scrape em by noon, den we could have a chitlin strut at de street to-night if you work fast an' get em cut up."

Heavy sorrow swiftly turned to noisy joy. The men whooped and shouted, women laughed with pleasure. Cun Hester lifted her arms to the sun, curtsied low and said:

"God don' fail to provide for his chillen."

Dead hogs spotted the shady hillside below the barnyard. Flies buzzed around half-open eyes of huge beasts breathing their last. One grunted feebly when Uncle Ben called her name.

"Sallie, honey, I would help you if I could," he moaned, but the plowmen laughed and whistled happily.

The wash pots were filled with water, and fires built under them. No axes were needed to stun the lifeless hogs, or sharp knives to slit the thick throats.

When a huge black sow was thrust head foremost into a barrel of boiling water Uncle Ben wept. "Just to think Melia's dead. E was de finest sow in dis country. Melia birthed two litters every year God sent. Melia had sense like people. E never ate a chicken in his life. God knows dis is one sad day."

"Melia was a fine sow for-true, but old Jack was de prize. Jack give Melia's pigs dat silky hair an' tender meat," Cun Fred answered.

Uncle Ben wanted to argufy but Cun Fred shouted:

"Let's move fast, mens! A big work is to do befo sundown. You won' have no chitlin strut lessen you turn like pulleys."

The barnyard seethed with haste and dust flew

under fast-stepping feet. Long stout poles mounted between tree limbs were filled with white carcasses and men clustered around them slitting open the clean fat bellies. The overhead sun beat down strong on the tubful of high-smelling chitterlings, to be cleaned and cooked for the strut to-night.

Cricket was with the children, roasting pig-tails in the ashes, eating them fast as they browned. Her hair was ruffled, her face greasy, her dress smutty.

Aun Missie looked up from a tub. "Quit eatin dem pig-tails. You ain' got strong insides like Cooch an' Toosio. Wait an' eat you some chitlins to-night. You needn' turn up you nose. When dey get fixed dey will pure be sweet as white violets."

"Dey's de best part of de hog," Aun Fan said. "Lord, yes."

"Dey is sweeter'n ham," "Better'n spare-ribs," a shower of answers agreed.

"Gi'me chitlins till I die," Cun Jule sang out, but Brer Dee rebuked her.

"Dat's a reel song, Sister. It'll make you have sin."

"God made de chitlins. It ain' no sin to praise em," Cun Jule answered.

"Maybe so, but you better praise God stead of chitlins." He lined out the hymn.

"God moves in a mysterious way His wonders to perform."

Everybody joined in and sang lustily, since singing ever helps work to go faster.

By first dark the meat was divided according to size of families, by sweaty men who boasted how they'd strut with their partners in the moonlight to-night.

CHAPTER XXI

THE moon was shining high in the sky and a great fire burned at the end of the street. Chitterlings hung on a framework of poles around it, sizzled and browned. Head-rags shone like gay blossoms as women bent near the flames roasting ash-cakes to eat with the rich smelling meat.

Big Pa stepped around with the aid of his stick and sweet-talked the ladies like a young man. Uncle Wes had not come to squeeze his accordion, but Uncle Ben played lively tunes on his fiddle and the people sang:

"Ham-bone, ham-bone, bite off de end.
Do, Mas John, don' do dat again."

or

"I don' care how you share em
So long as you share em even."

Every tongue fell silent when Brer Dee asked God's blessing and begged God's forgiveness if any Christian missed and crossed his feet enduring the strutting, but a thin scream, followed by a dog's mournful howl, floated down the road.

Cun Fred set off in a run and Blue let go Cooch's hand to follow at his heels, for Aun Missie stood in the road sending out screams.

"For God's sake, make haste, Cun Fred!" she cried. "Wes is gwine dead—dead!"

Uncle Wes sat quietly by the hearth with his arm around Cricket who sobbed like her heart would break. He looked up and smiled as more people rushed into the room.

"Nothin don' ail me. Missie just got eye-sighted because I was late comin home."

"Oh, my God!" Aun Missie lamented. "I been beggin Wes to keep out de skin games, but he wouldn' listen to me. I worked so hard to clean dem chitlins, now I can' go eat none."

"Go on an' eat de chitlins, Missie. Soon as I dress I'll fetch my 'cordion an' squeeze em for de people to strut." Uncle Wes was so pleasant the other people believed him and hurried back to the Quarters, but Cun Fred closed the front door and made Uncle Wes take off his shirt so he could examine the small hole in his middle.

"How-come you let somebody shot you, Wes?"

"I ain' shot. One of de boys stuck me wid a ice pick when I made em take dat ace out his sleeve. I'd 'a' killed em but e got away."

Cun Fred looked worried. "Who was it, Wes?"

"I ruther not tell, Al-fred."

"If I had a good sharp knife, I'd cut dis hole an' make em bleed."

Uncle Wes felt in his pocket and shook his head. "I left my knife in dat boy's neck, but I got a razor yonder on de shelf."

Cricket found the razor. Cun Fred opened it, felt its sharp blade, "I hate to cut in you belly, Wes, but it's de best thing to do."

He made a slice, then another. Beads of sweat stood on his forehead, his eyelids blinked fast, but Uncle Wes did not even wince.

"Now I'll pour turpentine in de hole an' cover em up."

"We ain' got a turpentine in de house."

"Hand me de lamp, Cricket," Cun Fred bade, but as Cricket lifted the lamp the glass shade fell on the floor with a crash.

"Great God!" Cun Fred cried. "Breakin a lamp-shade is de worst luck ever was."

"You too quick to look on the dark side," Uncle Wes said gently. He unscrewed the burner himself and poured a clear stream over the cuts. "My insides is tough as leather. I'll be well by to-morrow."

"You better get in de bed, Wes."

"Fill my pipe for me, Cricket," he answered.

The room swung before Blue's eyes. Everything got black. When he waked up, on the bed, Uncle Wes was leaning over him, "Is you all right now, son?" he asked kindly.

"Blue is too chicken-hearted for a boy," Cun Fred complained.

"I ain' got no fault to find of Blue. He ain' used to blood, not yet." Uncle Wes lifted the pillow to put under Blue's head and underneath it were the three small bags. "What dat is, Cricket?"

Cricket did not know and Blue dared not tell.

Uncle Wes staggered like he was drunk.

"Missie's cunjured me wid dem bags?"

"Let me see em, Wes."

Cun Fred looked scared, but Uncle Wes threw the bags in the fire.

"It ain' good to burn up a cunjure," Cun Fred said gloomily, and sure enough, the next morning Uncle Wes had bad indigestion. Big Pa drenched him with teas to help the pain, and Cun Fred begged him to stay in bed. Uncle Wes said a bed saps a man's strength. He would mend quicker if he sat up in a chair. His blood was in good order. By next week he would be sawing logs, sound as a silver dollar.

Before first dark, Aun Missie's screams and She-She's howls told the world Uncle Wes was bad sick.

The house was soon crowded and the road full of people coming. Aun Missie walked up and down in the front yard frantic with noisy grief.

"Oh, my God! Nobody can save Wes now! E's gwine dead. Yes, Lord, e's gwine dead! A man stuck em wid a pick an' de lamp-shade broke. De lamp-shade knowed death was comin!" She flung her apron over her head and beat on her breast with clenched fists.

Big Pa hobbled around the hearth boiling teas, but nobody mentioned the charm bags.

Uncle Wes lay on the bed and groaned with every breath. He writhed and twisted with agony as Cun Fred laved his swollen belly with cold cloths from a basin of water. When Big Pa

brought the long-necked bottle of hot root tea
to drench him again, his face twisted into a horrible pattern.

"For God's sake, let me be!" he cried. "I
can' swallow no more of dat bitter stuff! If I'm
cunjured, I'm cunjured an' drenchin makes me
worse. Missie done me wrong, wrong——"

Big Pa talked, argued, but Uncle Wes turned
his head away and clenched his teeth.

"Wes ain' in his right mind," Big Pa said.
"We got to hold em to drench em. Come on, mens.
We can' let a good man die."

"You can' drench me no more, I tell you."
Uncle Wes crouched on the bed like a wildcat
ready to spring. He grabbed at the china basin
to fight the men off, but it fell with a crash on the
floor. Brawny muscles in his naked shoulders
heaved and strained to be free from hands that
forced him back on the pillow. He ranted, cursed,
but the bottle poured root tea down his throat.

"Dat's bound to help em," Big Pa said cheerfully when the bottle's gurgling ceased. "It's
de strongest medicine I got."

A flood of nausea seized Uncle Wes. "Oh,
God! Have mercy," he whispered when it lulled,
for hiccoughs clicked in his throat like a shuttle in
a loom.

"Try to lie still, honey." Cricket lifted his
long limp hand and laid it against her cheek.

Aun Missie sat by the bed rocking from side
to side, praying God to have mercy. Aun Bina

stood beside her with tears pouring from her eyes.

Blue could endure it no longer. He crept outside where stranger-men sat on the wood-pile smoking, talking. How could they talk about pulling fodder when Uncle Wes was so near death?

The back door fell open, red light from the fire inside played over the black moon shadows. Old She-She raised her head, gave a long sorrowful howl and one of the men got up and went to see what had happened. He hurried back full of excitement. Uncle Wes was talking to dead people. Cun Hester was hanging a thorny limb on the head of the bed to keep death off, Big **Pa** was putting leeches on his temples, for blood leaked out of Wes's nose.

The other men shook their heads. Thorns and leeches could not save Wes now.

The poor fellow would go when the river tide ebbed.

A hooting owl lifted up his voice in the swamp. "Who-who-who are you?" he cried twice.

The men whispered together and got up. They knew the owl had spoken to death.

Blue climbed up and peeped in the window just as Cun Fred took the shadeless lamp and bent over the bed.

"Wes," he said. "I'm right here wid you, son."

The awful heaving in the naked bony breast lessened little by little. Cun Fred laid one hand over Uncle Wes's heart, held it there, took it up.

"E's gone. My best friend is gone, mens."

Cun Hester raised the first death-cry, a long keen wail full of sorrow. Other voices joined in until the house could not hold so much grief. Trees and buildings outside took the echoes and sent them over the world, to tell everybody Uncle Wes was dead.

Cun Andrew took out his red pocket handkerchief. "Better tie up de chin, Al-fred."

"I ain' got de heart." Cun Fred was crying.

"Come on outside, Missie, so de mens can do de last duty."

Cun Hester tried to lead her away, but Aun Missie butted the wall and pulled her own hair. "Oh, Wes! Oh, Wes!" She screamed his name over and over.

Cricket was the only one who made no sound. She crouched on the steps motionless and silent. She did not even lift her downcast head when Aun Fan said, "Try to holler, gal. Dry grief is awful unhealthy."

Man Jay came out of the room and fell on his knees beside Cricket and sobbed fit to break his heart. She put her arms around him but spoke no word.

"Cricket must be in a trance. His best friend is gone an' e don' so much as mourn."

"No, Fancy. It ain' in de gal's blood to holler an' carry on over dead people," Cun Hester said gently.

CHAPTER XXII

Aun Fan went home to make coffee for those who sat up. She hurried back for she wanted to see how Bury League Knights act with the dead. They spent most of the long night hours sitting on the door-steps or lying outside on the ground talking in low mumbling words. The meeting benches from the Quarters had been put in rows across the piazza to make narrow beds for the women, and the old bench legs creaked out wearily with the restless weight of those stretched upon them.

Once Cun Hester jumped out of a sound sleep and cried: "Do, Jesus, don' let me fall off dis bench an' broke my leg dis night."

The honeysuckle vine on the porch corner made the air stifling sweet, but as the night rolled on the scent of death crept out of the house and smothered every smell with its strength. The wailing had hushed for fear any racket would fret Uncle Wes's spirit and make it tarry near the house.

When the cocks crowed for middle night Aun Fan and Cun Hester got up and heated coffee in a wash pot in the yard since no fire burned in the chimney. The Knights drained one cup after another and the women finished what was left. So much hot coffee made sweat trickle down faces, but it drove sleep away and started words to weaving patterns.

Aun Missie's tongue was loosened at both ends. She told how Uncle Wes's people tried to keep him from marrying her because they were house servants and she was raised to do field work. She told how year after year she drank Big Pa's teas and wore his charms to make her bear children, for Uncle Wes craved somebody to keep his blood alive after he was gone. He went off with Bina and stayed three long years. When he came back his father was gone and Cricket's mother was dead. Wes hated the bright-skin child, but Cricket was too small to know and she throve on goat's milk and pot liquor. Big Pa got the tip of a buzzard's claw and hung it on a string around her neck to make her teeth easy. A blue-tailed lizard's toe tied on her leg made her walk before her first year passed, and the sweet way she tripped across the floor to meet Wes was enough to move a heart of rock. One day Wes cursed Cricket's Daddy, and his words fell on the child. She began to fail right away, and every time Wes came in the house Cricket's sad, blameful eyes followed him. Big Pa's remedies and Cun Hester's did her no good. Wes knew he was at fault and he almost went off his head with grief. He went all the way to town on the *Comanche* and brought back a bottle of spoon medicine. One dose put her to sleep so nobody could wake her.

The best conjure doctor in the land, next to Big Pa, lived away back in the pine lands. To reach him Wes had to pass a country where low-down white people had signs on trees telling niggers to read and run. That did not stop him.

He took his foot in his hand and started off with his gun before day was clean.

It took him three days to go and come, yet all he fetched back was a puppy named She-She, whelped by an old witch dog. The old conjure man said the puppy and Cricket must eat out of the same pan and if the puppy licked Cricket's mouth, she would live.

Wes fixed a pan of goat's milk weakened down with pot liquor and fed Cricket one spoonful and the puppy one. Cricket was like a different child after that first feed.

She would laugh and hold out her arms if Wes came in sight. As soon as she got strong on her legs she began to dance. Many was the night Wes sat patting his feet and clapping his hands while Cricket cut funny little steps. She was no higher than Wes's knee but he got crazy about her. He quit throwing his money away and buried every cent so Cricket could have everything nice when she grew up.

He was going to buy Cricket a Victoria this fall. Now he was gone——

"God knows what's best, Missie. Maybe if Wes had lived, Cricket would have sin," Aun Fan sighed.

Cun Hester disagreed. Wes was the finest man in the country. So kind-hearted, so free-handed. The plantation would never be the same.

Aun Missie sobbed that it hurt her to the heart to think Wes was in Hell to-night.

"You can' say for certain Wes is in Hell, Missie. Wes ever was a good boy," Cun Hester said gently.

"Wes never was baptized," Cun Andrew put in.

"Wes come from Methodist people, Andrew."

"Dat ain' no excuse. God says people must be dipped or be lost."

"God says judge not lessen you get judged, Andrew." Cun Hester stood up in the middle of the floor.

"Yunnah tell me dis," she said solemnly. "Did Wes ever mistreated a soul in his life?"

"Everybody loved Wes from de oldest to de youngest," Cun Fred answered warmly.

"Well, den, if we here loved em God ain' got reason to hate em."

The women stirred and the benches creaked, but Cun Hester stood her ground. "Looka dat star, chillen." She lifted her eyes to a red star hanging low in the sky. "Yonder's whe' Wes is. Cricket's Mammy come for Wes to-night; e is holdin to his hand right now, leadin em to de throne of God."

"Cricket's Mammy is in Hell." Aun Fan gave a snort.

"No, Fancy. Dat gal died birthin Cricket, an' birthin chillen is Jesus' business. When Jesus' great all-seein eyes falls on dat poor boy an' his sister such a long ways from home, e ain' gwine let God mistreat em."

"I believe you," Cun Fred agreed.

The argument waxed warm until Cun Hester shouted, "My Daddy knew more about God an' Jesus dan any preacher ever was. My Daddy was wise. An' straight talkin too. E belonged to white people but e didn' let nobody fool him." Cun Hester wiped her eyes. "I can' hardly talk to-night, my heart is so full."

A mocking-bird in the apple tree trilled for dawn while Cun Hester told how God made the first people out of dust. They were not black, not white, but the color of the dust of the ground. He put some in Africa where the sun was hot and it baked them black as tar. He put some in a country where winter-time covered the ground with snow. Cold weather bleached them white. The black people lived easy for fruit hung on the trees and fish swam in the rivers. The white people had a hard time; cold and hunger plagued them; they got mean and cross; they learned how to quarrel and kill. God got worried in his mind and sent an angel to make them behave. They were cold and hungry and they begged the angel for some way to keep warm.

Satan was walking around and heard all the racket. He came up and said he owned all the fire. God didn't have a piece to his name. They begged Satan to give them fire and food and Satan went off. He came back with a table piled up with fine victuals. Pork ham and turkey stuffed with oysters. Fruit cake and pound cake, ambrosia and pies. Everybody's mouth leaked water just to smell the seasoning. Satan would not let them taste the victuals until he made this trade. He would give them fire and all they could eat for their souls after they died. They were willing enough but the angel said the price was too big. Satan laughed and brought out three barrels of corn liquor. He gave everybody a drink and the angel took a taste to warm him up, for the poor creeter was cold and nervish. The liquor went to the angel's head. He let Satan swim a piece of Hell through seven rivers to cool it and show the white people how to rule it. The trade was made. Satan never let white people rest after that.

Before long, sweet little Jesus looked down from Heaven and saw Hell's burning lake piled up with white people and he asked his Pa to let him come tell the others how to escape torment. Jesus was black as a crow's wing, so the first place he went was Africa.

It was spring and the first woman he saw was planting corn. He made his manners and asked her what she was planting. She looked straight at him and frowned up her face.

"Is you vex as you look?" Jesus asked her just so.

The woman made answer, "A strappin young man like you ought to help me plant my crop."

"What you plantin?"

"I'm plantin rocks."

"Rocks let it be."

Jesus took the seed and dropped it. The corn made fine ears but every grain was a flint rock.

At the next house another woman was planting corn.

"What you plantin, Sister?" Jesus asked her.

"I'm plantin corn, but I ain' got a grain outside dis handful of seed in my gourd."

"I'm so hungry I thought you might bake me bread."

The woman studied a while then she said, "I'll divide what I got wid you." She took a few grains from the gourd and ground them between rocks. They made a small dough no bigger than a hickory nut, but she put it on the fire in a skillet and went back to her planting. While the bread baked, it swelled so big, it lifted the lid clean off the skillet. When she and Jesus ate all they could hold, plenty was left, and the new planted corn had grown tall as the house and full ears covered every stalk from top to bottom.

Jesus went on to the next house and asked that woman if she had any troubles. She said she was blessed in all but one thing. Rats were eating her out of house and home.

Jesus took off his black glove and threw it on the floor. It jumped up a cat and the dog on the hearth growled. "Just for dat," Jesus said, "dogs must ever stay out-of-doors in de weather but cats can sleep on de hearth."

Jesus went all through the world doing good, but when he got to white people he had a hard road.

White people had got rich and he told them to sell their goods and feed the poor. When he said that the white people got vexed and hung him on a cross alongside thieves and robbers. God sent a storm and earthquake to stop them but it was too late. Poor little Jesus!

"You reckon any white people is in Heaven, Cun Hester?"

"Mighty few, Fancy. White people traded dey souls for dat fire an' food. Dey fetched black people to dis country an' learnt em sinful ways. White people has much to account for."

Big Pa's breast heaved with sobs. "I wish I was back home in Africa."

"Don' fret, Big Pa. You ain' got much longer in dis country. You will soon be walkin on de golden streets," Cun Hester consoled him.

"I want to see my mudder befo I go. I ain' seen em in so long." Big Pa blubbered so Cun Hester patted his head and sang:

"Don' mourn, Big Pa. Don' mourn, Christians."

The Bury League Knights swelled the song until it filled the night.

> "Don' mourn, Christians,
> De big day is comin.
> When we'll meet all together,
> On de banks of de river,
> An' we'll walk for ever,
> On dem gold-en streets."

CHAPTER XXIII

BIRD songs filled the dawn when the Knights went inside to measure Uncle Wes for his fine store-bought box and his grave. Cun Fred took out a string from his pocket, but Aun Missie jerked it out of his hand.

"Nobody can measure Wes exceptin wid dey eyes. A string'll put bad luck on em."

Cun Fred argued that Wes was to have a fine store-bought box worth twenty-five dollars. The Knights wanted him to have a good fit and be comfortable in his grave.

Aun Missie was firm. She would bury Uncle Wes in his shroud sheet before a string should lie alongside him. She wept until her breath came and went like bellows.

"Don' take it so hard, Missie," Cun Fred comforted her. "You is a widow for-true, but Wes left you a good insurance. De Knights will pay you one hundred dollars a week from to-day. One hundred dollars will take care of you and Cricket as long as you live."

"It's two hundred dollars," Cun Andrew corrected.

"No, Andrew. Wes left Man Jay and Bina one hundred dollars insurance."

Aun Missie rent the air with shrieks and began butting the wall. How could Wes do such a thing! Since the day Wes joined the Knights she had

pinched and saved to keep up his monthly dues.
Man Jay and Bina would get that money over her
dead body. Cun Fred pulled her into the shed-
room where Uncle Wes lay on the bed with a sheet
stretched corner-wise to reach from his head to his
feet. When Cun Fred uncovered the dead face
Aun Missie sobbed, "I give in," and fled into the
back yard where Cricket sat on the wood-pile holding Big Pa's hand.

Poor old Big Pa, shrunken and tottering,
mumbled like somebody out of his senses when Aun
Missie laid her head on his knees and wailed, "Dat
charm were too strong—too strong——"

"You ought not to put all three of dem bags
under Wes's pillow, Missie. You done Wes
wrong. Dat's how come e died so hard."

Aun Fan and Cun Hester fell to cleaning up the
house. The floor was swept, the cold ashes taken
up and the pots turned upside down on the hearth
before the neighbors came to fetch food for Aun
Missie and red flowers for Uncle Wes.

Terror gripped Blue's heart every time Cun
Hester took people into the shed-room. He had
never seen a dead somebody before. He could
hardly believe Uncle Wes was stricken and silent,
unable to answer those who looked at his uncovered face and talked about his poor lost soul. A
silver quarter lay on each eyelid, his mouth smiled.

Everybody praised his looks. He had on his
Sunday clothes, his hair was clipped neatly, his
face shaven clean. A small white paper covered a

cut on his chin but Cun Hester said it would be taken off before he was put in his box.

Reverend Duncan and his wife drove their buggies around to the back door and Blue helped to hitch the bony nags to the apple tree. Reverend's face looked drawn and worried. He asked Blue if Uncle Wes prayed before he went.

"Uncle Wes been too sick to pray," Blue answered. "But e did say, God have mercy."

Reverend shook his head sadly and wabbled toward the benches which had been taken off the porch and placed in a square under the big oak tree. A table was set in the middle beside two blocks of wood. Women filled the benches and men stood or squatted in a circle outside them, talking low. Babies gurgled and cooed, children stared in wonderment at all that went on.

A stream of people flowed down the road. Hats, ribbons, colored dresses, red flowers, fluttered in the sunlight. Uncle Wes was a sinner and no white flowers could lie on his grave.

Noon came nearer and shadows grew short. Red flowers in cans of water wilted under the hot breeze that rose from the rice-fields. The white curtain in the shed-room window flowed out, trembled, fell back into place. Hushed voices wondered where the hearse could be. Aun Fan said the road was long and sandy, the ruts deep and dry, the hearse heavy. Big Pa groaned and said he hoped to God the hearse would broke clean down so the sun could set in the grave.

"I hope so myself," a strange woman answered.
She was Aun Missie's cousin, Olivia, who had
come all the way from across the river to pay her
respects to Uncle Wes. Her black skin was
smooth as a girl's but her naked gums and the
white wisps of hair that straggled from under
her head-rag told she had lived a long time. She
tried to keep Aun Missie in heart with cheerful
talk. She knew what it was to bury a lawful
gentleman. She had done it four times already
and the gentleman she had now would hardly last
through cotton-picking time.

Cun Hester made a wry face. "One husband
was enough for me. E was bad as any plague
God sent on Pharaoh. When e died an' left me
shet of em, I said to myself, 'God's will be done!' "

Olivia agreed that burying a husband is not
like losing a child. She had birthed twenty-six
head. Nineteen had come to full time, only eleven
were left. The girl-child with her was her gran.
She would soon be in her fourteenth year but she
had never travailed. It caused her to be spindly
and have a bad swinging in the head. Big Pa
looked at the girl's tongue, felt her pulse and said
he could brew a herb tea to set her straight.

"Better not make de tea strong," Aun Fan
warned.

"How's you trade dese days, Fancy?" Olivia
asked.

Aun Fan pulled a long face. "Triflin," she
grunted. "God knows what ails de women. I ain'

caught enough chillen dis year to pay for my
head-rags. Last year I caught forty-odd before de
crop was laid by.''

Big Pa told her to put some of his roots in the
springs and wells, they would start the women to
breeding.

"Missie tried dem roots. Dey ain' no-'count,"
Aun Fan answered sharply.

Big Pa straightened up and stared at Cricket
who walked up holding a bunch of white stars of
Bethlehem.

"Do Jesus! Look what dat gal went and done."

He jerked the flowers out of Cricket's hand,
threw them behind the wood-pile. "What you
mean, gal? Is you crazy?''

Cricket looked cut to the heart. "I didn'
thought you would mind me pickin em—Uncle Wes
ever loved dese white blossoms——''

"Don' talk hard at em, Big Pa. De gal didn'
aim to do wrong." Olivia took the corner of her
white apron and wiped Cricket's eyes. "When
I was a small girl, I done de same thing. Bad luck
ain' followed me," she said gently.

Big Pa explained to Cricket that after this when
anybody kin to her died, she must never break any
kind of growing thing until the burying was over.
Not a blade of grass must be plucked, not a wood
must be cut. No fire must burn in a dead man's
house, not even a pipe, lest smoke mix with his
spirit and scatter it. No kinsman can lay out the
dead or help dig the grave. No kinswoman can

wash a dead somebody's clothes. Cricket must go break some bread and put in a piece in Uncle Wes's hand to undo what she had done. Somebody cried the box was coming and he hurried Cricket into the house.

Cun Fred came down the road driving a pair of mules to a two-horse wagon. A crowd of men wearing white gloves sat on the long board box. Loud screams of grief rose to meet them, but Aun Fan kept saying, "Whe' is de hearse?" Cun Fred could hardly make her believe that the hearse had broken down and Uncle Wes must ride his last ride in a wagon.

One mule lifted his long head and gave a loud hungry *hee-haw-haw*. Cun Fred jerked him and told him to hush. This was no time to think of dinner.

The box cover was lifted, bright coffin handles cast sparkles of light on the black cloth cover. The white-gloved men lifted it out, carried it into the shed-room, closed the door behind them.

CHAPTER XXIV

Aun Missie put the long black veil Olivia brought over her black sailor hat. The shed-room door opened, Cun Fred stepped out and took her by the arm. "De time is come, Missie," he said.

She broke away shrieking, "No, no," at the top of her voice.

"For God's sake, Missie, don' tear my veil," Olivia cried above Reverend Duncan's booming words:

"De life of a man is like de path of de sun-in-de-sky—— E cometh up in de mornin."

The pall-bearers walked out slowly with their long heavy burden. Loud screams filled the house as they backed through the narrow door.

Cun Fred and Aun Missie went behind them, Man Jay and Aun Bina followed, then came Cricket holding to Big Pa's hand.

When the long box was put on the two low blocks Cun Jule whined like a dog but nobody paid her attention, for she was no rightful mourner. Aun Bina ran forward and fell across the box screaming Uncle Wes's name. Cun Andrew had to help Man Jay hold her when Reverend Duncan shouted with powerful words that no matter how right you live, you must be born again or go to Hell when you die. Wes had been warned ten thousand times. Every drop of sweat that fell off his brow said pray! Every

190

thunder that rolled begged him to make his peace
with God. His saw chanted through the trees,
"Pray, Wes! Pray, Wes!" but he gave no heed
to the warnings.

Aun Missie shook with sobs, and Cun Fred got
restless as a worm in hot ashes. He twisted about,
crossed one leg, then the other, blew his nose so
loud Aun Fan shook her head at him. Every time
Reverend Duncan shouted Uncle Wes was a miz-
zable man to-day, Cun Fred cleared his throat
and spat.

Cricket sat still as a stone. Her bright dry
eyes fastened on Reverend's face until his last
words died away.

Aun Bina's frantic howls could not equal Aun
Missie's now for the mourning time had come.

Reverend nodded to the men in white gloves and
they stood up. Cun Fred stood up too. "Wait
a minute, mens," he ordered. "I want to say a
few words before you move de body."

Everybody was dumb struck. Even Aun Missie
was speechless.

"Reverend," he began, "I know you is a good
honest man, but you made a bad mistake when
you preached Wes to Hell. I been knowin Wes
ever since e come in dis world. I wasn' but a
knee-high boy when I used to tote Wes on my back
to de Big House kitchen for his Mammy to suckle
em. I learnt Wes to walk. I learnt em to talk. I
stood in his weddin when e married to Missie. I
know all Wes done from den until now. I take my

stand to tell de world, God never made not a better man."

A heavy silence lay over the bewildered crowd. Cun Fred was not even a church-member, and he stood up before all the people talking bold as a preacher.

He paused a moment and went on. "Reverend, if I was settin home on my piazza to-day an' I seen Wes comin down de road, weary an' sick an' lost from home, I'd run wid joy to meet em. I'd tote em on my back same like I used to when e was a baby. I'd put em in my company bed to rest an' I'd give em de best victuals in my house."

A gentle wind fanned the red flowers and passed on by. Nobody stirred. Reverend listened in silence, Big Pa leaned forward and held a hand back of his ear.

"God is a better man dan I is, Reverend. E made Wes same like e made you an' every member of Heaven's Gate Church. When dat po' boy was wanderin around in de sky last night, not knowin which way to go, God didn' turn his back on em. No, suh, God done same like I would, same like you would. E opened de gate of Heaven and took Wes in."

"Juba-lee! Oh, yes! Dis is de year of Juba-lee when de sinners all gets home." Cun Hester's words hung alone in the stillness for a heart-beat.

Aun Missie threw her veil back, jumped up and danced shouting steps round and round the coffin. Now and then her hand struck hard on its black cloth, as she threw scraps of words into the lonely song.

"Juba-lee! Oh, yes! Dis is de year of Juba-lee when de sinners all gets home!"

Cun Hester stood at one end of the long box, singing and clapping her hands for Aun Missie to shout. Olivia took up the words and soon the whole crowd joined in: "Juba-lee! Oh, yes, Juba-lee! Dis is de year of Juba-lee."

The sun had dropped when the pall-bearers lifted the coffin and put it on the wagon. The hungry mule got contrary. He reared and pitched until Cun Fred called to the Knights, "Go get Wes's oxen and hitch em to Wes's own wagon."

It was done quickly, for the oxen were gentle. Side by side, they waited patiently until their master was loaded. Cun Fred climbed up on the box, took the rope lines, and the wheels creaked ahead. The white-gloved Knights walked behind, two by two.

Nobody spoke a word during the sad journey. Everybody seemed lost in solemn thought. When Heaven's Gate Church came in sight, so clean and white against the dark trees, Big Pa began weeping. Slowly, carefully, the oxen went past new graves, past others old and sunken. When they halted beside a gaping hole with two boards across it, Reverend Duncan got out of his buggy and chanted:

"De Lord gave, de Lord have taken em away, Blessed be de name of de Lord."

A great wailing burst forth when the long box was lifted up, then it hushed suddenly. The grave was too short. Cun Fred took off his hat and coat and got down in the deep hole to help the Knights shovel out dirt. People murmured and sighed for no such bad luck had ever befallen anybody in the country.

Only Big Pa was glad and he cried out happily, "Thank God. De sun will set in de grave; Wes'll sleep sweet to-night."

Cricket gazed at the shining west and her eyes were bright with tears, but her lips trembled into a little smile.

At last the grave was lengthened and long ropes lowered the box with a thud. Aun Missie tried to leap in behind it. She almost pulled her arms from the sockets, trying to get away from those who held her back. Torches lighted the dusk as spades poured in a hollow mumbling stream of earth. Aun Missie was on one side of the grave, Aun Bina on the other, both screaming for Uncle Wes to come back. Cun Fred smoothed the mound of earth, and Aun Fan picked up an armful of red flowers.

"No, Fancy," Cun Hester stopped her. "Red blossoms stands for a lost soul. Dis grave must lie naked except for what I got in dis basket." She handed the basket to Cricket who put the glass lamp at the head, the long-necked drenching bottle at the foot, and midway between them she placed a white china plate and cup and saucer.

Reverend Duncan lifted his arms and prayed for the widow and orphans while Aun Missie screamed, "Oh, Wes! I can' go home widout you!" and Aun Bina wailed shrilly:

"Me an' Man Jay ain' got nobody now. Po' me! Po' Man Jay!"

Cricket clung to Big Pa, but her face was hidden in his old patched coat.

CHAPTER XXV

THE harvest season came in full and rich. A young moon hung thin and bright but instead of lying straight to foretell fine weather, it stood on one sharp point saying all the water in the sky would pour out soon. Big Pa said the hot sunshine was deceiving. It was time for a storm. The wind had behaved for nigh ten years and something was due to happen. The people got uneasy over his forebodings, for the crops were good. The bottom of every cotton stalk was loaded with fruit in spite of boll-weevils which pestered the fields. A storm would be a calamity.

Cricket went with Aun Missie to the field every morning soon as the dew was dry, to pick cotton until sundown. Aun Missie made her wear Uncle Wes's old hat stuffed with leaves to keep the sun-hot from baking her brains, but soon as the shadows lengthened Cricket took it off and let her hair fly in the breeze. Her hands were so sore from pulling fodder she could not pick fast. She lagged behind Cooch and Toosio dragging her sack up and down the long rows. The big green cotton worms scared her; bending over so long made her shoulders ache. Except for Blue and Man Jay she would have been laughed to scorn.

Two long rows of cotton sheets edged the field and sunset found them piled high for Cun Fred paid the pickers fifty cents a hundred pounds.

Wagons hauled the cotton to the gin house fast
as Brer Dee weighed it. The wooden frame holding the steelyard was called "the horse." It had
two sturdy legs and a long stout pole for head and
back.

Cooch and Toosio always pouted when the
horse's weighing hook fastened into the knot of
Cricket's sheet, for its heavy weight made the
horse legs creak and the sheet's strong cloth
stretch and tear. Brer Dee would push the iron
pea forward and backward until a balance was
made, then shout Cricket's fine weight for everybody to hear before he wrote it down in a book.
Every day Blue and Man Jay took cotton from
their own sacks and put it on Cricket's sheet, for
they wanted her picking to weigh well even if
their own weights were short.

Cun Fred was busy from morning until night,
but he always went to see Aun Missie and Cricket
before he slept. He had promised Uncle Wes to
take care of them.

The big gin house trembled with the rumble of
gins long after dusk. White lint poured out in
two steady streams as the gin saws plucked out
seed and sent them pouring from a trough into
wagons. Fat cotton bales in a neat row on the
hillside showed clean white lint puffing out against
black iron bands which bound on the heavy bur-
lap.

Aun Missie had three bales in that row. She
said they were salty with her sweat, but she

thanked God for the dollars they would bring.
Everybody gave her high praise, and said she did
fine for a lone widow woman with only Cricket
to help her.

Her piazza roof was hidden under a thick layer
of peanuts for the sun-hot to sweeten and dry, her
sweet-potato patch promised enough to make
several earth covered banks.

One evening when the cotton was being weighed,
Cun Andrew stepped up and asked her to walk
out to meeting with him that night.

"Walk out wid who?" she asked angrily.
"Listen, Andrew; I is a widow for-true, but when
I walks out to meeting all de beau I wants is a
good fat light-wood knot. I can put em on de floor
until I'm ready to go home. All I got to do is pick
em up an' come. It ain' got no fat gal like Toosio
to pester me an' Cricket."

The cotton-pickers laughed boisterously, but
Ann Missie said she used to think when men
acted friendly they just meant to be friendly.
She had learned better. All men were a case. The
whole tribe of them. Deacons were bad as the
rest. All the husband she craved now was Jesus;
she was done with natural men.

When the cotton was gathered, molasses was
made from the sugar-cane, and wine from scupper-
nong arbors where ripe grapes filled the nights
with rich sweet smells.

On dark nights the men went to catch flounders
in the salt creeks by the sea, only four miles away,

and they brought back wagon-loads of oysters and clams. Sea bass were biting too, and a big bass stuffed with shrimp was good as any turkey.

Reverend Duncan wanted to thank God for these blessings with a revival meeting, but Cun Fred said that the surf was dark with mullet. Sharks chased big schools of them near the shore and made them hop out of the water so the dimmest eyes could see how fat they were. It would be foolish to waste time on a revival when mullet could be caught in a net and salted down for the winter. Spring was the time to pray. In the fall, people needed to pleasure after their year's hard work.

CHAPTER XXVI

THAT was the way sinners all talked, Aun Fan declared. They always wanted to wait for a more convenient time. It would take a whole bale of cotton to pay for a fish net. Who wanted salt mullet when plenty of good smoked herrings could be bought for fifteen cents a box? Satan ran the sea. He filled it with monsters. Shark's teeth almost bit a man's leg off last year. A stingaree shot his sting through another man's foot and gave him convulsions all night. Cun Fred had better look at the moon. It had blood spots on it and its misty ring made queer thin watery shadows.

Cun Fred was back-talking Aun Fan when Cun Hester came walking in.

"Al-fred," she said solemnly, "a vision come to me at sunset dis evenin. De spirit told me to come here an' make it known."

Her thin face was tense, her lips trembled, her hands clapped softly as she closed her eyes and prayed, "Sweet lil Jesus, help me tell Al-fred straight."

Surprise had taken Aun Fan's breath, but Cun Fred asked what the vision was.

"Son, I seen a white-wing angel when I was sayin my sundown prayer. E stood in a cloud an' waved his arms until my mind knew e was tellin me Judgment Day is at hand. Gabriel will stand wid one foot on de land an' one foot in God's holy sea roarin on de beach, to blow de last blast on his golden trumpet."

"Lord have mercy. Do, Master, look down," Aun Fan prayed.

"Listen to me, Al-fred." Cun Hester's voice rose higher. "What you gwine do when de sun an' moon crumbles? De rivers an' seas'll turn to blood, de ground will quake an' spew up de dead. Young an' old, rich an' poor, will stand before God's judgment bar. If you ain' ready, Al-fred, every tree an' rock, every grain of sand will rise up an' testify against you. For God's sake, pray before Satan drags you down to de bottomless pit, to burn you for ever. Not a drop o' water will cool you parch-ed tongue."

She swayed forward, backward, as her feet patted sharply on the floor.

"Judgment Day is comin. It's right round de corner. Is you ready to meet you God?"

"I want to be ready," Aun Fan quavered.

"Dat ain' de pint. Bein baptized won' save you, not lessen you live right. De graveyard is full of people wid dey mouth full o' dirt an' dey souls in Hell, because dey was lyin hypocrites."

Blue trembled with terror when he thought of his sins. He often lied to Aun Fan and he stole things from the store every time he had a chance. He sat with his head down until Cun Fred got up and took him by the hand.

"Don' let Cun Hester scare you, son. E's been

talkin bout Judgment Day ever since I can recollect. It ain' comin no time soon. Religion is a good thing for de ladies or old men wid one foot in de grave. We got plenty o' time left for prayin when we get too old to have pleasure. You go on to bed. We got to rise soon in de mornin.''

CHAPTER XXVII

BEFORE Aun Fan waked next morning Blue and Man Jay were walking to the beach with Cun Fred and a score of men. They carried camp things and the big net rented from the store man for half the catch of mullet. The morning was foggy. Not a shadow showed. Everything stood single and alone.

The small birds had nothing to say, but crows flew about cawing noisily. Now and then a stick crackled in a clump of myrtle, and Blue spied a buck or a startled doe guiding her fawn to safety. A big gobbler's fiery wattles shone under a sweet acorn oak. A shy fox squirrel with a bit of white on his throat peeped out from overhead branches. Cun Fred pointed to a great pine towering above its fellows and holding a bald eagle's nest. He said every brood was fed until the eaglets were able to fly, then the nest was filled with rocks to run them out and make them shift for themselves.

When the salt creeks and green marshes came in sight the fog had lifted into swift low-flying clouds. The tide was low and long-legged birds were gorging on shrimp and fish in the shallow winding creeks.

Stinging sand gnats got in Blue's eyes and nose, as he helped push dingy rowboats from the bank down into the water. These were loaded with pots, rations, quilts and the big lead-weighted net. Strong arms pulled the oars, the boats moved slowly along tide-driven stream past islands of marsh grass, mud-flats, oyster banks. The clear salt water blossomed with jelly fish, cool pale cups of pink, blue, purple. Oysters spurted out tiny jets of water and clicked their shells. Shrimps leaped up like grasshoppers in a pea-field. A smooth circle of water showed a stinga-ree's track, and Cun Fred told about a stingaree Big Pa's mullet net caught a long time ago. The creature was so big it took four men to lift its liver and the barbed sting on its tail was wide as a hand saw.

Blue shivered as the oars lifted and fell all together, guiding the boats along the channel, now in deep water where a big turtle's head showed and disappeared, now close to the marsh grass where a marsh hen's old nest, fastened to a tall grass stalk, could rise and fall with the tide. Sand-dunes crowned with yellow sea oats showed in the hazy distance. Cun Fred said the sea had gnawed a road through that narrow strip of land so the tide could come in to feed oysters and clams and water the marsh grass.

The boats were anchored in the main creek be-hind the dunes, and Blue hopped out and ran to get his first look at God's holy sea where Gabriel would stand when he blew the Judgment Day trumpet. Sand crabs put out spectacled eyes, stared and scurried into holes. Man Jay told them not to be scared for their shells had not

enough meat to fill a hollow tooth. The ᵔlean
yellow sand was ringed by white surf. Long lazy
waves rolled up with a crash and melted. Then
flocks of tiny birds hopped along the water's edge
snatching up bits of food.

As they picked up driftwood to build a fire,
Cun Fred called Blue and Man Jay to see a flock
of white gannets near the mouth of a creek. They
chattered harshly until their captain gave an
order, then they promptly formed a line across
the stream. Close together, wing to wing, their
legs made a fence to pen fish. The captain spoke,
the fence straightened, tightened, moved slowly
forward, while long gannet bills caught the leaping
fish.

Cun Fred said people think creatures are sense-
less, but the Bury League could not line up and
march to dinner more dignified than those wild
birds.

When a fire was started and a hand pump driven
in the sand, Blue went with Man Jay to a small
island facing the inlet to get shrimp and oysters.
The shrimp net opened like an umbrella when
Man Jay slung it in the water. A cord in the
middle drew up the lead-weighted edge, closed the
net like a bag and trapped the shrimps which
fluttered and struggled as Man Jay emptied them
into a bucket.

Small pools of water covered round holes where
stone crabs lived in the oyster banks. Sharp
billed oyster birds stopped feeding to stare when

Man Jay knelt beside a pool, felt it to see if the water was warm or cold.

"Dis old crab is home," he grinned and, leaning low, reached so deep into the hole that the pool wet his shoulder. He mumbled, grunted, gave a quick jerk, brought a huge crab up between his thumb and forefinger. "God bless! You's a big one!" he cried.

The crab sputtered and spit bubbles but Man Jay laughed. "You better pray stead o' cussin me. You time is out, son. If I didn' got you, you'd 'a' held me down till de tide rose an' drowned me." To show Blue how strong the crab was, he let one big claw seize the handle of the heavy bucket of shrimp. The claw held on as he raised the bucket clear off the ground.

"Try catchin one, Blue. It's fun."

Blue's heart gave a painful thump. "I got a pain in de belly, Man Jay. I can' bend over."

"You got a coward heart," Man Jay spat. "I been tellin Cricket so, an' e didn' believe me."

"You told em a lie," Blue yelled, but cold chills ran down his spine as he knelt by a water-covered hole.

"Run you hand deep, Blue. When you feel de crab, grab de small claws beside his eyes."

Blue shut his eyes and reached down, down until the tips of his finger felt something hard and sharp. He seized it for dear life's sake.

"God bless!" Man Jay cried when Blue dropped his crab on the ground. The furious creature ran sidewise reaching out a great scissors claw. Man Jay picked him up and tossed him in the bucket, where he clenched with his fellow crab.

"You is braver'n I had thought, Blue," he said carelessly, and knelt down by another pool.

The young flood tide rolled in from the sea, and Blue helped Man Jay row the boat-load of oysters, shrimps, crabs, back to camp. The oysters were stacked in a horseshoe to roast. Shrimps and crabs were put in pots to boil. Man Jay took a plug of tobacco from his pocket.

"How bout a chaw?"

Blue had never chewed, but he bit off a corner. It burned his tongue but tasted sweet.

"Better spit fast," Man Jay said as he gave Blue a pan of hot shrimp to pick.

Their whiskers were tangled, thorny bills stuck Blue's finger and their smell made a horrible dizziness blind him. He dropped the pan and leaned forward, wrung inside out with sickness.

Man Jay laughed but Cun Fred came running. He made Blue drink a cup of sea water and lie on the sand, ill unto death. Man Jay cast him a sly grin and held up the plug of tobacco. Blue's legs were hardly able to carry his weight, but he got up and staggered out of sight.

An east wind made the air chilly. A heavy surf pounded the beach. Great, curved, gray waves flung foam against the dunes, and the inlet was a hell of crazy water. Blue lay flat down full of misery and anger, until Man Jay came and showed

him starfish, bachelor buttons, long strings of
conch eggs, black sea-louse shells, shells colored
like blossoms, he had gathered to take to Cricket.
Curlews whistled mournfully overhead. Wil-
lets dived in the foam. A multitude of gulls
hovered anxiously over baby birds drowsing on
the sand, matching in color and quick movement
the golden heads of sea oats that quivered above
them. Man Jay said they had no mothers.
The eggs had been laid on the sand and hatched
by the sun. If they fell in the water the tiny
birds swam out as easily as they walked or
breathed, for they had no fear. Blue thought how
Uncle Wes had said, ''You can' be happy long as
you is afraid of anything in de world.''

He slept close to Man Jay that night and covered
his head with the quilt, for the overcast moon
rose red like blood and a strange green light lay on
the angry sea. Puffs of wind made sand sting
his face, before dawn a cold wind blew down
spikes of rain. Sea oats hissed, sea birds cried.
The sea thundered horribly and day-clean showed
no marsh grass, no oyster rocks.

Cun Fred gazed at the sky and waves. He
drew in his mouth when a mighty gust snatched
his hat off. ''Dis is awful cross weather, mens.
De wind is aloft now, but when it comes down,
it'll pure blow de buttons off we shirts.''

The men hurried to load the boats and get back
home before the storm broke. Blue thought about
Cun Hester's vision and got so weak he could

hardly wrap himself in a quilt and huddle down in a boat stern. Man Jay showed him a shark fin among the whitecaps beaten up by the gale and said if the boat capsized a shark would bite off Blue's legs. Blue could see himself legless in the seething water and bitter tears stung his eyes, ran down his cheeks with the rain-drops.

"How about a chaw?" Man Jay gave him a nudge.

Blue struck at him so hard the boat tilted.

"Does you want to turn de boat over?" Cun Fred shouted angrily above the roar of water and wind.

Blue covered up his head and closed his eyes. Maybe Judgment Day had come.

A school of porpoises bumped into the boat, the wind rushed dizzily over Blue's head driving rain through the quilt to freeze his skin. Never had he felt so desolate. Who would care when he drowned? Aun Fan would grieve for Cun Fred. Most of Cricket's tears would be for Man Jay. His mother, his father, would not know when he lay dead under the water with stingarees and sharks gnawing his bones. The ache in his heart swelled bigger, fiercer.

Oars creaked in the row-locks, rain pounded on his shoulders. Tears poured through his tight-shut eyelids. Cricket came before him as plain as day, dressed in her blue Children's Day dress and ribbons. Her little hands were full of Man Jay's sea-shells and a stone crab was running toward her

little feet. Blue tried to scream when she picked it
up and fondled it like a kitten.

"What you hollerin bout, Blue?"   Man Jay
shook him. "Wake up, boy. We done to de hill."

Blue could not believe his eyes when trees
showed through the driving rain. Wind and tide
helped drive the boats up on the bank and the big
net was loaded on two men's shoulders. The camp
things were left behind for walking was hard
empty-handed, in such rain and wind. Oak leaves
were whipped off, pine limbs crashed down. Blue
held fast to Cun Fred's coat tail and splashed
along in the water-filled road. Once he stepped
in a hole and floundered in water to his armpits.

Man Jay's voice rang out above the rush of
wind.

> "If you want to get to Heaven an' you
>   don' know how,
> Just keep you hand on the Gospel plow.
> Little David, play on you harp,
> Halle-loo! Halle-loo, little David,
> Play on you harp, Halle-loo!"

Blue thought as he plodded on that Aun Fan's
house would be heaven; Aun Fan would look like
an angel to his weary smarting eyes.

CHAPTER XXVIII

CUN FRED snored on the bed while the rain poured and the wind howled and whined. Blue sat by the fire with Aun Fan, telling about the beach. Hot towels had dried his skin and hot food warmed his blood. He boasted proudly he had caught a stone crab, and showed slices the oyster rocks cut in his soles. Aun Fan shamed him for having tender skin when he was old enough to have feet as tough as alligator hide. He should have gone to meeting and got saved. Cooch got religion soon after Toosio did. She squealed like a bee stung her when the spirit hit her, then fainted off in a trance. Meeting lasted until day-clean. Some of the mourners were seeking still.

"Is Cricket seekin?" Blue asked.

"Cricket started, but I doubt if e holds out to find peace. White blood don' mix good wid religion."

The next week proved Aun Fan wrong. Cricket got religion in a vision, and at Wednesday night prayer-meeting she and Cooch and Toosio gave in their experience to the deacons.

Cooch told a long tale about going down into a deep dark bottomless pit. She called on God to have mercy and a golden ladder came straight down from the sky. As she climbed it, lightning flashes played over her head. One flash hit her bang on the head. She knew no more.

211

"Ain' dat wonderful?" Cun Jule cried joyfully.
The deacons nodded solemnly.

Brer Dee stood up. "You have heard de experience of de candidate, Brother Deacons. What
must we do wid em?"

"I move we baptize em. De vision Cooch seen is
good proof of salvation," Cun Andrew answered.
The other deacons agreed that Cooch was saved.

Toosio stood up next to tell her experience.
She was climbing a high hill ĭn the night with a
turn of dirty clothes on her head. It got so heavy,
she fell flat down. She called on Jesus to help her.
A sudden bright light shone out and melted her
load. She felt light as air. A loud voice said,
"Go in peace, an' sin no more."

"What did you do when you heard de voice?"
Brer Dee asked.

"I started singin, I been so happy."

"What did you sing, daughter?"

Toosio could not exactly recollect. Seemed like
it was something about a gold crown.

"I'm gwine to wear a golden crown when I
walk dem golden streets?" Cun Andrew suggested, and Toosio nodded yes, that was her song.

"I move we baptize em," Brer Dee said, and the
deacons agreed again.

Cricket held her little head up high when she
faced the row of men. She spoke clearly, without
hesitation.

"My experience come in a dream."

"You mean you been sleepin?" Cun Andrew

frowned and shook his head, but Brer Dee asked kindly:

"What did you dream, daughter?"

"Seems like I was dyin, an' I was awful scared. Big Pa come to drench me, but somebody pushed de bottle out his hand an' give me a glassful of medicine white same like milk."

"Was de medicine sweet?" Cun Andrew asked.

"No, suh, it didn' had no taste."

"Go on, daughter, tell how you got saved," Brer Dee encouraged.

"Dat same somebody told me not to drink Big Pa's teas, neither take any kind o' medicine, long as I live."

"How did de somebody look?"

"I couldn' see em, but e talked like Uncle Wes." Cricket's eyes beamed with happy light.

"Like Wes?" Cun Andrew's face grew dark, but Cricket went on.

"When I drank de medicine, two lil white baby chillen come. Dey had gold hair and dey skin was white like de sun ain' never shine on em. Dey fastened two sets o' white wings on my back."

"What did dey say?"

"Dey been too small to talk."

"Did you flew?"

"Yes-suh. Seems like Uncle Wes was squeezing his 'cordion, so I flewed by de music, but my feet was on de floor."

"What tune did de music play?"

"De tune been *Sallie Ann*."

A silence fell over the room. Brer Dee bowed his head.

"How does you bretheren feel bout dis candidate's vision?" he asked presently.

Cun Andrew cleared his throat. *"Sallie Ann* is a reel song. It ain' no song for a Christian."

"Angels fastened wings on Cricket's back, Andrew," Brer Dee argued.

"White chillen might be angels if dey die befo dey have sin."

Brother Andrew looked doubtful.

"Jesus was black. Solomon said plain, I am but black but comely."

"Angels might change dey color to match de people what prays," Brer Dee argued and moved that the candidate be received and baptized. The other deacons looked at each other doubtfully.

"I'm gwine be a Methodist, Brer Dee," Cricket faltered.

"A Methodist? God says you must bury you sins in a watery grave, Cricket."

"My Mammy was a Methodist."

"You Mammy died in sin, Cricket. You ain' to step in his tracks." Aun Missie stood up to speak. The deacons nodded and she added, "You better follow Jesus wid me."

Cricket's head drooped and she walked back to her seat.

Cooch whispered something to Toosio, and Toosio shook with a smothered giggle but the deacons and members stood up to sing.

"I'm gwine to live so God can use me.
Anyhow, Lord, anyhow.
I'm gwine talk so God can use me,
Anyhow, Lord, anyhow."

"I'm gwine to moan, pray, die, so God can use
me." Many verses were sung but Cricket did not
crack her teeth.

On the fourth Sunday after their baptism Toosio
and Cooch stood in front of the pulpit at Heaven's
Gate Church while the members marched past,
gave them the right hand of fellowship and sang:

"Religion is a powerful chain,
Every link spells Jesus' name.
All you sin been taken away,
Glory, Hallelujah."

The Lord's supper followed. Brer Dee and Cun
Andrew passed the bread and wine to the two girls
first of all.

Toosio took too much wine and Brer Dee chided
her sharply.

"You ain' to drench you'self in de precious
blood of Jesus."

When all the members had taken a crumb of
bread and a sip of wine, the women tied their
heads with white cloth and slipped on white baptizing robes to dance the holy dance.

Hands were clasped above high held arms as

couples bent, swayed, circled, changed partners
and sang:

"Planted by de water,
I shall not be moved.
Don' let de world deceive you,
I shall not be moved.
I'm a tree planted by de water,
I shall not be moved."

The spirit came down. Women screamed out
with joy, fainted off in a trance, but the holy dance
did not halt.

"I'm on my way to Heaven,
I shall not be moved——"

Cooch danced with Cun Andrew, Brer Dee held
Toosio's hands.

"De time is come to wash feet," Reverend Duncan boomed out, and the deacons saluted their
partners, and went toward the barrel of water by
the pulpit. Cun Hester and Aun Fan got a pile of
tin pans and white folded clothes out of baskets
while Reverend Duncan told how Jesus washed
his disciples' feet.

"You feet is dirty, Blue, better go get em
washed," Man Jay whispered.

"Stop makin sport," Cricket whispered back.
"God'll strike you dead."

Men took off coats, shoes and socks, rolled
up breeches; women bared their feet. Basins

dipped water out of the barrel, were handed around. Men washed men's feet, women washed women's.

Aun Fan knelt before Aun Missie. Toosio knelt before Cooch.

As the water blackened it was thrown out of the windows and clean water dipped up from the barrel but the long white cloths got wetter, darker.

Reverend Duncan began unlacing his shoes. Whose feet would he wash? Who would wash his? The singing softened, everybody's eyes watched. "Come forward, Brother Kazoola," he thundered. "You was born in a heathen land, but you son preaches de holy Gospel. I'm proud to bend my knee before you an' wash you feet."

Big Pa went to the pulpit steps and sat down weeping, shaken. He had on no shoes to take off. Christians roared out:

"Jesus lit de candle on de waterside,
When I stepped in to be baptized.
Let's go down to de water.
Religion is so sweet."

When Reverend Duncan knelt before the old man, wild shrieks pierced the rhythm of the singing. Reverend leaned forward, spoke to Big Pa. A deep hush fell. Something was wrong.

"Someting ails Big Pa." Cricket screamed and ran down the aisle, but before she could reach him, Reverend stood up, lifted his arms.

"Kazoola is gone to a better land."

Cricket's voice rose high and shrill in a death-cry. Thin and piercing it cut through the racket. Reverend Duncan put his arms around her, tried to hush her, but she struggled loose and leaped about with wordless screams that rose above the mourning of women's voices.

Cun Fred and Cun Andrew held Big Pa's life-less body across their laps in the wagon, while Blue drove the mule home. The old man was laid out on Aun Fan's company bed and his clothes carefully buttoned up. His face had a peaceful look. Death had smoothed out wrinkles in his withered cheeks and left a gentle smile on his mouth.

It was Sunday, but Cun Fred sawed boards, planed them smooth and nailed them together so Big Pa need not sleep his last sleep in a store-bought box.

The next evening after sunset, he was laid in a grave close to Uncle Wes.

When the mound was smoothed Cricket laid a bunch of white snow on the mountain near by the old spade which Cun Fred stuck in the soft ground for a head marker.

CHAPTER XXIX

The years drifted slowly. Spring full of tender leaves and soft showers of rain strengthened into summer and scorching heat. Black thunder clouds full of sharp lightning cast hail-stones down to batter leaves off the crops; dry droughts parched blossoms and shriveled green fruit.

Winter was frosty but it brought ease from days of back-breaking labor and long nights to be filled with pleasure.

Aun Missie and Cricket were the only ones who took no part in gay birth-night suppers or parties. They went only to church and prayer-meeting.

A storm blew the old schoolhouse down so the teacher boarded at Aun Missie's and had school in the big front room. Cooch and Toosio went to town for schooling, but Cooch had returned Cricket's prize Testament. It had hard words, small print, but Cricket and Man Jay learned to read it. Aun Missie's favorite chapter was the story of Jesus on the cross. She rolled her eyes and sighed over his stripes, his crown of thorns, the cruel nails through his feet and hands, his death-cry when he tasted the vinegar. Cricket couldn't bear it. Whenever the teacher read it she went out on the piazza or into the yard.

Aun Missie's heart was set on Cricket's baptizement, but Cricket insisted she wanted to be a Methodist. Cricket had her own notions and no-

219

body could change them. She had grown tall as
Aun Missie, but she worked too hard and stayed
too slim for looks. All summer long she jerked
a hoe and sweated, fighting grass and weeds.

Boll-weevils destroyed most of the cotton, but
when Aun Missie's little barn was full of corn
Cricket picked peas enough to fill one end of the
piazza and tramped them out from the shells with
her bare feet.

Cun Fred had never let the two white oxen do a
lick of work since they carried Uncle Wes to his
grave and it fretted him to see Cricket sweat and
strain so hard. He talked hard to Aun Missie about
it, and she finally agreed to let Cricket go to the
Quarters and help Aun Bina sew. Cricket learned
to cut out frocks and make them with her fingers
as strong and stylish as Aun Bina could do. Her
own clothes took the shine off the other girls' altogether. Aun Missie was too stingy to buy cloth,
but Cun Hester gave her dresses packed away in
the Big House attic, and she made them over to
look like new. Aun Fan talked hard about
Cricket's spendthrift ways, but Cun Fred encouraged Cricket to dress up and look nice.

Every Monday night a dance was held at Singleton's Café, an old tumble-down shack near Big
Pa's house. Reverend Cato Singleton was a well-
to-do widower and a local preacher, who declared
he served God by having a decent place where
people could pleasure themselves in good order.

Every Monday night the café was crowded with

sinners and Christians for Reverend Cato declared
Christians could dance together without sin. Two
clean sheets can not soil each other. Cooch and
Toosio thought Cricket was too stuck up to go to
the café. But the truth was Aun Missie never let
Cricket go anywhere at night except to prayer-
meeting. She had to dance at home or not at all,
and even then Aun Missie kept close watch on her.

Singleton's café had two rooms. One had a
counter piled with crates of bottled drinks, shelves
filled with cans of salmon and sardines, boxes of
crackers and sweet cakes for the gentlemen to buy
and treat the ladies. The other room, the dance-
hall, had only a bench in the corner to hold the
musicianers. One picked a banjo and blew a
mouth-organ held to his mouth by a wire frame.
The other sang and beat time on a tin washboard,
tapped different sized frying-pans with thimbles
on his fingers.

In the storeroom a lantern hung over one end
of the counter where the money box stayed under
the hand of Reverend Singleton's daughter. The
dance-hall was lighted by tiny flames from cloth
strings in Coco-Cola bottles of kerosene set high
on the rafters.

Reverend Singleton's daughter was a cold dry
woman, black as tar. She never wore gay clothes,
beads, or jewelry, never bothered with men except to take money they paid to dance or for things
to eat and drink. She kept her mouth shut about
her business. Everybody wondered how much

money she and Reverend Singleton had and where
they kept it. Some people thought they buried it,
others believed they filled a barrel and anchored it
in the river.

Cooch's Daddy, Old Man Kelly Wright, had
moved into Big Pa's old house and he ran a liquor
still in a branch behind the café. Reverend Cato
furnished corn and molasses for the wooden vats
of mash which boiled and foamed like breakers
on the beach. Chips on the café wood-pile bulged
up with hidden glass jars of white lightning. Ten
cents bought a small drink, a dollar bought a
quart.

The café dances often ended in a row; the lights
were kicked over, scared people leaped out of
windows and doors, ran across the fields when
pistol shots banged behind them, but for all that,
they were fun.

Reverend Singleton said the still was a Christian business. Boll-weevils had destroyed the
cotton crops, people were poor and needed sale for
their corn. Jesus himself turned water into wine.

Uncle Kelly used mostly meal molasses and
china berries for his liquor mash; plugs of tobacco
were added to make the mess hot and strong. A
few shovels of old stable manure and sour bugs
made it work in a hurry. The still boiled the beer,
and the steam ran through little pipes laid in cold
branch water, then trickled out whisky. White
lightning made Blue sick, but all the other boys
drank it, so he bought it, gulped it down too. Like

the other boys he wrote the name of the girl he
wanted on a slip of paper and dropped it in one
of the vats. If the girl tasted the stuff she was
his, for Old Man Kelly put a charm on his liquor.
Blue tried several names with success and one day
he wrote Cricket's name on a piece of wrapping
paper. Man Jay's sharp eyes were quick.

"What you mean by dat, Blue?" Man Jay tried
to fish the paper out with a stick. When he could
not get it, he wrote Cricket's name on a slip himself, dropped it in and punched it down deep.

"Now we'll see who gets Cricket," he said so
fiercely that Blue knew it was a threat, but he
laughed carelessly. "It'll take a smart man to get
a drop o' liquor past Cricket's lips, close watch as
Aun Missie keeps on em."

Cun Hester had been getting ready for the grave
ever since an angel came to her in a dream and
told her she must soon take a long journey to a
far country. She sent for Brer Dee and Reverend
Duncan and told them the dream; they agreed the
angel meant she was soon going to Heaven.

Cun Hester said she wanted to be dressed right
when she met her Maker face to face. Mice had
gnawed holes in her old baptizing robe, and its
cloth was rotten with age. So she bought new
cloth for Cricket to make a brand-new robe for
her shroud. Cricket made the shroud and hemmed
a square of white muslin for a head-kerchief to
match it.

Cun Hester seemed quite well, but Cricket went
every day to sit with her and talk.

Blue wondered what those two talked about so
much, for Cun Hester's mind tarried on what was
over and gone. Maybe Cricket wanted to find out
all about those Big House white people. What
good would that do her? They were dead or gone.
Blue went to Cun Hester's one afternoon because
he knew Cricket was there. She was there. Man
Jay was too. Through the open door Blue could
see them.

Cricket sat bent over a white paper in her lap
and wrote words on it while Man Jay knelt beside
her, cautioning her to take her time and make the
letters plain. Cun Hester stood over them, her
eyes fixed on the paper. Her mouth was taut, her
forehead lined with worryation.

"Wet de pencil, Cricket. Make de words black.
Don' let you hand trimble, honey." Man Jay
glanced up and his jaw dropped, then he snapped
out:

"What you mean, Blue, sneakin up so nobody
couldn' hear you?"

Man Jay was not glad to see him, but Cricket's
eyes gave him a sweet come-on-in smile.

Her cheeks had that queer reddish tinge which
was always a sure sign that something had set her
blood to racing. "We ain' doin nothin wrongful,
Man Jay. Blue is my kinnery same as you."

"Blue better not tell," Cun Hester threatened,
and the lines in her forehead deepened.

"If you crack you teeth, if you open you blab mouth, I'll beat you to death," Man Jay declared angrily.

"Tell what?" Blue was puzzled and curious, and when he heard, he was dazed with amazement.

Cricket's voice broke as she told how she craved to go to school in town but Aun Missie would not send her. Cun Hester had thought up this plan. Cun Hester said she must write a letter—a letter to her white father. Cun Hester went to the store man and bought a stamped envelope. Cun Hester got the store man to write the name and the right place on it. Cricket held the white envelope up and it shivered in the tips of her little fingers.

"Man Jay is helpin me write dis letter to go inside em. It's done now, all but my name."

"Put you name down, honey," Cun Hester bade, and Cricket bent over the paper again.

"Honey," Cun Hester added, "if you don' get answer to dis letter, you mustn' forget God is you Father—God will provide for you—same like he does for de lil sparrow birds. God numbers de hairs on you head and e won' let you cravin's be vain."

"If you tell a soul bout dis letter, Blue, it will start all de people to talkin," Man Jay warned.

"Blue wouldn' tell a bit quicker'n you, Man Jay." Cricket spoke sharply and her eyes flashed.

"It ain' no use to get cross wid me, Cricket, I'm thinkin on you, not me."

"Blue won' tell, will you, Blue?" She smiled so

kindly Blue could hardly think whether she meant
him to say yes or no.

Months passed, the *Comanche* came and went,
but no answer came to Cricket's letter and she
ceased going to ask the store man for mail.

Cun Fred wanted to send her off to school for
she had learned all the teacher knew, but Aun
Missie would not consent for Cooch came home
and her baby was born soon afterward. The
deacons turned her out of the church but Cooch
said she was glad; she'd rather pleasure herself
than pray. Cun Jule's house became head-
quarters for frolicking and Cooch taught Blue
many things she learned in town.

Aun Missie declared Cooch was outrageous, and
scolded Blue for going with her when everybody
knew Cooch had that child for Man Jay. Maybe
she did and maybe she didn't. Cooch never would
say, and Man Jay just laughed when Blue asked
him.

Blue was seventeen when he first begged Cricket
to marry to him. He was young but he knew how
to work. She was young but she knew how to
housekeep. Cricket would not consent although
she answered him kindly. Every few weeks he
asked her again until she said no so firmly he
knew his hope to win her was wasted. He had
spells of leaving her alone, spells of begging her
to marry to him. She always refused but said she
loved him and Man Jay better than anybody else.

If Blue was ready to have wife, Cooch or Toosio would take him at the drop of a hat. Why not ask one of them? Blue argued that field work made her look rough and coarse; Uncle Wes would not rest in his grave if he knew she worked like a common field-hand. Cricket declared she loved to work, loved to be strong. When she and Aun Missie got enough money ahead, they might go to town to live. Then she would dress up and strut and her hands get as soft as anybody's.

One night at the café, Reverend Cato asked Blue why Cricket never came to the dances. He and Wes were friends as long as Wes lived; he thought the world of Aun Missie; Cricket was almost a woman; she would soon be ready to have husband; all the nice girls who came to the café caught beaux.

"Aun Missie is a widow woman, Reverend, an' you is a widow man. Whyn' you go talk to Aun Missie?" Blue answered.

"Eh, eh," Reverend Cato's one eye twinkled. "I ain' thought o' dat. I'll court de widow, you court de gal."

Reverend Cato came the next night to Aun Missie's and gave her a special invitation to come to the Monday-night dance. He would let her in free for he needed Christians to help him guide the young people.

Man Jay came too to say good-by, for he was going to town the next day to find work. He took Cricket and Blue off to one side and told Cricket

to keep away from the café. He said she and
Blue must not go to seed like the Quarters people.
Big Pa's Daddy was a king. Big Pa's son, Reverend Africa, their own Granddaddy, was the finest
preacher in the world. Man Jay talked solemn as
a preacher himself.

He was going to town and get a job. When he
got enough money ahead he would send for Aun
Bina and Cricket. Blue could fetch them and get
work himself. "You'll do it, won' you, Cricket?"

"I can' leave Aun Missie by himself." Cricket
shook her head sadly.

"I'm gwine be de foreman when Cun Fred gets
old," Blue boasted.

"De plantation ain' gwine need no foreman
soon. De store man told me some rich people up-
North wanted to buy it to hunt on in de winter.
If dey buys it, no tellin what'll happen. You can'
tell what white people will do. Looka Cricket's
own Daddy. E didn' much as answer dat latter."

Cricket's lips quivered and tears came in her
eyes. "I'd go wid you on de boat to-morrow if I
could. But Aun Missie gets vexed when I say
I'm weary stayin here home."

"Home is good enough for me." Blue tried to
sound cheerful. "Big Pa ever said de people
what goes off mostly comes home in a box. I ain'
scared o' strange white people. Dem Big House
spirits will keep em straight if dey comes here.
Dey won' pester me, neither Cricket. We won'
pay em no mind."

"Well," Man Jay straightened up, "I'm a done-talk man. You can do like you please. Stay or either go. But don' forget, Blue, you is responsible for Cricket when I ain' here to look after em."

Man Jay said good-by and Reverend began urging Aun Missie to come to the café and pleasure herself.

Aun Missie was all eye-sighted. She said she had not danced in years and three long miles on a dark road at night was too far to walk without a gentleman.

"Dat ain' no way for a pretty young widow to talk. If you say de word, I'll borrow a horse and buggy and ride you to de dance free o' charge."

Aun Missie said she had never gone to a dance when Uncle Wes was alive, people would talk if she started out now.

"Please let's go, Aun Missie," Cricket pleaded with her heart in her eyes.

"A buggy seat is too narrow for three people." Reverend's one eye winked at Blue who answered quickly:

"Cricket can walk wid me."

Aun Missie said she promised her God when Wes died, she would never let Cricket out of her sight after dark. She had respect for preachers but she mistrusted everybody else who wore breeches.

Reverend Cato stroked the sparse beard on his chin. "It ain' good to be too strict on a gal.

It'll make em want to break loose. You let Blue
fetch Cricket to de café. I got fine musicianers.
Christians' feet pure itch when dey play. De
Good Books says dancin ain' sinful if people don'
cross dey feets!''

Aun Missie sighed that Cricket was no Christian
yet.

"Find em a husband, Sister. Dat'll settle em
down. If I was a lil younger, Cricket would be
married befo Christmas." Reverend Cato's one
eye shone.

Cricket laughed. "You is plenty young enough,
Reverend."

"Shut you sassy mouth, Cricket. You ain' to
talk such brazen talk to a preacher," Aun Missie
scolded.

"How bout walkin out to meetin wid me to-
night, Sister Missie?"

Aun Missie's eyes dropped. "I ain' walked out
wid a gentleman in so long I wouldn' know how to
act, Reverend."

Reverend patted her shoulder.

"Too much grievin will broke you consecution.
I know by my own-self. I ain' eat a full meal of
victuals or slept a whole night through since my
lawful lady died last spring."

"Five months ain' like five years." Aun Missie
wiped her wet eyes.

The meeting bell rang out in the dusk calling
people to come worship God.

"Put on you hat, Sister Missie. Let's go join

de Christian band," Reverend Cato insisted.

"Come go wid me, Cricket," Aun Missie coaxed, but Cricket shook her head.

"You go wid de Reverend. Blue will stay wid me."

Aun Missie said no more, and soon her white apron-strings tied in a bow behind glimmered fainter and fainter in the moonlight as she walked to meeting with Reverend.

Cricket patted old She-She gently when a fox barked in the woods back of the house.

"Po' old She-She." She stroked the long floppy ears. "E's too deef to hear foxes any more. Everything is gone backward since Uncle Wes died."

"I ain' gone backward, Cricket. I made good money dis year diggin clams an' catchin shrimps. Mullet is runnin thick on de beach right now."

"Money don' make people happy, Blue."

"Money helps out a lot."

"It ain' money I crave. I want to go off an' see somebody new. If Uncle Wes had 'a' lived, I could 'a' gone off to school in town."

"You might got a baby like Cooch did."

Instead of flaring up as Blue expected, Cricket answered sadly, "I'm so weary doin de same old thing, hearin de same old talk, year in, year out. Sometimes I think Cooch is better off dan me."

"For God's sake, Cricket, shut you mouth. What de matter ail you to-night?"

"I don' know, Blue. I feel so unrestless here lately. I wish to God Aun Missie would marry to Reverend Cato. I ruther help Miss Sallie sell liquor dan to weary my life out pullin fodder an' pickin peas, sewin frocks for other gals to dance in."

"Whyn' you marry to somebody, Cricket?"

"It ain' nobody here I'd marry to," she sighed. Blue sat silent as she went on. "I want to see how a town looks, Blue. Cooch says it's pure beautiful at night with lights a-shinin, an' everybody walkin around on de streets. Cooch says de *Comanche* looks small by dem boats what crosses de sea."

Blue was in a deep study.

"If you got you heart set on town, I'll take you. De next excursion lasts two or three days."

"I can' go off wid you an' spend de night."

"How-come? Me an' you is two sisters' chillen."

"Aun Missie would fret an' people would talk."

"De excursion would make a nice weddin-trip, Cricket."

Cricket did not even lift her eyes.

"Cricket," his voice quivered. "Every cent I got buried, every time I put much as a dime in de ground, I say to myself, dis will help buy de boards an' nails for de house I'm gwine build for Cricket. I know you don' like Aun Fan. I wouldn' ask you to live in his house; but a lil new house— lumber don' cost much. I could build most of it myself. We could whitewash em—put papers on de walls to stop up de cracks——"

A silence followed Blue's husky words. He swallowed so hard that the tight collar of his Sunday shirt creaked.

"Town people ain' like we. I can' stand to think about you stayin mongst all dem river-rats an' drunk women."

He put a hot hand on her shoulder.

"If you don' want to give me a answer now, I can wait. But please don' think on town not no more."

"If I stay on here, Blue, nothin ain' ahead for me but to dry up an' get sour like Aun Missie. If I marry to you, Aun Fan would say you married beneath you. I'm a bright skin, Blue. People here holds it against me. Cooch says bright-skin people stands well in town."

It was no use to say anything more to her, and Blue sat silent while Cricket reminded him that Cun Jule said long time ago a bright skin had no place in the world. She used to believe it, but Cun Hester said that God made a place for everybody who did the best they could.

She had tried to do her best. She tried to have long patience with Aun Missie. Sometimes it was hard, sometimes she forgot and hurt Aun Missie's feelings. Aun Missie had forgotten how it felt to be young. She thought of nothing but pinching, saving, praying. She thought pleasure was sin, everything but back-breaking work was sin.

If Uncle Wes had lived, things would be different. But he was gone. Man Jay was gone. Like as not, Man Jay would get killed playing skin same as Uncle Wes did. She had nobody to depend on but herself and the place she belonged was not here. No. Her place must be somewhere else.

Blue let her talk herself out but deep in his heart he felt glad Man Jay was gone.

CHAPTER XXX

MONDAY evening fell cool and clear. By first dark Reverend Cato came with Nelly Blyne and Cun Fred's rickety buggy to take Aun Missie to the dance. He hitched the old horse to the apple tree, and sat on the porch with Blue while the ladies dressed. Groups of boys and girls in their best clothes laughed and chattered as they straggled past. Couples holding hands walked slowly. Aun Jule had a baby in her arms and a string of children trailing behind her.

"How you do, Sister?" Reverend Cato called. "You sho got a fine passel of chillen."

"Thank you kindly, Reverend," Cun Jule answered. "Dey's fine enough but dey sho is a lot of trouble. I don' know which is worse, a knee child or a arm baby." Cun Jule would have tarried to talk but Reverend's words cut off, for Cricket came dancing out, ready to go.

In spite of the shortness of her flowered silk skirt, she looked like a grown-up woman with her hair knotted on the back of her neck and a band of white ribbon around her head. No town girl could have looked better, although Cricket made the frock with her own fingers out of an old dress Cun Hester found in the Big House attic. Its tight-fitting waist showed every curve in her slim body. Thin white stockings and black slippers made her feet and ankles look very small and trim.

Reverend's eyes opened wide, gleamed like a cat's in the dark. "Here's de pick of all de gals in de country, Blue."

Cricket's teeth flashed in a laugh when Reverend took both her hands and drew her up to him, but when Reverend smacked her full on the mouth, she gave him a push that sent him reeling.

"Is you lost you mind, you old fool?" she asked angrily.

Blood roared in Blue's ears. He grabbed Reverend to choke him, but the old man yelled.

"I was just cuttin crazy for fun, Blue. I ain' meant no harm."

Aun Missie walked out smiling, and Blue came quickly to his senses but his heart throbbed and his breath panted. "What de matter ail you, Blue?" she asked.

"Blue got vexed wid de Reverend, but I been to blame, Aun Missie. De full moon ever goes to my head," Cricket explained quickly.

"Mind how you act, Cricket. Don' forget I raised you to be nice." Aun Missie looked better, younger than Blue had ever seen her. Instead of her black mourning dress, she wore a purple one spotted with white. She tittered when Reverend Cato took her arm to help her down the steps and her voice was fluttery like a young girl's when she called from the buggy. "Better wear you old shoes, Cricket. Sand will cut out de soles of dem new ones."

Cricket did, and Blue put her new black slippers

in his pocket, locked the front door and led the
way down the path.

The road narrowed and darkened with mud as
it wound through thick woods. At the two-mile
notch post near Big Pa's old house where plat-
eyes walk on moonlit nights, a buck crossed the
road and two does scampered after him. Cricket
gave a little frightened cry, and Blue took her
hand.

"Dey ain' plat-eyes, dey is deers headed for
somebody's peas-field. But don' never run from
a plat-eye or dey will run you to death."

"I ain' scared o' plat-eyes, but I'm scared o' Old
Kelly Wright. His liquor still is back in dem
woods."

Blue held fast to her hand although it burned
his palm like fire. "Cricket, honey," he blurted
out. "You pure look like a flower garden—you
smell sweeter'n a blossom."

Cricket answered with a light laugh. "Dat ain'
me you smell. Dat's cologne Man Jay sent me
from town." Her indifference stung him so he
dropped her hand and plodded across mud to the
other side of the road. His heart was pure sick
for Cricket and she treated him like a child. She
did not know how to love. She expected devotion,
and wanted to give nothing for it. Cooch said
Cricket was thin-blooded and that bright-skin gals
were ever cold as clabber. Maybe Cooch was
right. Maybe she was wrong. Aun Missie had
taught Cricket that love is sinful unless people are

married together. Maybe that was why Cricket
acted so. She was always kind to him. Blue knew
she trusted him, yet if he tried to kiss her or hug
her close, she got vexed.

The river was full of silver ripples and soft mist
made a white cloud over the willows.

"How can you be down-in-de-heart, Blue, when
de night is so shiny and beautiful?"

"I feel weary, Cricket. Let's sit down on dis
log and rest." He caught her arm, but she pushed
his eager hand away and walked on.

The café was whitewashed and moonlight made
it gleam through the trees. Carts and oxen, mules
and wagons filled the yard. Music banged through
open door and windows. A soft yellow light from
the lantern shone on Aun Missie's happy face as
she watched Reverend Cato sell boiled peanuts and
bottle drinks.

"For God's sake, looka Aun Missie. I'd have to
move myself to catch de Reverend now." Cricket
laughed as Blue took her arm and guided her
toward the wood-pile where she sat on a log to
change her old shoes for Sunday ones. Blue put
the old ones in his pocket and said gently:

"Don' dance wid no strange mens. Some awful
rough ones works at de still. Dey don' have no
respect for a gal."

"What de matter ail you, Blue?" she said fret-
fully. "You talk like you is old as Nelly Blyne."
The old horse had been unharnessed and was
wandering about eating grass.

"Nothin don' ail me but lovin you so hard when you don' love me none."

The musicianers sang out merrily:

"Say, young gals, won't you come out to-night,
Come out to-night,
Come out to-night,
Say, young gals, won't you come out to-night,
An' dance by de light off de moon."

Cloth wicks in the Coco-Cola bottles cast a poor flickering light and the dancers were a mass of black shadows. But the floor planks slapped the sills with the beating of joyful vigorous feet. Some danced alone, some danced in couples, two women as often as two men. The dance was more important than the partner.

Cricket's little feet stepped off smoothly with Blue's. He held her close on account of the crowd. With his arms tight around her, her cool cheek pressed against his hot one, they became like one person. A strange heavy-set man and short bow-legged girl bumped into them. The girl looked at Cricket and whispered to her partner. Both laughed boisterously and danced on, bowing, bending, flinging legs and arms, taking up far more than their share of room. Blue gave the girl a vicious kick on the leg. She stopped to make an ugly face at him, but her partner pulled his hat lower over his eyes, grabbed her and shouted:

"Come on, gal, an' do you stuff! Don' be

foolin wid me to-night! Dis ain' no time to
weaken!''

The girl leaped into his arms. Their feet beat
like drums. "God bless," Cricket laughed.
"Come on, Blue, don' let em outdo us."

"Let's stop," Blue answered. "We can' dance
good in dis crowd."

The room was close, the air heavy with smoke
and smell. Blue took her outside and boys crowded
around quickly asking her to dance. She said
she was thirsty and Blue went to buy a bottle
drink.

Down the road came two shining lights and a
roar like the ocean's voice. Excited people shouted
an automobile was coming, and hurried to see it
pass, but it halted among the wagons and carts.
Blue's mouth fell ajar when a tall yellow man
stepped out. He had long black gloves on his
hands.

The music stopped short, musicianers and
dancers poured into the yard and joined the throng
around the car. Everybody wanted to know who
the stranger was. He took off his white straw hat
and bowed.

"Good evenin to you all," he said pleasantly and
his gold teeth glittered under a small black
mustache.

"Good evenin," answers rose in a questioning
tone.

Blue pushed through the jam. "What might
be you name?" he asked.

"I'm a stranger in dis country, but Reverend Cato invited me to de dance, so I thought I'd come. I hope it's agreeable to everybody."

Reverend Cato held out his hand. "I'm glad to see you, Mr. Weeks. Come right in and make you'self at home. De ladies will be proud to meet you."

There was no need to tell him that. He looked as much at home as Reverend Cato himself. His ease of manner, his clothes, showed plainly he was from town. He was as tall as Man Jay and as broad-shouldered, but his skin was as bright as Cricket's. Reverend Cato introduced him.

"Ladies and gentlemen, meet Mr. Cæsar Weeks. I done told em we is glad to have em in our midst. De Good Book says strangers is often angels unawares."

The man's bold eyes strayed over the faces, fell on Cricket, tarried with a slow smile. Her soft lips slowly answered and a strange cold fear crept up Blue's spine, lingered in the roots of his hair. Not that the stranger showed signs of wrongness. Nobody could have been more mannersable. His voice was pleasant as he greeted Aun Missie and asked for a dope. He took a roll of green bills from his pocket and pulled off the top one to pay for it. The people filed slowly past, going inside to dance again. The music sang out a quick measure. The stranger stepped up to Cricket, murmured something that made her smile.

"Come on, Cricket. Let's dance," Blue said.
"Dis lady has agree' to dance de next set wid
me," the stranger answered as he took her arm
and led her away.

CHAPTER XXXI

BLUE stood with his eyes on that white straw hat glimmering above the dark heads. The burning end of a long cigar flared red above Cricket's hair, a puff of its smoke floated over her laughing eyes.

The music stopped and the stranger called Reverend to fetch two bottles of dope. Blue cursed Cricket under his breath. How could she face the crowd with that stranger-man's arm around her, looking happy like she found Jesus himself. Who was that man? What business had he here? Where did Reverend Cato find him? Fury burned in Blue's heart as he went to tell Aun Missie how Cricket was acting. Aun Missie went to the door and looked, rolled up her eyes with delight.

"Wouldn' it be grand if Cricket could catch dat man for husband?" she said. "Reverend Cato says e's pure lousy wid money."

Cricket hardly tasted her bottled drink, but the man gulped his down thirstily. The music struck up a tune. He handed both the bottles to Reverend with a bow, then gathered Cricket up in his long arms. Off they whirled into a shadowy corner. Cricket must have got dizzy for she threw out an arm to catch her balance. He laughed and put it up around his neck, danced toward the door and halted. His two big hands lifted Cricket up and set her outside on the ground.

If Man Jay was here, he would put a stop to Cricket's carrying on in a hurry. Helpless rage stung Blue to the marrow of his bones as he followed Cricket and the stranger to see where they were going. The night was cool but the white straw hat fanned Cricket's face briskly as they walked toward the automobile.

One long yellow hand held the bare flesh of Cricket's arm. The other opened the door, spread a white pocket handkerchief over the seat and helped her in. Blue looked around for a stick, found a barrel stave and stood in a shadow to see and hear. If that man cracked his teeth to Cricket in the wrong way, he would get his head smashed to a pulp.

"It's funny to see mens dance wid dey hats on. Where I come from, people thinks it's not polite to de ladies." The white straw hat fanned Cricket lazily.

"Somebody might steal you hat if you take em off here," Cricket explained. "Rough people comes to de dances sometime."

"I paid five solid bucks for dis hat in Charleston de day I left."

"You bought em in Charleston?" Cricket was amazed.

"Sho thing, honey. It's a long ways off too. It took me two weeks to get here. I never seen such roads. So much mud an' sand mighty nigh ruint de cyar."

"Whe' you gwine from here?"

"I might go down south an' spend de winters at a hotel in Florida."

"We has a lot o' pleasure here in de wintertime, wid birth-night suppers, an' all kinds o' plays."

"Lord, child, I wouldn' live here if you give me de whole country. How-come you don' go to Florida wid me? I could get you a job easy, a good-looker like you. Not a maid at de hotel is got a thing on you."

"I wouldn' know how to act in Florida. I ain' never been nowhere but here home."

"I'll learn you how to act if you'll go wid me. I'll take you through Charleston an' Savannah an' South Ca'lina an' Georgia. Lord, it would take me until day after to-morrow to tell you all de places we would pass through. Soon as me an' de Reverend gets our little business straight, I'll hit de road. Better come on an' see de big world."

"You ain' scared to roam round mongst strangers?"

"Scared?" He laughed. "I don' know what scared means. I been cut up wid a razor about ten times, I been shot wid a pistol ball five times. I'm hot-stuff man, honey. Nothin can' kill me." Cricket sat silent until he added, "But if I had to live in dis God forsake' place I reckon I'd die."

"We got rich land here. You ought to see de hay an' corn."

"I ain' seen de hay but I tasted de corn. It

most knocked my head off. White lightnin is
de right name for em.'' He put his arm up on the
seat behind her. "How bout a lil nip wid me
now? I got a flask in my pocket.''

"I don' like mens to drink.'' Cricket sat up
straight.

"Aw, honey. I was just makin a little joke. I
don' hardly ever drink. I'm a workin man. I been
a butler for rich white folks. I been a painter an'
a cyarpenter, a porter on a Pullman train. I can
cook or press clothes——'' His arm slipped
around Cricket's shoulders. "I'm a pure greasy
streak of lightning. Me an' lovin is twin buddies.''
His lips were against her hair.

"Cricket,'' Blue called, "git out dat cyar!''

The stranger looked around and his eyes
glittered at Blue. The engine roared out. The
car snorted and leaped into the road.

Blue ran to tell Aun Missie but instead of being
angry, she laughed in his face.

Blue's heart seethed with hate. How could Aun
Missie stand behind that counter smiling, bowing
to people when Cricket had gone God only knew
where with a stranger-man in an automobile that
might blow up and kill her any minute?

Blue sat on the wood-pile so hot with fury that
sweat poured off his face.

Girls passed back and forth, asked why he did
not dance. When he made some flimsy excuse
Toosio giggled. "Cricket loves de fleas on old
She-She's back better'n you, Blue.''

Cooch came up and took his hand. "How-come
you craves a bright-skin gal, black as you is?
Come on, boy, let's walk down de road a piece."
She put an arm around his neck, but he gave her
a push, fled into the café, bought a dime's worth of
white lightning, and swallowed it down.

"How-come you ain' dancin, son?" Reverend
Cato asked kindly.

"I don' like to dance in such a jam o' people."

"Is you vexed as you look?" Aun Missie smiled.

"I'm vexeder dan I look. I'm pure vexed to
de heart."

"What got you so heated up, son?" Reverend,
the old hypocrite, made like he did not know.

"Blue is jealous-hearted, Reverend, dat's what
ails em," Aun Missie laughed.

"A jealous heart is a pizen thing, son. De Good
Book says it's sharper'n a serpent tooth. Don'
set you heart on one gal ahead of all de rest. Dey
is all alike, more or less. De Good Book says
women is a vain thing for safety."

CHAPTER XXXII

AFTER the dance Cricket's behavior set every tongue in the country to wagging. Some people said she must have lost her mind to take up with that liquor-making man. Every day God sent, she rode with him to the new still he had put up near the river. The automobile spouted steam as it rattled and bumped over the road, terrifying gentle well-broken beasts until they broke shafts and harness, turned wagons and buggies upside down. Other people blamed Cricket's bright skin, and declared they ever knew she would break loose sooner or later.

Blue made up his mind to try to forget her. He dug up his buried savings and bought a new buggy so he could drive Nelly Blyne's colt and ride Cooch out on Sunday afternoons. They were crossing a bridge one day and the automobile came around the bend in the road. Instead of backing out of the way, Blue flicked the colt with the whip. The poor frightened beast went crazy, reared up, leaped aside off the bridge into the creek, carrying the buggy, Cooch and Blue. The colt's neck was broken, the buggy ruined, Cooch almost killed, Blue's Sunday clothes spoiled with water and mud.

He was crazed with anger but instead of siding with him, Cun Fred took the stranger's part. He said Blue should have pulled out of the road and waited for the automobile to pass. Blue swore he would get out of nobody's way when he drove on the road in a horse and buggy. He told Cun Fred to his teeth that the plantation foreman had no business letting a stranger-man put up a still on Big Pa's land. Cun Fred said Blue should be glad the plantation could sell corn for good money, and have clean whisky to drink instead of the filthy stuff Uncle Kelly made.

Uncle Ben had raised that colt and he grieved when it died. He thought Cun Fred should make the automobile leave the country, but Cun Fred held that the roads were free and Blue was to blame for the colt's death.

Aun Fan made no complaint, for Cun Fred gave her part of the roll of green money the stranger paid for the dead colt and broken harness, and Cun Andrew mended the buggy at the blacksmith shop.

Blue had seen the glass jars of white whisky Cun Fred kept in the barn out of her sight. He knew why Cun Fred went to the barn and came back with loosened tongue to talk about old days when the plantation was rich, and the stables full of horses that could outrun any automobile ever made. He gave orders to the plow-hands every morning when they came at day-clean, but by sunup he forgot what he had told them and hurried to the field to tell them something else.

Blue resolved to waylay the stranger and slit his throat with a razor some night, but the auto-

mobile tarried in Aun Missie's yard whenever it
was not rolling around the country and Cricket sat
on the front seat as if she owned the whole world.
Lord, how she had changed. She never did a lick
of work but pleasured from morning until night.
From a steady hard-working girl she had become
a shirking gadabout. She sought people she used
to scorn and mistreated those who loved her best.
What would Uncle Wes think if he knew? And
Big Pa? And Man Jay?

Aun Missie was not like the same woman. She
talked of nothing but the fine automobile and
Cricket's wedding. She boasted that Cricket's
beau was vast-rich. When he married Cricket she
would go to town with them and live at a fine hotel.
She was done with work and skimping and saving,
done with sorrow and trouble. Cricket's beau
did pay her way and Aun Bina's to go to town
and help Cricket buy wedding-clothes. They came
back loaded with bundles of cloth which they cut
and sewed into garments. Aun Missie had gone
clean crazy. Her garden was not planted. Her
hungry pigs rooted up the neighbors' potato
patches. She laughed when other women wrung
field straw for brooms and bragged how she
would use stick brooms in town.

The whole country was upset, yet the stranger
was so mannersable and pleasant, nobody mistreated him. Blue did nothing but refuse to speak
to him. Old Man Kelly made a few threats but
nobody paid him any mind, for liquor from the

new still was better. Making it and taking it in
boats to town gave work to many idle men.

Blue sulked around like a bad-tempered dog,
wondering what he would do the rest of his life
without Cricket. He could not forget her to save
life and he tried drinking more, working harder
than ever to get relief from his misery. He
gathered oysters and clams, caught mullet and
salted them down for the *Comanche* to take to town
and sell. Liquor made him sick, staying wet and
cold made him thin and ashy. He came home
Saturday nights and slept all he could on Sundays
for the idle hours left on his hands were long and
painful. Cooch tried to cheer him up, but he had
lost his taste for her. She and Toosio met him
at the store one night and asked him to go with
them to a party. When he refused, Cooch looked
vexed but Toosio giggled.

How coarse Toosio was with her fat bulging
breasts. They shook like great bags of jelly when
she laughed. Her nose was flat, her lips thick as
sausages, her feet like hams.

"Would you dance wid Blue at a party in dem
old ragged clothes e's got on?" she asked Cooch.

"Old clothes? You just wait till I buy what I
come to buy." Blue had meant to buy only a cigar,
but he got a bottle-green box coat and peg-top
purple pants, a blue shirt and a stick pin with a
red stone.

"Looka dem beautiful gloves, Blue," Toosio
whispered. "Dey ain' cotton gloves neither."

She spread her fat hands out and sighed. "Cricket's beau bought em a pair just like em."

"How much dey cost?" Blue asked her.

"A dollar and a half." Toosio's eyes brightened hopefully.

Blue reached in his pocket and got out a handful of money. He laid a dollar bill and two quarters in her hand. Toosio might as well spend his money. He had no reason to save it now.

"Buy you some gloves like Cricket's own," he said, and gave Cooch a sidelong smile, but she looked cross and walked away. He made haste to catch up with her and gave her more than the gloves cost to make her forgive him. Women were pests, all of them.

The next morning Toosio came to Aun Fan's with the gloves on her hands.

"Whe'd you git em, Toosio?" Aun Fan asked.

Toosio covered her face with them and shook with fat giggles.

"I ain' got de heart to tell you, Aun Fan."

"Is you eengaged to somebody?" Aun Fan pressed her.

"Pa asked me dat same thing." Toosio peeped at Blue through the glove fingers.

Blue was furious with the silly girl and ashamed of what he had done.

"Whe' you gwine in such a hurry?" Aun Fan laughed.

"I'm gwine whe' I'm gwine, dat's whe' I'm gwine." He stamped his feet to emphasize his

words as he strode away down the road, going
God knew where.

For once, the automobile was not at Aun
Missie's. He stopped, looked in at the open door.
Cricket was squeezing the accordion and her soft
wailing voice sang, "By and by, when de morn-
in' comes." The music suddenly hushed and
Cricket called.

"Come on in, Blue." He hesitated but she came
out and took him by the arm, led him into the house.
His heart thumped painfully when she looked
straight in his eyes and said with a catch in her
voice, "De sight of you is pure good for my eyes,
Blue. I ain' seen you in too long."

"I stays on de beach workin, Cricket. I don'
have time to pleasure."

She looked at the palm of his hand, stroked its
hard ridges with her little fingers. "I love every
corn on dis hand," she said gently, but Blue drew
his hand away for Cricket's gold bracelet glittered
in his eyes.

"Whe' is Aun Missie, Cricket?"

"E went in de auto-mobile wid Cun Jule to a
funeral sermon down de country."

Before he knew it, Cricket had him laughing at
Cun Jule's efforts to get on one of Aun Missie's
new frocks and wear it to her daughter's funeral
sermon. The child had been buried two years, but
the sermon had never been preached because the
child's Daddy could not come before now. Cun
Jule wanted him to see her dressed fine, and

Cricket had helped pull her corset strings until she was slim as Aun Missie. She wore Aun Missie's new hat too, and lord, how the shiny black bunch of grapes on the hat did shake and bob when Cun Jule practised in front of the looking-glass the cold way she would bow when she saw her dead child's Daddy. She would not start early, for she wanted him to be at the church when she rode up in the automobile. She practised getting in and out of the car, then strutted to show how her dress would switch when she walked up the aisle in the church.

"Cun Jule was ever a heavy case," Blue laughed.

"Cun Jule is right to put de best foot foremost. No woman wants a man to see em look down-in-de-heart because e took em an' left em," Cricket answered soberly.

"All de mens Cun Jule had in his life would make a army big as Pharaoh's."

"Maybe so, but God made Cun Jule like e is. E ain' to blame."

"You sho is changed, Cricket. You used to be down on Cun Jule. Now you take up for em."

"I know, Blue, but now since I'm leavin home I feel different bout de people. Cun Jule is mighty kind to de sick an' e lays out de dead sure grand. I'll miss em when I'm livin mongst strangers."

"When is you weddin to be, Cricket?"

"When is yours, Blue?" The little smile she gave him was somehow sad.

"What you mean, my weddin?"

"Toosio showed me his gloves dis mornin."

"My God! How I hate a blab-mouth gal!" Blue flung it at her as if she were the blab-mouth.

"Toosio told me e was engaged to you."

"Toosio was just mouth-talkin. Toosio knows I'd marry to Satan first."

"I thought so, because Cooch already showed me de piece of you shirt-tail e cut off to put a charm on you." A mocking-bird in the apple tree broke into a laughing song, but Cricket's eyes were on Blue, accusing, questioning.

"Half de gals round here has cut cloth off my shirt-tail, Cricket. Cooch ain' de only one. I don' care nothin bout none of em. I bought Toosio de gloves, but I just done it because I ain' got nobody to buy nothin for not no more——"

"Whe' is Cooch?"

"I don' love Cooch—— Sometimes I hate him too. I ain' never loved no gal but you, Cricket— you know it too—an' you done me wrong—you went back on me——"

Blue's racked nerves gave away, a great sob rose from the pit of his stomach. Cricket put her hand on his shoulder, and the sob burst. She patted his face, smoothed his forehead with her cool hands.

"Please don' cry, Blue——"

"You don' care nothin bout me——"

"I does care about you, honey. I love you same as ever. I had wanted you to stand in my

weddin an' give me away but you acted so strange,
I didn' know if to ask you or not.''

"I can' do it, Cricket. I can' stand to see you
married to dat man an' go off wid em.''

"Big Pa is dead, Uncle Wes is dead, Man Jay
is gone off—you is de only blood kin I got left.''
Tears shone in her eyes. Blue turned his head.
He never could stand to see her cry.

"You say you love me, Blue, but when I need
you, you cast me off. If Uncle Wes was livin——''
She got no further. "I'll do it, Cricket. I'll
give you away if I drop dead doin it.'' Blood
beat hot in his temples. He pushed Cricket's hand
from where it nestled on his arm and hurried out
through the back door.

Uncle Ben was the only one to whom Blue could
talk freely about his troubles. The old man never
drank, yet he never talked hard about those who
did; he never gambled or rambled, but he held
that every man must live according to his notion.

Uncle Ben was a church-member, but instead
of going to church on fourth Sundays he claimed
he served God by staying home and seeing that
the beasts which worked hard all the week were fed
well and watered.

His chief joy in life was to fetch little David
to the barnyard and show him how to do everything there, from shucking the corn to cleaning
the stables. David was lifting a new-born calf,
for Uncle Ben had told him if he lifted it every day

he would be able to lift it when the calf was a full-grown bull.

David was six or seven, the oldest child Cun Jule had after she married to Uncle Ben. The others were husky and well grown, but little David was Uncle Ben's heart-string.

"What you studyin bout so hard dis mornin, Uncle Ben?" Blue asked, for the old man's blood-shot eyes were gloomy.

"I'm in deep water, son. I don' know which way to turn."

"Is you frettin bout Cun Jule ridin in de auto-mobile?"

"No, son, I ain' got dat in de back part o' my head."

"A funeral is a sad thing. Thinkin on dead people makes me low in de mind, too."

"People has to die, Blue. It's de will of God. Jule's dead gal don' worry me none."

"Cun Jule was just jokin bout puttin on airs before dat dead gal's Daddy. Cun Jule ain' got dat man to study bout."

Uncle Ben heaved a deep sigh. "I ain' never been a jealous-hearted man, Blue. Jule is welcome to put on all de airs e can."

"What's got you down, Uncle? I never seen you look like dis before."

"I'm in trouble, Blue. My old heart is well-nigh broke."

"Better talk it out. I tried shuttin trouble up tight in my heart an' it liken to busted em open.

Dat's how-come I tell you all my worryations."

"1 reckon you right, son. Dis trouble I got now has pure pizened me until I can' eat, neither sleep."

"Is it Old Uncle Kelly Wright?"

"No, Jesus! I don' pay dat old sinner no mind. Jule is too scared of em to much as talk wid em. It's lil David got me upset."

"What lil David done?"

Uncle Ben made a place for Blue on the bale of hay. "Set here by me, Blue. Dis is mighty close talk I'm gwine tell you. I don' want it to get out, by it would make people think hard of David."

Blue promised never to breathe a word of what was told him, and Uncle Ben began.

Dicey, his first wife, died the year before Blue came. But everybody in the country said she was the best woman ever lived. God did not bless her with children, and she turned her love on other things, especially things that were weak or feeble. If a pig or a lamb was runty, Dicey would nurse it faithful as if it were a people baby. Dicey taught him, big and rough as he was, to have tender feeling for helpless things.

He was happy until Dicey got down sick, not that she complained overmuch, but he could not bear for her to suffer. Everybody helped him nurse her, Jule was the faithfullest one. When Dicey died, Jule laid her out. Jule grieved like her own sister was dead. Jule said she loved Dicey. Maybe she did.

After Dicey was buried, the house was so lonesome he could not stay home. Jule said she was lonesome, too. Maybe she was. Anyhow, it looked like it was best to marry to Jule. She said she would be proud to have him for her lawful gentleman. Some people thought he ought to wait until Dicey got cold in her grave, but Jule said Dicey was dead as she ever would be. And she was. Jule said Dicey would fret to see him live alone with nobody to cook or keep him company. And Dicey would.

Reverend Duncan came and married them together. They had a quiet wedding, two weeks after Dicey died. Jule treated him fine and when little David was born he thought God had blessed him more than his due.

The first time he took little David in his two hands, they pure trembled with joy until they most dropped him. He had pure trembled with joy over David for nigh on to seven years. And now all his joy was gone.

"David stands like a nice boy to me, Uncle Ben. What's e done to fret you so?"

"Jule told me last night David ain' my own. Jule says none o' dem last chillen is my own. Jule says e is tired livin wid a old no-'count man. E wants me to go back to Dicey's house an' stay."

"I would go, Uncle Ben. I wouldn' tarry a minute after Cun Jule said dat."

"I'd leave de country to-morrow, Blue, but I ain' got de heart to leave David wid Jule. It

would be leavin a lamb wid a wildcat. If David
didn' love me same like I love him, I might could
stand it, but David do love me. David is raven
bout me. Jule won' give em to me. E wants
David his-self. Long as Jule keeps David, I can'
go nowhere."

"Who Cun Jule had David for?"

"I asked em, but e won' tell me. E just laughs
an' makes sport when I try to find out de name
of David's Pa."

"Cun Jule is just plaguin you. E don' mean
what e says. David is de pure spittin image of
you, Uncle Ben."

"You think so?"

"Sho e is."

"I don' know, Blue. Sometimes I think de boy
favors Al-fred. Al-fred makes a mighty lot of
David, always givin em things, buyin em clothes."

"Cun Fred is de foreman. It's his business to
look after de chillen on de place, specialty de
boy-chillen. Cun Fred thinks too much o' you to
trick you, Uncle Ben. Cun Fred ain' no common
man."

"I hope you is right, Blue. I'd hate to think
Al-fred done me wrong."

"What you two mens got you heads so close
together bout?" Cun Fred was standing so near
that Blue wondered if he heard anything.

"I just come to tell Uncle Ben Cricket asked
me to give em away when e marries."

"What did you tell Cricket?"

"I told em I would."

"Dat's right, Blue. You ain' to fail Cricket in nothin. Cricket is a fine gal. E's gettin a fine husband too." Cun Fred spat cheerfully but Uncle Ben sighed.

"I'll be glad when de weddin is over an' Cricket takes his husband off. I don' like de things Old Man Kelly's been sayin'. Old Man Kelly lives yonder in Big Pa's house wid a lot o' cunjure things. E might put a bad hand on somebody. Uncle Kelly is awful cross bout dat new liquor still. E would as soon drop pizen in de mash as not. Better mind how you drink dat whisky, Al-fred. I wouldn' trust to taste em after all Uncle Kelly said."

Cun Fred smiled.

"Better take a drink wid me now, Ben." He reached up and got his jar off the joist. "You don' look so spry to-day. What's got you fretted?"

"Not a God's thing don' fret me. I was just settin down to rest a while, by Jule is gone off to his dead gal's sermon."

CHAPTER XXXIII

BLUE waked early on the morning of Cricket's wedding-day. His heart throbbed in his breast for he had never given a bride away before now. He dressed hurriedly and went to Aun Missie's.

The world was asleep except for a few little birds that twittered over plans for the day. He found Cricket dressed, but Aun Missie was still snoring. Cricket said Aun Missie was weary for she had given herself no rest until everything for the wedding was fixed exactly to her notion. The house had an empty look with the trunk packed up ready to go, and the wedding-cakes covered over with a sheet so no flies or dust could get on them. All the walls were fresh papered with pretty colored pages from the catalogues and magazines Aun Missie got in town. Some showed ladies' dresses, hats, shoes; others showed cooking stoves, sewing machines, organs. A piece of plain paper cut into pretty scallops covered the mantel-shelf where water glasses stood in a shining row waiting to hold the wedding-wine.

The day was fine and fair. A fine wedding it would be, for Aun Missie had invited everybody for miles around. Cricket stood with Blue on the little front piazza and looked out at the bright world. She said she would be sorry to leave this pleasant house where she had known so much joy. She could hardly believe her childhood was over.

If only Uncle Wes could be here to see the nice man she had. Uncle Wes would be proud to know she had done so well. He would be glad she could live easy the rest of her life. No more hoeing in the field to blister her hands and make her back ache, no more fighting boll-weevils off cotton, trying to make money enough to live decent.

"I thought de groom stayed here last night," Blue said.

Cricket said the groom spent the night at the café with Reverend Cato. He would go this morning to the crossroads store for the license.

She would not have bothered about any license, but Aun Missie insisted she must marry by the law. It seemed a pity to waste a whole dollar for a piece of paper. If Reverend Duncan read over them out of the book and they made promises to each other, that ought to be enough. But Aun Missie's heart was set on having the wedding stylish, and she wanted to please Aun Missie in everything.

Blue took the buckets and went with her to the spring for water. They tarried long talking over old times. When they got back Aun Missie had breakfast ready and, to Blue's surprise, she did not scold but made Cricket sit down with Blue at the table while she waited on them both. She said a bride is not to work on her wedding-day. When the breakfast was eaten, Aun Missie insisted on washing all the things and putting them away by herself. Cricket must rest.

Aun Bina had made paper flowers to fill the vases, but Cricket wanted some fresh blossoms too. Blue held them as she picked them. Dewdrops fell softly from the petals as she broke the stems and piled Blue's arms with red roses, zinnias, marigolds. Aun Missie came to the door and watched. She had taken off her work clothes and put on a clean dress and apron to be ready in case somebody came to look at Cricket's pretty wedding-dress and underclothes.

"I wonder whe' Man Jay is, Cricket?"

"God knows. E ain' wrote nobody a letter not lately."

Aun Missie held up a hand to shield her eyes, as she looked down the road.

"Who's dat comin?"

"It looks like Cooch to me."

"Whe's Cooch gwine so soon? E better keep dat baby home out of the dew," Aun Missie said between tight lips. "Jule give em a ten-cent bottle of paragoric yesterday and it ain' done no good."

Cooch looked strangely down-in-the-heart. Her shoulders huddled over the sleeping child in her arms when she halted in front of Aun Missie's.

"Whe' you gwine, Cooch?" Aun Missie asked.

"I'm gwine," Cooch moistened her lips with her tongue, "to de store to buy de baby some shoes and stockins for de weddin." Cooch's voice was husky and Aun Missie asked if she had a cold. "Not a God's thing don' ail me."

Cooch's eyes were on a fly which tried to light on the baby's face.

"How-come you walkin out so soon, Cooch? Whe' you gwine dis time o' day?"

"My Daddy said last night e was gwine to town to-day. I want em to fetch de baby some medicine if e is comin back. E said e might, den again e might not."

"Uncle Kelly was just talkin. E ain' gwine to stay in town," Blue said.

"I don' know. Pa says de new still ruint his liquor trade." She gave Cricket a dark look.

"A gal is a fool in dis world," Aun Missie grumbled as Cooch walked away.

"What you mean, Aun Missie? Old Man Kelly is Cooch's Daddy."

"I mean what I mean, dat's what I mean." Aun Missie said no more.

The morning hours went by and the groom did not come. Cricket's fresh roses in jars of cool water refused to stand up. She broke their stems shorter but they hung their heads. As time wore on neighbors came and went. Blue listened to their chatter, noticed their sly smiles, as they prophesied how many children Cricket would have. She would soon make up for Aun Missie's lack.

"Cricket needn' fret about havin too many chillen," Aun Jule said. "I have hearsay bright-skin people don' breed fast."

"Is you scared, Cricket?" Aun Fan asked.

"Not yet," Cricket answered quietly.

"De groom looked kinder ashy yesterday evenin when I seen em at de store."

"Grooms always be scareder dan brides. A bride don' know what's ahead of em." Aun Missie smiled.

"Who don' know?" Aun Jule laughed. "Show me de bride what don' know."

"Don' start none of you lip here to-day, Jule," Aun Missie snorted. "Cricket sho don' know. I ain' raised Cricket to have loose ways."

"For God's sake don' start no rip rap, Jule. A wedding-day ought to be peaceable," Cun Hester chided.

The neighbors went home to dress for the wedding, and the midday sun blazed down hot. Shadows grew short and clouds melted out of sight. Cricket said she was dry for a drink of cool water and went to the spring. Aun Missie went to the door and sent a long hard look down the empty road before she took Olivia, who had come to the wedding, into the shed-room and showed her the wedding-clothes. Olivia looked at garment after garment, examined the stitches, agreed that Cricket sewed as well as any sewing machine. Aun Missie lifted the sheet to show the wedding-cakes all iced and sprinkled with candies. Olivia smacked her lips with approval, then she drew out the corn-cob stopper from the jugs of wedding-wine, sniffed the sweet rich smell and rolled up her eyes.

In between times Aun Missie kept casting her

eyes toward the door. In the pretense of spitting, she went out on the front porch to search the distance for some sign of the groom.

"I wonder why de groom don' come on?" Aun Missie whispered to Blue, and cast her eyes up at the middle day sun.

Cun Fred walked slowly up the path, called Aun Missie to come outside.

They stood in the yard and their words were low. Aun Missie's back was turned so Blue could not see her face, but her stiffly folded arms could not hide a droop which fell over her shoulders.

Cun Fred beckoned to Blue and told him the automobile stood in the old road near Big Pa's house. Nobody was in it. Uncle Kelly was not home, nobody was at the still.

"You go tell Cricket, Blue. I ain' got de heart."

Blue found her by the old play-house. Her hands trembled when he took them and held them close.

"Is e come?" She tried to smile, but her hands were as cold as ice. When Blue shook his head she stumbled quickly to her feet. Aun Missie was coming. Cun Fred too. Aun Missie was wiping her eyes.

Cricket tottered, held tight to Blue's arm for support.

"Is de automobile killed em?" she whispered.

"Something must 'a' happened, Cricket." Cun Fred's voice was husky, his skin sweaty, his eyes shifty.

"Is e dead?"

"God knows whe' e is," Cun Fred gulped and halted. "De automobile is in de road. Nobody ain' in it."

"Is e dead?" Cricket asked again.

"E might be fell in de river. Reverend Cato says e was drinkin last night."

"Whe' is Uncle Kelly?"

"I couldn' find em."

"I'll kill em myself if e went off an' fooled Cricket!" Aun Missie cried.

Cun Fred laid a hand on her shoulder.

"Hush, Missie. You ain' to talk such a talk now."

A thin scream leaped from Aun Missie's throat, leading the way for others that followed with every breath. Her rigid arms stretched upward, her feet stamped the ground. "Oh, Jesus," she yelled. "Get out my way, Al-fred! I got to mourn, mourn, I tell you! I can' hold in no longer. Dat man is fooled me. E fooled my Cricket!"

Her heels beat time with her words which fell into a mournful tune. Cricket swayed forward, Blue caught her, held her while Cun Fred got the water gourd and poured cold spring water all over her head and shoulders.

"Don' let Cricket dead! Don' let em dead here to-day!" Aun Missie screamed.

Blue carried Cricket's limp body through the back door and laid her on the shed-room bed beside her wedding-dress. Olivia put a cold cloth on her forehead, and Cun Fred took Aun Missie out of the room.

Cricket's eyes fluttered open and her pale lips whispered, "Is e dead?"

"No, honey," Olivia answered. "E ain' dead. Drink dis good weddin-wine, den lay still an' rest."

"May as well tell em de truth, Olivia," Cun Fred spoke up.

"Nobody knows whe' e is, honey, but e ain' come not yet."

Cricket closed her eyes. If she breathed Blue could not see it.

Cun Jule cracked the door open. "How Cricket is now?" She came in to stand by the bed. "No use to fret, Cricket. Plenty good fish is left in de sea. Dat's what I told Cooch when e come home from school lookin like raised bread. I told em to hold up his head even if e had disgracement."

"Cricket ain' like Cooch. No—no! Cooch ever was a devil just like Old Man Kelly Wright," Aun Missie wailed.

Olivia moved about quietly putting things in place, telling Aun Missie she must bear up. To grieve over what had happened was foolish. If the groom did not want Cricket it was better for him to go before he took her for wife. Cricket would see it before long. Cricket was no fool.

The sadness which filled the house was unbearable. Cricket buried her face in the pillow while Aun Missie moaned and wrung her hands. "Looka de cake, looka de wine, looka de weddin-dress all ready for de weddin, an' no groom to marry to Cricket. What'll I tell de people? What will dey think? If Wes was here e would know what to do. I ain' got nobody to stand by me now."

An idea flashed into Blue's head, thrilled down his spine. He took Aun Missie aside. "If Cricket will have me, I'll marry to em. Dat'll stop de people from talkin."

"Why, Blue!" She looked amazed, then pleased.

"You know I ever did want Cricket, Aun Missie."

"Wes ever hoped you would have em too."

Cricket shook with sobs while Aun Missie coaxed and argued. "De preacher is comin, de people is comin. Could you stand em to see you in disgracement?"

"It's de God's truth." Olivia's face brightened. "Blue's got sense like people, Cricket. You better go on and take em.

"God bless you, son." Olivia patted his shoulder.

"I can tell de people you changed you mind at de last minute," Aun Missie said.

Cricket made no answer at all.

"Think bout Uncle Wes, Cricket. E was a proudful man. E couldn' rest easy in his grave if I let you down and let dat man fool you befo de whole country."

Blue poured out pleading words. His heart-

beats shook them, made them low and mumbling.
Cricket's face was drawn, her lips quivered. Her
eyes were scorching bright, like a trapped creature.

"Don' hang you head an' cry no more, Cricket.
Maybe it's all for de best," Aun Missie said.
"We might 'a' got killed in dat automobile gwine
to Flurida."

Cricket burst into such a deep despairing sob
that Blue's heart was rent.

"If you don' want me, I won' have hard feelins, Cricket."

Her little cold hands clung to his. "I'll stop
cryin in a minute," she whispered.

Blue waited, silent.

"I can' stand for people to pity me, Blue."

"I know dat, Cricket. Uncle Wes was proudful de same way."

"You is doin dis now by you pity me." The
look she gave him sank deep in Blue's heart,
stirred a pity in him he had never felt before.

"No, Cricket. An' if you don' want to give
answer now, I'll go home an' dress. When I
come back you can say yes or either no, whatever
you mind tells you to say."

While he dressed, Aun Fan groaned, called him
a fool, told him Cricket was making a convenience
of him. Blue was crazy to tie himself to a wife
whose heart was set on another man. Cricket was
no better than her mother. No wonder she got
treated like her mother. Cricket's blood was wild.
Blue had better stop and think.

BRIGHT SKIN

Cun Fred shifted the wad of tobacco in his cheek and spat in the fireplace.

"Leave Blue alone, Fancy. E wouldn' be satisfy to do else but what's e doin."

"You will rue dis day if you marry to Cricket," Aun Fan cried, but Blue hurried away full of hope.

Cricket had on her white wedding-dress and a thin mosquito net veiled her face. The yard was full of silent people. Curious eyes stared, knowing looks were cast when Aun Missie explained how Cricket could not bear to leave home and go off to Flurida. The automobile was ailing, likely to blow up any minute. Cricket had changed her mind and decided to take Blue for husband.

Everybody stood up when Blue walked out on the piazza with Cricket on his arm. Reverend read out of the Book, said a long prayer. Cricket said, "I will," firmly, then whispered, "Say 'I will,' Blue," and he did. Together they knelt down. Reverend's hands rested on their heads as he asked God to bless them, make them one, and pronounced them man and wife.

Cricket was shaking so that Blue had to help her get up off her knees.

"Salute you bride, Blue," Reverend bade.

Blue lifted the net, kissed her gently on the cheek, but Reverend threw the net back from her face, kissed her mouth with a loud smack, shook Blue's hand warmly. "God bless you all two," he said and wiped his eyes.

Blue stood by her side as the people came forward. Some kissed Blue, all kissed Cricket.

Cun Fred kissed her and said, "I ruther see Blue marry to you dan to any gal in de world. Dis is a happy day for me," but his sorrowful face belied his words.

So much wine was drunk, a little laughter fluttered when the presents were brought forward and put on the table at the end of the piazza. Pieces of money, china, glass, clinked cheerfully against the painful uneasiness. The people left early, went out quietly as people leave a house of death, without singing or dancing or tarrying to make merry.

Aun Missie went home with Cun Fred and Aun Fan so the bride and groom could be alone.

Cricket dropped in a chair in front of the fire. The room was shadowy, silent.

"How you feelin, Cricket?" Blue tried to speak cheerfully. "It all went off nice I think."

Big tears slid down her cheeks, fell in her lap. She did not lift a hand to hide them, and Blue dried her eyes gently with his new white pocket handkerchief. He tried to make her smile, but all he did, said, was fruitless and he turned away, hurt and angry. He would have left the house, but he could not go now and leave her alone. He went into the shed-room and flung himself across the bed. Firelight came through the open door, flickered on the whitewashed wall. Cricket did not want him and he had sworn before God he

would stay with her until death parted them from
each other.

He tried to sleep but his quivering flesh would
not let him. He called himself a fool and a coward
heart to let her tears scare him off from a woman
who was his by right. What if she did cry for
somebody else. She belonged to him now. His
craving for her stung him to the quick.

"Cricket," he called, "get up and go to bed.
I ain' gwine bother you."

When she did not answer, he went to her.

"You make me have surprise, Cricket, actin like
dis. Anybody would think I had mistreated you
instead savin you from disgracement."

Her big sad eyes looked up at him and he
knelt beside her, drew her wet cheek against his,
tried to comfort her as he would comfort a heart-
broken child.

The next night, he lay alone on the shed-room
bed with strange thoughts throbbing in his head.
He was a married man but his bride lay huddled
on Aun Missie's bed with a hard chill making her
teeth chatter. Dark lines lay under her eyes,
white rims showed around the great black pupils.
Her cheek-bones stood out, her lips were thin and
pinched. Aun Fan and Cun Hester helped Aun
Missie work on her, trying to get her warm. Every
time Blue went near her, her eyes got glassy and
strange. Before morning, she had fever, inward
fever, Cun Hester said. It was caused by too
much eye-sightment.

CHAPTER XXXIV

WEEKS dragged by, but no news came from Cricket's beau. The automobile, pushed out in the corn-field, sat like a strange silent ghost. The still was deserted. Reverend Cato's Monday-night dances ceased while he held a revival across the river, but Miss Sallie kept the store open.

On the way home from the beach one sundown, Blue stopped to buy some sweet cakes to tempt Cricket's appetite. The store door was open but Miss Sallie was not in. He took a box of the cakes off the shelf, left fifteen cents on the counter and started off. Miss Sallie rushed in, her face all twisted with horror.

"Something is in de corn-field, Blue." She could hardly talk for panting. "Dogs was barkin and growlin, I thought dey had a possum or a coon so I went to look."

"Maybe dey got a wildcat or a bear."

"It's somebody, Blue, sho as my name is Sallie."

Her eyes were fit to pop out of her head as she led Blue gingerly past the automobile, through tangled weeds in ripe corn rows. Dog voices quarreled and disputed, but it was no possum or coon they had.

"Don' go no closer, Miss Sallie. It might be a spook or a plat-eye. Me an' you couldn' deal wid dem. Let me run home an' get Cun Fred an' some of de mens."

Miss Sallie would not be left behind. Cun Fred listened to her queer talk and said she was drunk, but he called some of the men to fetch pitch-forks from the haystacks. Blue started off with them, but when that automobile came in sight he changed his mind and told Cun Fred he had promised Aun Missie to come home early and fetch the cakes for Cricket's supper.

He gave a sigh of relief when the men hurried on without him. Dealing with a plat-eye or spirits, even a rattlesnake or wildcat, was scary business after the sun dropped, for darkness hides many strange things.

Aun Missie's sharp eyes saw at once that something was on Blue's mind, and questioned him. He did not want to excite Cricket, and made some excuse to get Aun Missie out in the yard.

"Miss Sallie is drunk again," Aun Missie laughed when Blue told her the news.

"I ain' drunk an' I heard dem dogs. Dey didn' sound natural, Aun Missie." She shamed him for fearing a dog fight and he a married man too. Blue could hardly eat supper. He listened for Cun Fred's return, for the evening was still and sound traveled far.

Old She-She lifted her head and gave a long howl and tottered down the path on uncertain legs. Cricket asked what was wrong with She-She. Blue said She-She barked at the moon, that was all, then he slipped out of the house and hurried toward the corn-field. Fast running feet thudded, and two of the farm-hands hove in sight, racing like death chased them. One bellowed hoarsely, "Great God, Blue, dat's a awful sight yonder in de corn-field."

They choked with horror as they told about leg bones, arm bones, clothes, even a hat.

"Whose hat it is?"

They thought it belonged to Cricket's beau. The leg bones belonged to a high-standing man too.

"Was de clothes his own?"

They did not know. They did not stop to see.

Blue went home and sat on the steps, watching dim forms hurry by in the darkness. Waving skirts and white aprons, chattering voices of men, women, made haste to the corn-field. He warned Aun Missie not to tell Cricket for fear it would make her worse.

She was sleeping peacefully the next morning when Blue went with Cun Fred to lay the bones in the graveyard. Cricket's beau was dead, thank God.

Cooch walked home with Blue after the burying and she gave a low laugh when they got in sight of Aun Missie's.

"Does you know who killed em, Blue?"

Blue said he did not know.

"Don' crack you teeth to nobody, Blue. I got plenty on my hands like it is." She moistened her dark lips with a pointed red tongue. "Dat man thought e could outdo Pa sellin liquor. Pa fixed em. But if you tell I'll fix you."

Cooch's eyes glittered mean as they searched his face.

"Is you gwine tell?"

"But, Cooch——"

"If you tell, I'll say, 'How-come Blue married to Cricket so quick? How come e didn' wait? Somebody killed dat man. E ain' died a natural death in dat corn-field!' "

Blue swore solemnly he would never tell.

"How did Old Man Kelly kill em, Cooch?"

"You keep you mouth off my Daddy," she said fiercely, and her eyes held a wicked sparkle.

Little David, with Cooch's baby on his back, came galloping down the road. He shied, kicked up his heels, pranced around like a horse afraid of an automobile.

"Stop you doins, David!" Cooch screamed at him. "You'll jar de life out dat child."

David laughed and stamped, gave a vicious snort. Cooch picked up a stick.

"Git on home! First thing you know de plat-eyes'll be ridin you to death."

It was hard not to drop a word when the sheriff came on the *Comanche* and held an inquest in Miss Sallie's store. Everybody was sworn, questioned, cross-questioned.

Where was Kelly Wright? The sheriff's eyes glared at the witnesses.

Nobody knew.

Who saw the yellow man last?

Nobody knew.

Was it true he killed a horse for Al-fred and broke up a buggy and harness?

Yes, it was true but he paid for all the damage he did.

Was it true he had a still and a boat to haul liquor down the river?

Nobody knew.

Who pushed the automobile out of the road?

Nobody knew.

Who heard the dogs first?

Miss Sallie admitted that she did, but the body had been dead for days.

Where was the still!

Nobody knew.

Reverend Cato declared he was a servant of God who tried to have decent dances. Cun Fred swore that so far as he knew everybody liked the yellow stranger and was glad to see Cricket marry to him.

Why did she marry to Blue so sudden?

Blue's mouth got as dry as a bone, but Cun Fred spat and answered that Blue was ever accommodating. It seemed a pity to waste so much good wine and cake without a wedding. Blue was Cricket's cousin. They were ever friends. Blue had aimed to give the bride away and when the groom failed to show up, he just married to her himself.

The sheriff got cross, cursed everybody for a pack of liars, threatened to put them all on the chain gang, looked at his fine gold watch and

said he had to catch the *Comanche* and get back
to town where he had important business.

That ended the inquest, but not the talk. People lingered, cast suspicious looks at Blue, at
Cooch, at Cun Fred.

Cun Fred stood up, cleared his throat.

"Nobody never killed dat man, an' it ain' no
use to try to put blame on a soul.

"What you think killed em?" Brer Dee asked.

"God knows. God-self might be struck em
dead."

"A rattlesnake bite is as bad as a bullet."

"A plat-eye can kill you quick as lightnin if you
fight em."

Old Man Kelly had some strong roots in that
house, maybe the man drank poisoned liquor and
died. Many roads to death were mentioned, but
Blue rejoiced that suspicion did not rest on him.

CHAPTER XXXV

CRICKET stayed poorly and Blue consoled himself with hard work and left her in the hands of those who were wiser about sickness. On Thanksgiving Day he lifted her in his arms, put her in Uncle Wes's big chair on the piazza. She sat looking across the big field for a minute, then she said slowly:

"You been a good friend to me, Blue."

Blue vowed he would always be that, all he craved was to see her well.

She had put on flesh, her eyes seemed less big and hollow, but she sat looking at nothing, saying nothing. Blue could tell her heart was far away.

People came to see her, fetched her chickens and eggs, wild ducks and rice birds. She answered whatever questions they asked listlessly, thanked them wearily.

Blue quit working on the beach and sawed logs in the river swamp so he could come home every night. At dawn, Aun Missie had his breakfast on the table and his dinner in a bucket ready to take with him. Nothing was ever out of place in the shed-room where he slept alone in Cricket's bed. Aun Missie kept his clothes washed and mended, folded neatly in Uncle Wes's trunk. He had no complaint of her treatment. Cricket never asked him where he went, what he did, when he came home. She never spoke about the yellow scoundrel.

281

Blue wondered what she knew about the bones. Cooch came to see her. Toosio too. Girls are mighty blab-mouth people.

One Saturday afternoon in the Christmas Aun Missie took a basket of eggs to the store to sell and Blue was alone with Cricket. She seemed uneasy as though something was on her mind.

Blue took her hand. "What de matter ail you, honey?" he asked gently as he could, but she dropped her eyes.

"I try awful hard to please you, Cricket. If I'm doin anything wrongful just tell me an' I'll stop."

Her lips twisted. "You ain' done wrongful. I'm de one."

"What you done, Cricket?"

She made no answer, would not meet his eyes.

"I ain' got sense like you, honey, but I'd do anything in God's world to make you happy. Long as I been married to you, I ain' laid hands on you except to tote you like a baby."

"I know it, Blue. I thank you for it too."

Her voice was shaky, her eyes were afraid. Why was Cricket afraid of him? It pure hurt him to the heart.

"Don' think on me like dat, Cricket. I ain' never gwine push myself on you."

She laid a trembling hand on Blue's arm. "Blue, you got to have long patience wid me now."

"Why, Cricket? What you mean?"

A little vein in her neck beat fast. "Don' think too hard of me, Blue."

"Think hard? Why, honey? I think you is de finest thing in de country."

She shook her head slowly.

"Listen, Cricket," he took her hand. "I promised God when I married to you, I'd take care of you long as life lasts. I meant it den, I mean it now. Nothin could change me. Either sick, either well, you belongst to me. I'll do de best I can by you too."

She threw off the quilt and staggered across the floor into the shed-room. Blue could hear her sobbing, and he dropped his head down on his folded arms. Aun Missie came in, asked what ailed him. He told her he had swinging in the head. She went in the shed-room, came out in a hurry. She said Cricket was bad sick. He must fetch Aun Fan in a hurry.

"Cricket ain' sick. E's just worried in his mind, same like I is, Aun Missie."

"Like you is? I wish to God you had Cricket's ailment stead o' Cricket." She turned on him angrily. Her eyes narrowed, her lips shook with fury and Blue sped away.

Through the long night hours he could hear the women's voices trying to quiet Cricket's moans. He walked round the yard, smoked, sat down, walked around again. Thoughts whirled in his head until it ached fit to burst. Cocks were crowing far down when Aun Fan came to the door.

"Blue——" His heart filled his breast. "It's come, son, but it ain' old enough to be people not yet. Go get Cun Hester. Cricket don' do so well."

Off Blue went; back he came with Cun Hester, who did her best to comfort him.

"Cheer up, son, disapp'intment comes to everybody. Woman sickness is new to you now, but you'll get used to em if you live."

Day was clean, people were going to the field for the day's work. Blue went inside to avoid being seen. Aun Fan came out of Cricket's room in great haste.

"God willin, I'll catch plenty of full-time chillen for Cricket before I leaves dis world." She poured water out of the kettle and mixed a cup of warm soapsuds. "Dis'll float em out," she said cheerfully and hurried away.

"Please, let me die," he heard Cricket cry. "I ruther die."

Blue got up. "Whyn' you leave em alone?" He shook Aun Fan's arm.

"Cricket's got to drink dis soapsuds, Blue. Every woman drinks em."

"Try an' swallow em down," Aun Missie urged.

Cricket took the cup and drained it.

"Everything will be all right now," Aun Fan said pleasantly.

"Don' look so down-in-de-heart, Blue. You'll have better luck next time." Aun Missie gave him a dry smile.

The news of Cricket's sickness spread and women crowded in to see Cricket give thanks for life.

"So much people will fret em to death," Blue cried, for they stood thick all around her bed. Two of them took Cricket by her shoulders, two by the feet, and stretched her until she screamed.

"What you doin, Aun Fan?" Blue howled.

"Hush you racket, Blue. Dis'll make de gal have room for you next chillen."

"Please, please, leave me to rest," Cricket begged, but the women lifted her off the bed and held her clear of the floor.

"Hist you arms three times, Cricket," Aun Fan ordered.

Cricket was too weak, her limp arms had to be lifted. High they went, three times, while the women shouted at the top of their voices, "Praise to de Father, praise to de Son, praise to de Holy Ghost."

Blue fled outside, followed the branch into the deep dark woods to get out of sight, out of hearing. He lay flat on the ground and strange thoughts roared dizzily through his head. Aun Fan believed Cricket lost his child. Aun Missie believed it, everybody believed it. Cricket let them think it. He would tell the truth. But if he told, what good would it do him or her or anybody else? He was married to Cricket—married——

Red and white toadstools had sprung from the damp leaf mold. They smelled of death and he

wrung their heads off, squeezed them so tight
their bruised blood wet his fingers.

When he woke night had fallen. The dewy
woods were sweet now but the smell of Cricket's
room stung his nostrils. He could not stand to
go near it again. Where could he go? What must
he do?

Somebody whooped his name. "Blue—oo! Oh,
Blue!" It was Cun Fred. Blue got up. His legs
were numb, his heart sick.

"Yes-suh, I'm comin," he answered wearily.

Cun Fred met him and took his hand. "I'm
sorry, Blue, but Cricket's young. E will birth
chillen better when e gets full grown. It ain' no
use to fret because e lost you first one."

Blue longed to blurt out the shameful truth,
but his tongue lay dumb in his mouth.

Everybody expressed sorrow over Blue's misfortune. Everybody wished him better luck next
time. Cun Jule ever had heard bright-skin women
bore children hard, often lost them. Aun Fan ever
had heard bright-skin women mend slowly, and
she made Cricket stay abed longer than the three
days she allowed her black patients.

Aun Missie's sharp eyes watched Blue whenever
he came in the house. If he failed to ask how
Cricket was, she said impatiently, "You is de
slackest husband I ever seen, Blue. You made
Cricket think you was raven bout em. Now you
act like Cricket throwed you child away on a
purpose."

What could he say?

The few times he went into Cricket's room, his heart faltered and his words were stiff, in spite of her pleading eyes. The days passed quickly enough but the nights were endless. If Blue sat by the fire the big drum beat for birth-night suppers or the Christians sang at meeting and mocked his bitter lonesomeness. If he went to bed misery kept him awake for hours.

Everybody else was happy and pleasuring. He was left out of everything. Nobody cared how lonesome he was or how weary and down-in-the-heart, nobody but Cooch.

CHAPTER XXXVI

PRIDE kept Blue from telling a soul of the ache that burned in his heart. When Aun Missie scolded him for indifference to Cricket, he put on his hat and left. Sometimes to the store, sometimes to play skin, sometimes to wander about the roads and fields. If he went for a bit of talk with Cun Fred, Aun Fan made him unhappy with her talk of how Cricket should be up and about instead of creeping around the house like an old woman with no husband or crop to tend. Look at Cooch. Less than a week after she birthed her child she was as sound as ever. Cooch was no trifling bright-skin to loll around waiting for somebody to cook her dainty food. Cooch had her faults, but laziness was not one of them. Blue ought to teach Cricket a lesson. She was not the only girl in the country. Plenty of them would jump up and crack their heels with joy if God blessed them with a steady hard-working gentleman like Blue.

Blue tried to speak up. He said he lacked for nothing. Aun Missie treated him like a son, gave him the best of everything, let him come and go without a word. But all the time he felt like Aun Fan spoke the truth. Little by little his mind spoke to him, told him he was a fool to waste his life moping, fretting, thinking over what lay between him and Cricket, sticking home like a burr on a mule's tail or sneaking around to get pleasure

288

that he craved lest people think ill of him or her.

Cooch invited him to a dance one night and he made some flimsy excuse. He knew Cooch could cheer him up better than anybody else, but he went to see Cun Fred instead.

"How is Cricket?" Aun Fan asked.

He told her Cricket was up and about.

"A good sound frammin would bring Cricket to his senses," Aun Fan declared.

Cun Fred was horrified. "Fram Cricket? Great God, Fancy. You forgot who Cricket is?"

"Many a better woman dan Cricket has got frammed for not doin his duty. Blue ain' hard enough on em, Al-fred. A bright skin needs beatin same like other people."

Blue looked at the clock. It was not late. Aun Fan was right. He was a fool.

"I come here now to tell you I'm gwine to a dance to-night. I done quit hanging round home."

"A dance? Whe' de dance is, Blue?" Cun Fred looked surprised.

"Cooch is havin a birth-night supper for his baby."

"You better go slow, Blue."

"I'm glad Blue's gwine, Al-fred," Aun Fan said. "It'll learn Cricket some sense."

As Blue passed Aun Missie's he paused. Through the open door he could see Aun Missie smoking her pipe, and Cricket sitting with her chin in her hands gazing at the fire. She must have felt his eyes on her for she got up and came

to the door. He could not go on without a word.
"How you feelin, Cricket?"

"Is dat you, Blue? You come home early to-
night."

She said it gently, without a hint of blame for
other nights when he came in late or not at all.

"Cricket," he feared to say the words on his
lips. "Cooch is havin a dance. I'm gwine to it."
She made no answer. Blue felt awkward, somehow ashamed. "Whyn' you come go too, Cricket?
We needn' stay long. We needn' dance lessen you
want to."

"Is you lost you mind, Blue?" Aun Missie cried
fiercely, but Cricket answered quietly:

"I been thinkin all day bout a dream I had last
night. Uncle Wes come an' brought me a glass of
dat same white medicine what e give me when I
was seekin. E told me to drink em an' it would
make me well. I drank em an' dem same two
white baby angels come an' fastened two sets
o' wings on my back. I danced light on my feet
same as ever. Uncle Wes told me not to fret no
more about nothin. E was watchin over me."

Aun Missie sat open-mouthed as Cricket went
on.

"Blue has been mighty faithful. If e wants to
pleasure, Aun Missie, I ain' de one to hold em
back. Seems like dancin might help me too now
since I know Uncle Wes don' hold nothin against
me."

She got out her dance frock. It was wrinkled.

Aun Missie said it looked a sight. Cricket laughed.
Nobody would look at wrinkles.

"Everybody will look at em, Cricket. Dey will
think hard too if you go dressed like a hag."

"Wear de weddin-dress, Cricket," Blue suggested. "I'll put on my weddin-clothes."

Cricket hesitated for a heart-beat, then got out
the dress. Blue helped her put it on, tied the
ribbon bow in the back for her. Aun Missie
did not come. She was ever a kill-joy, ever glad to
agonize over something.

"You pure look like a ghost, Cricket," she complained. "Dis night air gwine make you sick, an'
I'm done wore out now wid nursin you."

Blue felt like choking her. "I'll nurse em, Aun
Missie, if e gets sick again."

"Good old Blue." Cricket gave a soft little
laugh and the dimples twinkled in her thin cheeks.
"You won' have to nurse me no more. Uncle
Wes's medicine'll keep me well." Her eyes brightened with tears, but she quickly wiped them away.
"I ain' cryin, Blue. I'm just eye-sighted over
facin all de people again."

"Don' fret about facin nobody when I'm wid
you," he said quickly.

She took up the lamp and held it by the head
to look at herself in the glass. "I look like a ghost
for true."

"Ghost nothin," Blue answered. "You pure
look like a star-lily." The words slipped out before he knew it.

How slim she was in the tight-waisted dress
with no veil flowing down around her shoulders or
over the cloudy skirt. Her hair was drawn back
smooth from her forehead and made a tight
little knot on the back of her small head. Her
skin looked bleached from lack of sun; his two
hands could have spanned her waist, but her eyes
were bright, her steps quick and light.

They spoke few words as they walked along the
dark road. Cricket breathed deep, smelling the
night. "Thank God for life," she sighed, and Blue
wondered if she knew how near death she had been.

The music was playing a quick measure, dancers
filled the floor but a group stood outside around
the door. They were dumb-struck at the sight of
Cricket, at her cheerful greeting, "How yunnah
do, to-night?"

"Great God, gal. I thought you was a sperit,"
Cooch cried, but the others crowded around
saying how glad they were to see her.

The room was gay as a flower garden with so
many bright dresses flashing around in the firelight. Every eye fastened on Cricket, but she
took no notice of astonished looks, open mouths,
whispers behind hands. She held up her head,
laughed, talked like she had never known sickness
or heartache. She could not sit back against the
wall when so many of the boys begged her to
dance. Blue took her out on the floor for the first
set and she floated around the room like a cool light
cloud, hardly resting on his arms. She took

another partner for the second set and Blue went
to dance with Cooch.

While the musicianers tuned up Cricket prom-
enaded around the room, her arm hooked in her
partner's.

"Cricket don' look like e been sick," Cooch said.

"E sho don'," Blue answered. He would have
said more but the music rang out. He put his
arm tight around Cooch and danced off to the
maddening music. He could feel the strength in
Cooch's firm lithe body. Her stiff sweet-smelling
hair brushed against his cheek and a chill shivered
over his skin. Her feet beat like hammers, her
body was hot, her full chest rose and fell against
his breast. He danced blindly on until Cooch
panted:

"Let's go outside an' catch some air, Blue."
The warm flesh of her bare arm was sweet to his
hand.

"Whe' you gwine, Blue?" Cricket asked as they
went past her.

"To cool out a minute."

"Don' cool out too fast or you'll catch cold."

Cricket's steady voice somehow brought back
his senses. He walked to the end of the street with
Cooch and turned back. Anybody could have
heard the few words passed between them.

"Is you ready to go, Cricket?" Blue asked.

"I'm ready if you is."

He borrowed a shawl from Cooch to put around
her and they said good night. Cricket stepped

along far more quickly than she came. She said dancing had done her good, limbered her up, made her feel like somebody new.

"You look like somebody new, Cricket."

"Maybe I is, Blue," she whispered and squeezed his hand.

They tiptoed into the house but Aun Missie called, "I ain' closed my eyes since you left, Cricket. I been too fretted."

Cricket went in the room where she was, murmured low words, came out, closing the door gently behind her.

Blue's heart stood still when she came toward him in her cloudy white wedding-dress.

CHAPTER XXXVII

BLUE was late getting to work and his fellow sawyers twitted him, but he answered their teasing without anger. His heart was at peace, quiet as the dawn, brave as the tall gums and cypresses that lifted heads to the sky above. Tender leaves danced and fluttered as the light slowly brightened. They had no care. Great dark roots sunk deep in the mud faithfully sucked up food and water to give them life and color.

Saw-saw, saw-saw, Blue pulled one end of the flat sharp-toothed blade. It ate through the strong wood, spat out clean sawdust scented with the great tree's breath. Blue wondered if the tree felt pain or fear now that its end was near.

In front of him a slow black creek meandered past, without hurry to reach the river. A flock of goats minced quietly along its grass-covered edge. Hogs rooted for worms, grunted friendly words when the big white bull came to browse near them. His pointed horns gleamed, his sleek hide lay smooth on his powerful body, his sharp hoofs cut tracks in the carpet of blue violets. The cows followed him, eating along without crowding or jostling. The bell on the neck of the old lead cow tinkled, calling the others to come munch in a choice grass patch. Calves tasted tender blades, kicked up heels to play. Little birds preened their feathers. Larger water birds waded knee-deep in the water. Squirrels raced up trunks, scampered from limb to limb.

Everything was happy in this shadowy world. Its gentle peace held no weary or downcast heart. Its creatures felt no jealousy or meanness, no hate or wish for vengeance. People ought to be satisfied too.

"What you doin, Blue? Wake up, boy! Pull dat saw! Stop you dreamin." His partner's harsh words broke the spell, and Blue tightened his muscles, pulled faster, harder. The saw's drone stiffened, the great trunk cracked and shivered. A loud cry burst from its solid heart, as the tottering limbs tore a path to the ground through vines and tangled branches. A deep silence followed. Blue could hear startled wings flit away as a strange sweet scent of the tree's life filled the air.

"Dis old tree will make five good logs. Let's get on em, Blue."

The saw droned again, through bark and wood. The shade felt steamy, for thick vines and undergrowth let in no air. Gnats danced in swarms, mosquitoes sang. The green-watermelon scent of a poison snake drifted in from a palmetto clump near by.

The old bull bellowed, the young bull answered. Heavy feet trampled, calves bleated, the lead cow's bell rang out a sharp rebuke. Her husband and son were fighting. Each craved to head the herd, now that spring had come.

Saw-saw, saw-saw. The steel teeth got dull and

a file rasped them sharp. Thoughts droned through Blue's head, making no sense, giving no answers. He got up, drank water, sweated it out. Hunger gnawed at his insides. If noon ever came, he would go home to eat dinner with Cricket. How would she meet him, what would she say?

She was only half awake when he left this morning. He had whispered to Aun Missie to let her sleep on.

The hours crept by but at last the sawmill whistle sounded near the landing. Noon had come. A good morning's work was done. Blue had one whole hour and a half to go home, eat and come back.

He took a short-cut through the woods. Mud clung to his feet, briar patches tore his overalls, vines dropped nooses over his head but nothing could hinder his haste to-day.

A little blue flower bell caught his eyes. Its name was traveler's joy. White star-lilies shone near the creek, but they were frail things, quick to wilt, easy to bruise. Cricket could put the little traveler's joy in water and it would last for days. He picked it and hurried on.

She stood in the door waiting for him. Joy made him forget she was not strong and he gave her a squeeze fit to crack her bones. She cried out but he laughed until she showed him dark mud stains on her clean dress and filthy mud tracks his feet left on Aun Missie's clean floor.

A good thing Aun Missie had gone off for the

day. She would be cross if she saw. He hugged
Cricket again, but she wiped her mouth, dusted
her hands off as if his filth clung to them too.

"I ain' had time to wash, Cricket."

"Dat's all right, Blue," she said gently. "Come
eat you dinner."

He hardly knew what he ate from the full plate
she placed on the table for him. He sat chewing,
swallowing, with his eyes on her mouth when
she talked, on her eyes when she smiled. She sat
across from him, cool, clean, talking about things
she had done since morning, fingering the little
traveler's joy which stood in a glass of water between them.

When his plate was empty, he wiped his mouth
on his sleeve and got up. Cricket got up too and
shuddered. Blue knew something was amiss.
"What's wrong, Cricket?"

"Look in de glass, Blue."

His shirt was soaked with sweat, his dingy old
overalls ragged and dirty. No wonder Cricket
shrank from him, fresh and sweet as her garments
were.

That evening he stopped at Miss Sallie's store
and bought soap. Not the bar turpentine soap he
ever used but a pretty sweet-scented pink cake. He
wiped mud off his feet on the grass before he
went in the house, then he hurried to the branch
and rid his whole body of sweat, dressed in fresh
clothes from the skin out so she would not shiver
when he touched her.

At the end of the week he drew his pay and hurried home to give every cent to Cricket. He told her all he made was hers to keep or spend. If she spent it freely, all the better.

Her smiling eyes looked up at him, and something like wishfulness filled them. Aun Missie laughed out with pleasure and said Cricket must bury the money with what little was left in the chimney corner. Blue told her his money was not to be buried but kept handy in case Cricket thought of something she wanted. Maybe a dress or new shoes or a ribbon.

"Cricket's got plenty clothes and shoes already. I spent money like water getting em things to wear in town when e was married."

The words stuck thorns in Blue's heart, but Cricket said it was he who must have clothes. The only underclothes he had to his name could hardly hold their patches.

"Did you tell Blue bout you letter, Cricket?"

Aun Missie gave Blue a narrow look.

"A letter? You got a letter, Cricket?" Blue's heart ceased beating.

She nodded, took an envelope out of her apron pocket, handed it to him.

"Who wrote you a letter?"

"Man Jay."

"Man Jay? Whe' Man Jay is?"

"At New York."

"Well, I declare. I'm sho glad Man Jay is livin."

Blue held the letter but his hand shook so he handed it back. "Read em to me, Cricket. It's got me all dizzy to know Man Jay ain' dead."

She opened the single page and read slowly.

"New York.

"Dear Cricket: I take my seat and take my pen in hand to tell you I am well and hope you are the same. I live at Harlem. I keep a place to shot crap. I go on they bond if the police get them. I I got money. I want you to come here. Write me a answer. Keep sweet. I was passin time with Cooch. She ain' for me. Don' listen to Cooch. Tell Aun Missie heaper howdy.

"Yours truly,
MAN JAY."

"Man Jay don' know you is married."

"No, Man Jay don' know." Cricket spoke very softly.

"I ever did know Cooch had dat child for Man Jay."

"Why so, Aun Missie?"

"I got my reasons." Aun Missie gave Blue a knowing look.

Cricket folded the letter, put it in the envelope, into her apron pocket.

"You must write Man Jay an' tell em you married to me."

"I is gwine write em. I'm gwine to de store dis evenin to buy some paper an' a pencil." For some reason Blue thought of those slips of paper holding Cricket's name, he and Man Jay had dropped in the liquor vat. Man Jay's had not worked, thank God.

Early the next morning Cricket's letter sat upon the mantel-shelf, its envelope fat with pages inside. Blue did not ask what she wrote, why she wrote so much, or when she would mail it. The letter was gone when he came home from work.

Planting time had come, and Blue took time off from the swamp work to plow the land. He loved to watch the soft rich earth turn, making furrows for the seed Aun Missie planted.

Cricket kept the house and she began to sing at her work. On her way to the spring, she tapped the bottom of the bucket to keep time to the words as Man Jay used to do. Blue smiled when he heard her wailing, "Why was I born so black and so blue?" or "Po' boy, long ways from home." Aun Missie resented such a waste of time, but Blue reminded her that Cricket was hardly grown yet. Girls need to pleasure when their work is done.

Man Jay answered Cricket's letter promptly. He wished Cricket joy, a gal and a boy, hoped she and Blue would live like Isaac and Rebecca.

He sent a package too, a paper box wrapped and tied with stout string, and on it was written, "Mrs. Cricket Goodwine, River Bend, S. C."

Inside wrapped together and marked "Cricket" were a tiny bottle of cologne, gold hoop earrings, gold beads, a tiny folded fan that could open up and show a pretty lady wearing a full-skirted red

dress. Red socks and a red cravat were marked
"Blue." Four small handkerchiefs with colored
hems, and a pair of black stockings were marked
"Aun Missie."

The day seemed like Christmas. Cricket stood
in front of the glass to put on the beads and earrings; then she opened the cologne and touched
Blue's cheek with the wet stopper. She laughed
happily when he said it smelled too sickening
sweet, put some on the front of his shirt and
fanned the scent up in his face.

Blue slept poorly that night and Cricket talked
in her sleep. Next morning she put on the beads
and earrings before she dressed. Blue came
home from work, weary from the heat and strain
of sawing all day, but Cricket would not rest until
he washed, dressed, put on his new socks and cravat
and took her to a dance at Toosio's.

Next morning she hummed dance tunes over
fixing breakfast and smashed one of Aun Missie's
china plates. Aun Missie fussed and said losing
sleep ever made Cricket nervish. She must quit
pleasuring or keep her hands off the dishes.

Cricket looked straight at Aun Missie. "If you
don' like how I do, me an' Blue can go live somewhere else."

Blue expected a furious outburst, but instead
Aun Missie gave Cricket a hard look and left the
room.

"What ails you dis mornin, Cricket?" Blue
asked.

"You keep you mouth out o' dis, Blue," she blazed out. "Brokin a plate ain' no sin. Aun Missie quarrels at all I do, here lately."

"Back-talkin' Aun Missie don' sound nice from you. You hurt his feelings, Cricket."

"E hurts my-own every day God sends."

"You is Aun Missie's heart-string, Cricket. Don' forget dat. Aun Missie ain' young like e used to be."

Cricket stood in the middle of the floor and tossed the broken bits of china far back into the chimney one by one and wiped her fingers on her apron.

"I tries to have long patience, Blue. You don' know how hard I tries. Aun Missie fussed at Uncle Wes de same way. I'm done wore out wid it, Blue. Clean wore out. I'm wore out wid everything here home."

"God knows you pleasure when you want to."

"Pleasure? Does you think it pleasures me to dance wid dem black sweaty mens? My God! I'd as soon dance wid a bunch o' ram goats." She stood in the door looking far away. The sun poured yellow light over her face, her earrings, her beads. Her mouth was hard, her eyes cold.

"I got to go, Cricket. I'm done lated now." Blue took up his bucket, his hat. "I got to help float a raft of logs down de river to-day. I won' get home before next week." He waited, but she made no answer.

A great desire to know what she was thinking

came over him. Questions welled up in his heart
but how could he ask anything when she looked
like that.

"If you say de word, Cricket, I'll build we a
house. Den you could go an' come when you
please."

"Go where? It ain' no place to go exceptin
whe' I done been till I'm weary."

"I say I won' be home to-night, Cricket. I'm
gwine down de river on a raft of ash logs."

She did not even turn her head.

"Does you want me to fetch you something
from town?"

She heaved a sigh. "I wish to God I was a ash
log."

"Honey, honey, don' talk like dat. Kiss me
good-by."

"Oh, Blue, I feel so un-restless. What'll I do
till you come back?"

"Whyn' you walk out to de store an' pleasure
you'self? Dat's what my money is for." He
kissed her and hurried away.

CHAPTER XXXVIII

BLUE stood up on the raft when it needed guiding, sat down when it drifted with the current and listened to the other men talk. One said the ash logs would make bodies for automobiles, another said ash logs were used to make bodies for engines that flew in the sky.

People out in the world had strange fearful ways. Blue sat silent and pondered over them.

"Who you reckon killed Cricket's beau?" The question startled him.

The inquest was discussed, acted. Boisterous laughter followed a take-off of Reverend Cato's testimony that he never could remember anything since a mule butted him in the head when he was a knee-high boy.

Blue resolved to tell Cricket the whole story when he got home. He would break down every wall that stood between them. She could not lean on him and pull away from him too. That yellow man was dead. She might as well put him out of mind. She must act like a married woman instead of keeping her thoughts secret from him. Even if her skin was bright he would make her quit her big-doings talk, calling the black men ram goats. While he thought it something in his heart rose up and told him he could never talk hard to Cricket. She had made a mistake for true, but she paid dear for it. She was not like Cooch or

Toosio in ways any more than in looks. She was
as far above them as the sky was above the river.
He must try to have patience with her. Long patience. Bright-skin women are different from
black ones. He had luck to be Cricket's husband.
Any man in the country would jump up and
crack his heels to take her around and show
her off, much less live with her. She had been
mighty sick. Maybe she was not over it. He
would make her rest more and get stronger.

Nigh a week would pass before he saw her again.
The men would want to tarry in town a day or
more. The boats tied to the raft to take them home
must be pulled with oars at three miles an hour,
four miles if a rising tide helped. A day and a
half going down, another day to load the logs on
a schooner, a day to rest and look around, a day
for the homeward journey, maybe more. What
should he take Cricket? Not beads or earrings,
not cologne or a fan. Man Jay had sent her those.
Not shoes, for her wedding-shoes were new. He
could not think of a thing Cricket lacked. The
Comanche hove in sight with a load of excursioners
going to town, and the raft had to be pulled out
of its way. Handkerchiefs waved, voices called—
but Blue had no time to look, for the raft was heavy
and contrary.

When town was reached at last and the logs
loaded on a schooner Blue was weary but the
pocket in his overalls held his pay in a little tobacco sack.

On the water-front, men naked to the waist un-
loaded bananas, bales of cotton, heavy boxes,
carried them through doors in the straight backs
of stores edging the river bank. Some stores were
brick, others wood. Counters and shelves were
piled with things to sell: clothes, food, shoes,
jewelry, many things strange to Blue. The streets,
squares, alleys were full of people, vehicles, beasts.
The day was circus day besides Saturday and prod-
uce from the country was brought in to be sold.
The sidewalks were crowded. Blue elbowed his
way through groups of black men and women,
stepped aside for white ones to pass him. On he
walked until the whole length of street was behind
him. Ahead stood the depot, railroad tracks,
people waiting for an incoming train. The great
iron engine halted, hissed steam. Car doors
opened to let passengers out, and in. A bell rang,
the big engine wheels turned and the train rolled
away. A child's scream came from the depot and
a policeman walked out dragging a little black
boy by the arm.

"Shut you mouth." The policeman shook him
and the boy shrieked louder than ever. Poor little
wretch, dressed in his Sunday clothes too. Who
should come hurrying up but Uncle Ben, and Blue
saw at once that the boy was little David.

"What David done, suh? Please for God sake
don' jail em." Uncle Ben was frantic.

"Oh, Pa!" David gave a great despairing sob.

"What you left dis boy here for?"

Uncle Ben met the policeman's question with pitiful heart-wringing, broken words: "I had just went across de street to buy a seegar. David never seen town neither a train befo, suh. I just fetched em on de boat excursion to de circus. We had aim to go home dis evenin. I can' go home widout David."

The policeman grunted. "He ain' quite big enough for the chain gang yet. I reckon I'll wait until he grows."

"What David done, suh?" Uncle Ben asked instead of fleeing.

"He went in the white people's toilet, Uncle. I ought to jail him, but I'll let him off this time. It's his first offense, I reckon. Better let it be the last."

"David wouldn' harm nothin on a purpose, suh."

"He would 'a' if I hadn' seen him."

"Whe' de white people had dey toys, suh?"

The policeman laughed, slung his club round and round by the leather strap and walked away. Blue and Uncle Ben hurried with David between them to the opposite sidewalk. David could hardly talk for crying, but little by little he made it clear that seeing the train got him so eye-sighted, he needed to go to the bushes. There were no bushes. He didn't know what to do. A lady told him to run inside the depot and he would see the place. He ran in. He saw a door. He opened the door and the policeman came in.

"Don' cry no more, son. Nobody ain' gwine harm you, now." Uncle Ben consoled him. "We'll go to de circus after we eat de rations I brought from home."

"I want to go to de bushes," David sobbed.

Uncle Ben stopped short, looked around. "I don' see none, but yonder's a tree. Go git behind em. It can' be against de law to stand side a tree. Even a dog ought to could do dat widout gettin arrested."

Blue left them and went from store to store, not buying, but looking until his eyes ached. What must he take to Cricket? How could he choose from so many beautiful things? Shining cloth of every color was suspended on poles to tempt him. Show cases blazed with ribbon, flowers, feathers, glittering ornaments, ladies' shoes. He glimpsed David and Uncle Ben at a counter filled with marbles, mouth-organs, whistles, jackstones as he went to look at the ladies' shoes. Cricket had black shoes, but here were white, blue, red ones made of cloth that looked like silk. The heels were high, the toes narrow, but Cricket's little feet were slim.

He chose a blue pair as soft as gloves. The price seemed dear, but he had money in his pocket to pay it. He reached in, reached deep, felt around, searched among strings, nails. That paper money was paid him only this morning, now it was gone. He had not a cent left except a few small coins. Where could it be? His pocket was solid. Aun

Missie patched these overalls and her stitches were
strong. He staggered back to the schooner, and
told one of the men who explained that town people
picked money out of pockets same like country
niggers picked cotton out of bolls. Policemen
don't care. No use for Blue to rave and rant. If
he made a racket he would go to jail like as not.
He'd better come go to the circus. Blue shivered
with a chill although the day was close and hot.
He borrowed some money and bought liquor from
a woman who had a shack in an alley. He got
drunk enough to sing as he stumbled away:

> "My gal is a high born lady.
> Not black but a lil bit shady——"

Two women were fighting not far off. Blue
laughed and watched their bodies reel, as they
clenched, bit, scratched, tore clothes to rags. One
was bigger than the other. It was not fair. Blue
slapped a cheek, cut a lip with his knuckles, walked
off arm in arm with the smaller woman, leaving
the other one prone. His friends found him with
her, took him away and got him into one of the
rowboats. They abused him roundly for being
too drunk to help them row home, told him he
had better keep away from yellow town women.
They were worse than black cats for bad luck.

"Don' tell Cricket on me," he said with a thick
drunken tongue.

They understood and promised.

A cold rain on the river sobered him, but his head ached. His heart ached too. He lay still and pretended to sleep. The oars, lifted, fell, with long steady pulls, the oarsmen laughed, sang, talked of adventures in town. Some of them had been to the circus, others to dance-halls, or games. Some won money, others lost, but packages wrapped in paper filled the bow. Every man had some present to take home. Blue felt ashamed to go with empty hands back to Cricket. Water splashed mournfully as the boat moved slowly up the river past willows sleeping on the bank in the drizzle of rain. Misery gnawed at Blue's insides, hate for town people gnawed at his heart. May Satan get them all and burn them for ever, with their jails and stores, policemens and thieves.

When he got home Aun Missie met him at the door. In a few cold words she said Cricket had gone off.

Gone off? That was good. Before she came back, he would get himself clean, fed, able to tell what happened. He was too weary now to talk.

"Is you hear me say Cricket's gone off?" Aun Missie repeated presently.

"Whe's e gone?"

"E went to town on de excursion wid Bina. E said e would see you at de circus."

"When's e comin back? How-come Uncle Ben ain' told me Cricket was in town?"

"God knows. Cricket just said e was gwine an' e went. I couldn' stop em. Cooch lent em de

loan of a valise to pack up his things. Uncle Ben
must 'a' thought you knew e was in town.''

"I wonder why e didn' come home wid Uncle
Ben an' David?''

"Nobody can tell what Cricket'll do dese days.
I never seen nobody changed like Cricket since e
married. Instead o' settlin down e has pure gone
wild. I can' tell what to make of em.''

"A lil trip will do em good, Aun Missie. People
get pen-sick if dey stay home too long, same like
pigs shut up in a pen.''

Blue sat down to rest after he had dressed and
eaten.

"Better go cut some wood, Blue. Night's comin
an' I got to feed up an' milk.''

As he cut, the sun sank behind bloody clouds.
The afterglow reddened the sky and faded. First
dark filled the world with shadows. The Quarters houses melted behind the dark trees, open
doors and windows made big bright stars. Only
Aun Missie's house looked gloomy, empty. She
had supper on the table, but he had lately eaten
dinner and was not hungry.

"How is town?'' she asked with her mouth full.
He would have told her about his misfortune but
her face was already dark. She would call him
a fool to lose all his money.

"Town is same as ever, full o' people. If you
crack you teeth policemen put you in jail.''

"I told Cricket so, but he wouldn' listen to me.
Cricket thinks Bina could fight off Satan his-self.''

"Cricket won' stay in town long. E don' like drinkin, an' dat's all town people do exceptin steal an' fight——"

"Why you didn' go to de circus, Blue? Ben said de circus had lions an' tigers an' all kind o' wild things. It's got a snake can swallow a man."

"Not me. I wouldn' spend my money to see no snake ever was. Plenty o' dangerous things is here home. One of us alligators could swallow a lion. Us snakes is pizen as anybody's."

"I told Cricket to stay home. I'm scared to death o' snakes, but e took every last cent e had, an' all his best clothes. I been most dead wid worryation ever since de *Comanche* turned de bend in de river."

"No use to fret. Aun Bina knows town like I know de swamp. E will take care o' Cricket an' fetch em home soon as de money gives out."

Blue sat wondering where Cricket was while Aun Missie sewed quilt squares and talked of trials she had come through: Uncle Wes's faithlessness, his gambling and wastefulness; her struggles to provide for Cricket since his death. Cricket was born for luck, but she ever tramped it down in the ground. Sometimes she did well enough, but lately she moped around and hardly spoke a friendly word. It was high time for Cricket to come to her senses. She was sixteen years old, not a child any more. True enough, Cricket had wild blood in her, from both sides, but she had been raised better than any girl in the

country. Man Jay ought to quit writing letters to
upset her. Wes ought to quit talking to her in her
sleep.

"Is Man Jay wrote Cricket another letter?"

"E's wrote em two. God only knows what e
said. Cricket didn' tell me an' I wouldn' press
em."

"How come you didn' told me before now?"

"I'd be de last one to make trouble between
you an' Cricket, Blue. You is de one to rule
Cricket, not me."

She would have talked on and on, but Blue got
up and went outside. As he walked up the road
toward the Quarters a dog bayed in the distance,
a man's lonely song sounded far off in the
night.

Where was Cricket now? What was she doing?
Like as not all dressed up and dancing, her eyes
shining like stars on some stranger-man while
her mouth laughed that pretty childish bubbling
laugh.

He meant to sit only a little while at Cun Jule's
house, hear a little cheerful talk and come home.
Cooch was not cheerful. Her baby had been sick
and cried all day. She had just got him off to
sleep.

"Talkin might wake em. We better go sit on de
steps," she said.

Blue said he better go home, but Cooch held to
his hand.

"It ain' no use to go home. Cricket's gone off.

Let's me an' you walk outside. I been in dis house till I'm weary."

Fowls roosting on the fig-tree limbs moved uneasily when Cooch stumbled over a broken wagon wheel in the path, almost fell.

"I'm gwine kill David," she ranted. "E ever leaves something in my way. Now I done scratch up my good shoes."

"You mouth is too sweet to talk such a talk, gal."

Cooch nestled against him. "How does you know if it's sweet or not? It's been a long time since you tried em."

"My God, Cooch, hush you crazy talk," Blue gasped, but Cooch laughed and pulled his head down, put her mouth up and clung to him. Blue sat down with her on the damp grass behind the castor-bean bushes and told her what happened to him in town. She was full of sympathy, told him not to fret, she knew how those town people acted.

A bruised gourd vine under Blue's feet gave out an evil smell, the pig-pen near by was no better. They went to sit in the barn door. The shucks inside were sweet, clean. When Blue left her, cocks were crowing for dawn.

CHAPTER XXXIX

CRICKET did not come on the next boat, but sent a letter saying she was out of money. Blue got Cooch to answer it for him. He gave her a five-dollar bill to put in the letter and two cents for a stamp. He met the next boat, but Cricket did not come. Weeks went by, day was added to day. Life went on with its work, sleeping, waking, three meals a day. Blue listened coldly to Aun Missie's bitter complaints of Cricket. He had heard them too many times to be stirred. Cricket had gone, left him behind. She did not answer Cooch's letter or thank him for the money. Cooch said he was a fool to give Cricket another thought.

Aun Missie said he should go find her. How could he find her in town with those miles of streets and houses? No, he would stay here home. When she came back—the thought turned him hot and cold—he would be here waiting for her. If she stayed away he would have to make out without her. He had sent her money to come home. That was all he could do.

A letter came at last and he tore it open with a feeling of dread. If Cricket came home now she would surely hear about Cooch and himself. He would tell her it was her fault. A man can not live satisfied alone after he has had a wife. Even Uncle Ben, the best man on the place, married Cun Jule to escape loneliness before his wife got cold

in her grave. Cricket could not blame him for anything.

Her letter was long and hard to read. Blue took
it to Cooch who could read writing as fast as
printed words. The letter said Cricket was in
Harlem with Aun Bina and Man Jay. Reverend
Africa was there, too. Blue should come to New
York. It was like Heaven. Man Jay could get him
a job.

Cooch said Cricket was crazy, plain crazy, to
think he would follow her now. Maybe Cooch was
right.

The next boat brought a package. Cricket sent
him six shirts, and Aun Missie a dress ready made.
He did not write to thank her. Once he started
a letter, but the pencil was awkward in his work-
hardened hands. He wrote, "Dere Cricket, I re-
ceive you letter and the shurts." He got no
further. What was the use to write when she
thought nothing of his feelings? She left him
without cause. She forgot he married her to save
disgracement. He was a fool. Cricket had used
him to shield herself. Yes, he was a fool. But
it was no use to tell on her now. Nobody would
believe him. People would think he was sore.
The only thing to do now was forget her, as Cooch
said. He gave part of his wages to Aun Missie
who still cooked his victuals, washed and mended
his clothes; the rest he gave to Cooch. Let people
say what they liked, it made no difference to him.
Cooch liked him. Cricket was gone to stay.

Another letter came and Cooch read it for him. Cricket said New York was Heaven and Reverend Africa was the finest preacher in Harlem. He had a tabernacle where people got sanctified. Blue must come to New York. Man Jay would get him a job. If he would come, she would send him a ticket.

"Let's me an' you all-two go," Cooch said.

"You ain' in no shape to go now, if what you say is de truth."

"Sho it's de truth, but I could drink some strong cotton-root tea. Dat would make me throw em away."

"I'll quit you if you do," Blue threatened. "I ain' got a use for no woman what throws my chillen way."

That ended Cooch's talk of their going, and Cricket's letter was never answered.

When Cooch was about to have the child, she insisted that Blue must marry to her. Blue argued that he had a wife already. Cooch declared that a woman who left her husband without cause was no lawful wife.

Blue was torn between hope that Cricket would come back and interest in the child Cooch would bear him. Early one Sunday morning, he went to talk it over with Cun Fred. Cun Fred said Cooch was Jule's gal and a chip off the old block. If Blue did not watch out he would be in Uncle Ben's shoes. The only reason for marrying Cooch or any other woman would be to get her. If he could have Cooch without marrying, Blue would be a fool to tie himself up. Times had changed. Blue was too easy-going. If he took up with Cooch he better slap her teeth out if she crooked. Cooch learned town women's ways when she went off to school. She would need a lot of knocking, a lot of rough talk.

Blue said he was willing to knock Cooch and talk rough too, but he had ever heard how the law said a man had no right to knock any woman unless she was his lawful lady.

"Do like you please, Blue. It's you business, not my own." Cun Fred spat, and Blue resolved not to marry to Cooch for the present.

As he walked away, he passed Uncle Ben at the pasture gate talking to the sheep as he let them through one at a time. He patted one ewe's broad woolly back. "Go ahead, gal. You can eat grass wid you sisters to-day. Maybe to-morrow too." To another he said, "No, gal, you better stay home to-day. De orchard is de best place for you now." The ewe bleated and tried to go on, but he held her back with gentle words. "De clover is green in de orchard, gal. I'll put you in some corn an' water. You must try to take it easy now. De milk is sprung in you breast. You lamb'll be here befo mornin."

Blue walked on with a softened heart. Cooch needed gentleness too, now that her time was near. He went straight to her and told her he would stand by her long as she stood by him. Cooch

swore she loved him worser than she had ever
loved any man in her life.

"If you two-time me, gal, I'll give you de worse
knockin ever was."

Cooch laughed. "Dat's all right, Blue. It ain'
no man livin I ruther have to knock me."

"You think by I'm small I can' knock hard."

"No, Blue. I don' think dat. I just mean I
ruther you to knock me dan for most to love me.
But, for God's sake, don' look at me vexed. I
never seen a man could look pizen as you can."

The next day Blue left Aun Missie's and moved
with Cooch into Big Pa's house.

He daubed up holes in the chimney with mud
and got fire from Cun Hester to start the blaze
that would make light and cook food for them in
the days ahead. He built a little fowl house,
patched up the old barn, fixed a stable, a cow pen,
a pig pen to fatten the shoat Cun Fred gave them.
Cooch dressed the house with newspapers, strung
eggshells together and hung them by the fireplace
to make the hens lay fast. She was heavy on her
feet, but she planted every seed in the vegetable
garden herself for seed dropped by a woman with
child bear fourfold. Cooch wanted to fetch her
other child to live with them, but Blue persuaded
her to leave him with Cun Jule. He was a tall
skinny child with a head too big for his neck.
His hair was thin, dry, and lay in nappy tufts on
his skull. His eyes were big and soft like Man
Jay's and he fretted unless his fingers were busy

putting bread in his mouth. But no matter how much he ate, his belly looked hollow and his spirit seemed heavy. Cooch had named him Kazoola and called him Jay-bird for short. Blue did not want Jay-bird in his house lest Cooch mark his own child by hearing him whine for food.

Blue asked Cooch to write to Cricket and tell her she need not bother about coming home now. Cooch said she was too nervish to hold a pencil. After her baby was born she would write Cricket the news.

Cun Jule thought several signs foretold that Cooch would have twins. One of her hens had laid an egg with twin yolks. The same day Cooch dropped her scissors so both points stuck straight in the floor. Those two things had happened before Cun Jule's twins were born.

Blue was sorry. Two babies would be hard to manage. A man needs children to help work his crops, to keep his name alive, to care for him when he is old, but having them by twos sounded rash somehow.

Cooch laughed and said Blue was jealous; Blue thought she would have less time to do things for him with two twins in the house; Blue always wanted clean clothes to put on, good victuals to eat; Blue was pure rotten spoiled. But the truth was Cooch had got lazy. She thought only of eating and sleeping, and cared nothing for how she looked. Nobody expected her to dress up, but she could wash her face and fix her hair and put

on a clean apron sometimes. Blue told her so and
shamed her for not scouring the dirty floor. It
hurt Cooch's feelings and made her cry. Blue
quickly took it all back, begged her pardon and
declared she looked like a flowers garden no matter
what she had on.

The winter had been cold and the little wild
beasts in the woods put on extra thick coats of fur.
White people made a law against trapping them
and the store man offered steel traps for sale at
half-price. Blue bought several and set them.
They caught coons and minks, now and then an
otter. Every hide was worth money, especially
the otter's.

Before long the sunny side of the house was
spotted with salted skins, stretched and tacked up
to dry. Cooch's pots on the hearth stayed full
of wild meats and she ate so much her face got
broad as Cun Jule's. Cun Jule had to make her
the loan of clothes to wear because none of her
own would meet on her body. Cooch looked a
sight, poor thing. Blue made up his mind that
soon as the birthing was over he would take her to
town and dress her up nice. He needed clothes
himself. All his breeches had holes in the seats.
He begged Cooch to patch him one pair so he could
go decent on Sundays, but she ever made some excuse: she had no black thread, or her needle was
blunt, or sewing dark cloth hurt her eyes. Cooch
was a schemy girl. She was afraid he would dress
up and go pleasuring without her. A few weeks

more and things would be different. The hides
would buy Cooch's dress and a new suit for himself. He would get a pinch-back coat, or a double-
breasted box coat, with peg-top breeches like the
town sports wear. He still had the fine shirts
Cricket sent him. Things were going well enough,
when a letter came. Cooch tore open the envelope
and read:

"Dear Blue: I take my seat and take my pen
in hand to say that I am well and hope you are the
same. Me and Reverend Africa all both wants
Cricket to get a divorce. It will be better for her
and you too to have respect for the law. If you
will come here she can get it easy by your help.
I will send you ticket when I hear from you that
you will come.
                               "Yours truly,
                                 "MAN JAY."

Cooch read the letter easily, all but one word.
She spelled it over and over. D-i-v-o-r-c-e.
Neither she nor Blue knew what it meant.

Blue took the letter to the Quarters and got
Brer Dee and Cun Andrew to read it, but the
same word stalled them.

In the back of Cun Andrew's new Bible was a
list of every word in the world. He found *divers*
and *diverse* but not *divorce*. He found a chapter
about a girl named Vashti whose people drank
wine according to the law in vessels of gold, and
those vessels were diverse. That settled it. Man
Jay had spelled the word wrong. But if Reverend

Africa wanted Cricket to drink wine out of a gold
cup, why didn't he buy her one? He had more
money than Blue. Blue said Cun Andrew was
wrong. Cricket never used to drink wine. Divorce
must mean something else.

Cun Andrew searched again and found a verse
about divers, but that meant a wool and linen garment. Cun Fred thought Blue ought to go and find
out the truth. It would be a fine trip on a free
ticket. And after all Cricket was Blue's lawful
lady. If she asked a favor of him even now Blue
was due to grant it.

Blue was all for going. He craved to see how
up-North looked and besides that he wanted to
shun Cooch's birthing. He had never forgotten
Cricket's groans, her drinking that warm soapsuds, her giving thanks for life.

Aun Fan joined Cun Fred in urging him to go.
She promised to see Cooch safely through her
trial, and said Cooch was a strong black girl, not
a weakly bright skin. Cooch would birth that
child easy as pop her finger.

Blue hurried home and told Cooch all that was
said. Big tears began rolling down her cheeks.
She said Man Jay's letter was nothing but a trick.
Like as not Cricket wrote it herself, to toll Blue
up-North so she could make him take her back. If
Blue went away now and left her she would die of
worryation. He would never see her alive any
more.

Cooch talked so pitiful Blue had not the heart

to cross her. He spoke right up and said he would
not think of going. He had no clothes to wear anyhow.

That night as he slept beside Cooch a foolish
dream brought Cricket back plain as life. She
stood at the door in her wedding-dress, squeezing
the old accordion and singing softly "De hog-eye
gal am de hell of a gal——" He was so horrified
to hear those wicked words on her lips he yelled
out and tried to grab her.

"What de matter ail you, Blue?" Cooch shook
him awake. "You sound like Satan's after you."

The room was pitch dark, the door was shut
tight, Cricket was not here at all.

Blue sat up. "God knows what ails me. I'm
pure dry for water. It must be all dat rich possum
meat I had for supper."

He got up and drank, then stood in the open
door for a breath of fresh cool air. Cocks flapped
their wings and crowed for middle night. His
coon dog barked answers to a lone hound baying in
the distance.

"You'll catch cold, Blue. Better get back in de
bed," Cooch said gently.

He did and she came close to him, sought his
mouth with her hot lips. He told her he was weary,
and she turned away. Her breathing soon showed
she was sound asleep, but his dream kept him
awake and worried his mind so he could not sleep.
Maybe Cricket was in trouble again. Maybe——
Maybe she wanted him to come and fetch her

home. Maybe since she had been away and had
time to think things out, maybe she loved him. If
that was so—Cooch would have to face it. Cricket
was his lawful lady. Nobody could change that.
Cooch had a child for Man Jay. Nobody could
change that either. The more Blue thought, the
more his heart stung. What would he do with
Cooch's twins? How would Cricket feel about
them? Why had he let Cooch snare him like this?

Why had he left Aun Missie's? He had been a
fool not to see Cooch had cunjured him. She was
to blame for the whole mess. When her twins were
born he would get some new clothes and go up-
North. He would have a straight talk with Cricket,
make a clean breast of everything.

Since the first day he saw her picking violets by
the branch, Cricket had been his heart-string. She
knew she could twist him around her little finger,
and when she got in trouble she used him to shield
herself. She knew he would never crack his teeth
about any wrong thing she had done. But after
he slaved for her until she was well and gave her
every cent he made, she threw him down. He had
done ten times more for her than Man Jay ever
had. All he asked in return was a little kind treatment. Any man has a right to ask that much.

Morning came at last with a full day's work
ahead. Other days came, slipped past. Little by
little Blue's heart grew calmer, for Man Jay wrote
no more.

Sometimes after supper people came to the

house, and Blue did his best to join in their chatter and laughter, to make merry answers when they asked if he had heard any more about that curious thing Cricket wanted.

One night Cun Jule spoke up and said whatever it was Blue could be sure it was nothing for his good. Cricket was ever quick to take without giving a thing in return. More than likely Cricket had heard how Blue made money selling hides and wanted to get her hands on it.

"You needn' judge Cricket by your own self, Cun Jule," Blue blurted out angrily. "Cricket ain' no greedy common somebody."

Cun Jule darted him a bitter look and whispered behind her hand to Cooch, but she dared not answer a word out loud.

"You is too quick to vex, Blue," Aun Fan chided. "Jule ain' meant no harm. Everybody knows Cricket done you wrong."

Blue tingled with anger from head to heels, his fists clenched into knots, but he held his tongue and left the room. He knew he would be no match for all these people in a quarrel about Cricket. Outside in the yard he could hear the buzz of their voices. He knew they were laughing at him. He felt cut off, helpless, devoured with anger against them. They were his own people. He was bound to some of them by ties of blood, and Cooch now had him tethered so he could not break loose. Nobody thought of his feelings, cared if he was worried. If Cricket was here, she would understand. Whether she loved him or not she ever took his part and sided with him right or wrong. Cooch was no more like Cricket than night was like day. Cooch thought Cun Jule was Jesus. She thought every word Cun Jule spoke was Bible truth. If he only had a bold spirit like Cun Fred he would tell Cun Jule to keep her mouth off Cricket or he would cut her tongue out by the roots. But his spirit was not bold. And his heart was pure weighted down with misery.

Blue was in the swamp robbing his traps the next afternoon when he heard David calling him. He hurried away thinking maybe Cooch was down. Aun Fan said her time would come before this growing moon waned.

David had run so fast his breath was gone, but his face showed that something exciting had happened.

"Is Cooch down?" Blue shouted. "What de matter ail you, boy? Whyn' you talk?"

"Dey is come, suh. Dey come on de boat dis evenin," David sputtered.

"Who is come?"

"It's Cricket an' Man Jay an' a stranger gentleman."

The sky was clear but sharp lightnings flashed before Blue's eyes. The world was so dim he could hardly see to walk. He stumbled into a briar patch that scratched his face and hands. His blood ran cold and hot like a fever, his legs tottered so he had to halt for breath. He could see Aun

Missie's house far across the field and the whole
yard was full of people. He could hear their loud
talk and laughter.

His heart gave a sudden leap for somebody in a
red dress was coming across the field. It was
Cricket sure as the world. Nobody else in this
world walked like that. Joy lifted him up and
carried him along swiftly to meet her. Dead cotton stalks tried to trip him. His legs almost gave
way, his breath cut off when she waved her hand
and called:

"Hey, Blue, how you do?"

"Hey, star-lily," he called back and tears
blurred his sight. He was too weak to stand
up when she reached him. He just dropped on his
knees and put both arms tight around her. He
could feel her little hands on his head, but his brain
whirled around in his skull and he could not speak
a word.

She bent over and asked gently:

"Blue, is you sick?"

He tried to answer, tried to tell her he was
dumbstruck with joy, but his tongue would not
move.

"Get up, honey. Let's go to de house so you can
lay down." She helped him to his feet, and stood
looking up into his eyes with a smile so tender
his soul all but melted away.

"I hope you ain' sorry I come?" she whispered.

He tried to pull himself together for he saw she
was troubled.

"Cricket, honey, seein you so onexpected is got me pure addled. But I'm dat glad you come I could pure kiss de dirt under you feets."

When he took both her hands and held them her eyes smiled as though nothing had ever come between them.

The sweet scent that rose from her made blood rush to his head. He would have gathered her into his arms but she held back and said slowly:

"Wait, Blue, I got to talk some close talk wid you. Maybe I ought not to come, but I couldn' stand to be away off so far, when Man Jay was here wid you all."

Man Jay's name made a sharp pain gnaw at his heart.

"Don' say dat, Cricket. You ought to had come home when I sent you de money."

"Money? You never sent me no money, Blue."

"You forgot, honey. When Cooch wrote de letter tellin you to come on home, I give em a five-dollar bill to put inside em besides two cents more to buy de stamp."

"Dat letter told me to stay where I was by you loved Cooch better'n me. Not a cent was inside em."

Blue could not believe his ears. Had Cooch dared to write that lie and keep his money too?

"You ain' tryin to fool me, is you, Cricket?"

Cricket shook her head. She was talking straight talk. Cooch had written those very words. Blue broke out in cold sweat as the truth dawned

on him. Cooch had tricked him. She had tricked
Cricket too.

"I'll cut Cooch's heart out for dis what e done!"
Blue bellowed loud enough to rouse the dead.

Cricket shook his arm.

"Hush, Blue. De people'll hear you. Dey will
think you is quarrelin wid me."

"Let em hear. I mean all what I'm sayin. I'll
stomp em long as I can see a piece of his dress."

Cricket caught his clenched fist, held it tight.

"No, you won't. You wouldn' have de heart to
mistreat Cooch now, when e's lookin to birth you
baby any day."

"Who told you dat?"

"Aun Missie told me soon as I come."

Shame stabbed his heart like a knife, but it
spurred him to defend himself.

"I ain' de first man Cooch had a child for.
Cooch had his first child for Man Jay."

Cricket made no answer.

"Cooch knows me an' you is married together.
Cooch knows I ever loved you better'n life. Thank
God, you come home at last."

"Did you got Man Jay's letter, Blue?"
Cricket's words sounded cold.

"Sho I got it, but I just couldn' get to New York
right den. I ain' had decent clothes an' things
here home was all tangled up——" He felt so
guilty he turned his head to shun Cricket's steady
gaze.

"You needn' feel bad, Blue. I don' see de use

of bothern bout no deevoce, but Man Jay's raven
bout bein lawful.''

"What's a deevoce, Cricket?"

Her eyes widened with surprise.

"You don' know what a deevoce is?"

"Not ezactly. Cun Andrew thought it might
be a gold cup or either silk cloth for a dress.''

Cricket burst out laughing, then her face got
solemn all of a sudden.

"You didn' know a deevoce is a paper what
unmarries people?''

"Why, Cricket, nothin could unmarry people
after a preacher reads over em out of de Book.''

"In New York people unmarries every day by
a deevoce.''

"Dat is pure heathenish doins. Decent people
don' act so.''

"No, Blue. You is wrong. De lawyer Man Jay
fetched here is fixin a paper now to unmarry me
an' you.''

"Fixin what? Is you lost you mind?"

Her eyes met his without a flicker.

"I may as well tell you de truth.'' She caught
her breath, then added, ''Soon as I get my deevoce,
I'm gwine to marry to Man Jay.''

Her words were a thunderbolt. His hair stood
on end as anger beyond endurance seized him. A
scream of rage tore through his throat, ''You can'
marry to nobody long as I'm livin. Man Jay is
a Judas. E's a lyin scoundrel. E thinks I'm a
fool but e's barkin up de wrong tree.'' Blue called

Man Jay foul names until his tongue got dry. He swore God would send some awful curse on Cricket if she did such a wicked thing.

At first she stood as if she did not hear a word, then big tears started rolling out of her eyes.

"I didn' thought you would act dis way," she sobbed brokenly.

Blue never could bear to see her cry, and now her pitiful, quick-drawn breaths of grief brought him back to his senses. For a few heart-beats the silence was broken only by her bitter weeping.

"Cricket—lil Cricket—honey." His teeth chattered as he drew her to him. He put his arms around her and held her close. His own tears fell on her head.

"Cun Jule says come home quick as you can, Blue. Cooch is gone down." David's voice broke the spell that had fallen upon Blue and called him back to what was.

"I got to go, Cricket." His whisper was husky and strangled.

"It hurts me to my heart for you to hold hard feelins against me, Blue."

He laid his lips gently on her hair, then took her little lace pocket handkerchief and wiped her wet cheeks. "I got to leave you now, honey, but I'll see you before I sleep."

CHAPTER XL

Aun Fan was with Cooch when he got home and she was all upset.

"It's just like Cooch to go down when I had fixed a fine supper yonder home for Cricket an' Man Jay to-night. I got a good mind to let Cooch birth dis child by his-self. I never was so disappint in my life."

Cun Jule was cross as two sticks. "You better say it's just like Cricket to come home when nobody wants to see em."

"Al-fred made me kill de best pullet chickens I had on de yard. Missie won' cook em fit to eat," Aun Fan flung back.

The two women grumbled on and on as they made things ready. Blue built up the fire, filled all the buckets with water, but he hardly heard what they said. Even Cooch's moans seemed far away.

"You look like you gone in a trance, Blue." Cun Jule's eyes held a mean sparkle.

"Blue's got enough to fret him to-day wid Cooch birthin an' Cricket here too. But I want em to go help Missie fix supper. E will be in de way here now."

"Is you seen Cricket yet?" Cooch asked from the bed, and Aun Fan answered quickly:

"Yes, lord, an' I hardly knew em e was dressed so fine. You better fix yourself up, Blue. Man

Jay looks fine as any preacher. You'll feel shame
if you don' look nice.''

"I ain' got a decent pair o' breeches to put on.''

"If you keep your back turned nobody can' see
dem holes in you seat,'' Aun Fan consoled him
when he got his old wedding pants out of the trunk
and held them up to show her.

Blue made haste to dress, but she urged him
to hurry faster and go see that Missie got the
chickens done and did not let the bread burn.

When he walked in the house his heart throbbed
fit to break loose for Cricket was already there
helping Aun Missie fix the supper. One of Aun
Fan's big aprons covered most of her dress, a
white one with shiny beads on the sleeves, but,
lord, how sweet she looked.

"You is just in time to help me set de table,
Blue.''

The way she smiled sent a thrill down his spine,
as he went to get the tablecloth Aun Fan kept for
company.

"How's Cooch feelin?'' Aun Missie asked
coolly.

"E was feelin better when I left em,'' Blue
mumbled as he pulled the table out into the middle
of the room and spread the red and white cloth
over it. Aun Missie was a mean old jade. She
thought to shame him before Cricket, but he would
show her different. Little was said until they
heard Cun Fred coming with Man Jay, then supper
was quickly taken up and put on the table.

Blue could hardly bear to face Man Jay, but he made up his mind to be mannersable no matter how Man Jay acted.

In they came, Cun Fred, Man Jay and a stranger-man.

Jesus himself could not have dressed finer than Man Jay with a round black hat, a salt and pepper suit, shiny black shoes. He had changed his way of talking. Blue could hardly make out what he said until he turned to the stranger. "Meet lawyer Brown, Blue."

Lawyer Brown bowed nice as could be and said something Blue could not understand.

Brown was the right name for him. It was the color of his skin, clothes, cravat, shoes. Even the handkerchief in his breast pocket showed a brown border.

"Well, Blue, how's everything with you?" Man Jay took the blue scarf off his neck and laid it with his hat on the shelf.

"Fine as silk. How you gettin on dese days?" Blue answered cockily.

"I have no cause to complain. Business is good. Things are coming my way." Man Jay rubbed his long hands together and held them out to the fire. "A open fire sho is a pretty thing. We don't have em up-North."

"How you keep warm? Didn' you say de ground is covered wid snow?" Cun Fred asked.

"We have steam heat wid a boiler in the cellar, underneath de house."

"Dat sounds mighty dangerous to me."

"Better come eat befo de supper gets cold."
Aun Missie sounded sweet as pie, and Cun Fred
sat down at the end of the table with Cricket on
one side and Lawyer Brown on the other.

"Where will you sit, Aun Missie?" Man Jay
asked.

"I don' like to eat right after I finish cookin a
meal o' victuals. I ruther pass things round an'
take time to cool out."

Man Jay sat next Cricket and Blue took the
place next Lawyer Brown. Aun Missie passed one
full dish after another. Plates were piled and
everybody ate in silence.

When Cun Fred's appetite was satisfied he
pushed his chair back. "Now tell me some more
bout New York, Man Jay."

Man Jay's mouth was full but he swallowed
quickly. "You ought to come see it. You can
make de trip in two days. Heaven ain' got a
thing on New York."

"You say de buildins is piled high as de sky?"

"Lord, yes, an' de streets pure jammed wid
automobiles an' people."

"But it ain' got no trees, Cun Fred," Cricket
spoke up. "You can go all day an' not see a blade
o' grass or a leaf. But de worse things is subways,
dem trains what run under de ground." She had
hardly touched the things on her plate, but she
pushed it away with a laugh and told how scared
Aun Bina got the first time Man Jay took her

down under the street to get on a subway. Aun
Bina stood up and hollered so loud Man Jay
threatened to call a policeman if she didn't hush.

"We hardly ever ride de subway now," Man
Jay broke in. "Reverend Africa has two fine
cars we can use." Man Jay told a lot about
Reverend Africa, how rich he was and how holy;
how kind he had been to Aun Bina and Cricket;
how he owned a tabernacle where people got religion, and a place called Night Club where sinners
pleasure themselves.

"You'd be crazy about Reverend Africa, Blue.
E pure treats us grand," Cricket said. "E looks
like Big Pa and Uncle Wes, all two."

Man Jay said Reverend Africa had changed a
lot since that time Aun Bina bought his picture
to cure her cough, but he still made money by the
barrelful. Tin basins took up the collection at his
tabernacle and were filled with money every night.

Man Jay helped Reverend Africa with his
money business. Reverend Africa owned a whole
building. The bottom floor was a dance-hall, and
every night it was crowded with people who paid
to dance and eat and drink.

The next floor had medicine doctors' offices,
tooth dentist rooms, but the top floor was a big
hall full of seats where black Jew people had
church.

"Black Jews? Whoever heard of such a thing?
Everybody knows Jews are white." Cun Fred
sucked his teeth but Man Jay laughed.

"You is wrong, Cun Fred. Reverend Africa says Jesus was a Jew and he was black same like we. All them white people what calls theyself Jews is just puttin on airs, tryin to be stylish."

Man Jay sounded as if he knew and Cun Fred said no more. Aun Missie sat down to listen better.

Man Jay said he had to keep a big double-jointed man with him all the time so people would not rob him. Plenty of them would kill a man for a dollar, and his pockets were ever stuffed with money, for he collected rents, and took charge of the dance-hall money too.

Cun Fred asked where the policemen were but Man Jay said up-North policemen cared nothing about well people. All they did was to take those who got cut or shot to the hospital. You could run to the corner and ask a policeman to send for the ambulance and he would do it, but if you asked him to come stop a fight he would laugh and walk off.

Man Jay said the dance-hall never got rough. It was different from Reverend Cato's altogether. Cun Fred would think he struck Heaven if he could hear that music and see all those white ladies dressed up like angels sitting mongst the colored people.

"Dey must be white trash," Cun Fred told him just so, but Man Jay laughed and said up-North white people were rich and grand. They had so much money he charged them a dollar and a half for a ten-cent bottle of ginger ale to mix with their

liquor. They didn't care. They liked black
people. They liked to dance with them too. They
were not scornful like the white people down-
South.

"Tell about de Princess Kazoola." Lawyer
Brown looked at Cricket and smiled.

"You tell em, Cricket," Man Jay urged.

"Let's don' talk bout dat." Cricket looked
quickly at Aun Missie and asked:

"What's become of Reverend Singleton and
Miss Sallie?"

"Aw, now, don' be shamefaced, Cricket," Man
Jay laughed. "Not when you is de finest dancer in
Harlem."

"Cricket ever could dance nice, but I had hoped
e was a church-member by now," Aun Missie
sighed.

"Cricket has changed his name, Aun Missie,"
Man Jay said.

"Changed his name? How-come Cricket done
dat?"

"Reverend Africa says Pinesett ain' no fitten
name for high-bredded people like we is. He
named Cricket de Princess Kazoola."

Blue wanted to say Cricket's name was never
Pinesett after she married to him, but what was
the use? Man Jay was not listening, he was busy
explaining that Cricket had taken that for her
dancing name,—The Princess Kazoola. Kazoola
means you belong to the family of a king. Big
Pa's Daddy was a king. That made Cricket the

great granddaughter of a king. Reverend Africa said Big Pa's people were bredded fine as any white people in the world.

"Jesus, Master!" Cun Fred turned and spat in the fire.

"You needn' look so surprised," Man Jay laughed. "I learned a lot about white people since I left here. Now since I run de Night Club I dance wid white ladies every night God sends."

"Mind now, Man Jay, don' start tellin lies," Cun Fred warned him.

"If you don' believe me ask Cricket, ask Brown." Aun Missie's mouth flew open as Man Jay added: "I'd rather dance wid a colored lady any time. De white ones are stiff in de legs. Dey ain' limber enough in the hips to do all de latest steps right."

Cun Fred told Man Jay he knew better than to talk such talk. He would get himself lynched if he did not mind. But Man Jay declared the white ladies were heavy cases. They gave him more trouble than all the black ones put together. They thought because it was a colored Night Club they could come there and cut monkeyshines. The doorman would not let one come in unless she had a white man with her to take her home.

"Leave de white ladies alone and tell about the Princess Kazoola," Lawyer Brown broke in, for Cun Fred was plainly vexed by Man Jay's brazen talk.

Man Jay smiled and felt in his breast pocket,

took out a picture and handed it to Cun Fred.

"Dis is de Princess Kazoola in dancin clothes."

Cun Fred squinted so Man Jay struck a match and held it close to the picture.

"You don' mean a white lady would go befo people like dis?" Cun Fred's eyes blinked with amazement.

"Dat ain't no white lady. It's Cricket." Man Jay laughed.

"My God, you don' mean Cricket had his picture took buck naked?" Cun Fred bawled.

Aun Missie jumped up, snatched the picture from his hand and held it close to the lamp. The light shone bright on a slim-bodied girl stark naked except for small circles over her breasts and a narrow band around her thighs. Her arms were outspread and her lips were parted in a shameless smile. "You don' mean dis is Cricket!" Aun Missie screamed. "Not dis naked slut!"

"You don' understand, Aun Missie. Dat's de way all de best dancers dress, in New York," Man Jay tried to explain.

"Well, it ain' decent, I don' care who does it. What would Wes say? Lord, have mercy. Wes would pure rise up out his grave. Is you gone back to heathen, Cricket?"

"But, Aun Missie——"

"Shut you mouth, Man Jay. I know what I'm sayin, I have shame to look at dis picture befo mens."

Man Jay tried to hush her, but she threw back

her shoulders and shouted him down in a voice
that shook the cups in the saucers. If people here
knew what Cricket did, they wouldn't let her come
on the place much less go inside their houses. If
this was how she acted she better go to Africa and
live mongst Big Pa's heathen kinnery. They went
naked but they never even heard of God or Jesus.
Cricket knew better. She was raised to be decent.

Cricket uttered no word, made no defense, even
when Aun Missie seized her shoulders and bawled:

"I got a good mind to tear you frock off you
back an' lick you until de blood comes."

"Hush, Missie," Cun Fred ordered, "you forgot Cricket's grown."

Aun Missie screamed and ranted until her
breath failed and she tottered so she would have
fallen except that Cricket held her up.

"Come on, Aun Missie, let's go home. You got
you'self all eye-sighted," Cricket said gently.

"Go where?" Aun Missie hissed. "You can'
come in my house." She gave Cricket a push that
sent her reeling into Cun Fred's arms.

"I got plenty o' room for you, Cricket. You
stay right here. I'll take Missie home. E ain' been
so well lately. Man Jay ought not to plague em.
Missie can' take a joke, and e got upset over dat
picture by thinkin it was you for-true."

Aun Missie straightened up and reached for her
hat and shawl. Cricket got them and helped her
put them on.

"Good night, Aun Missie," she whispered.

Aun Missie's toothless jaws worked fast but not
a sound came from them.

Nobody spoke a word as she held to Cun Fred's
arm and went out into the night. Man Jay glanced
at Lawyer Brown and smiled, but Cricket stood at
the door looking at the night.

"Po' Aun Missie," she sighed. "E cooked all
dat good supper an' e ain' tasted a bite."

Blue longed to go stand beside her and try to
comfort her misery, but Man Jay's eyes were on
him, cold, sneering. What if she had gone wrong
again? Man Jay was to blame. He used her to
fill his pockets with money. Poor little Cricket.
A naked dancer.

"Long as Blue is here we better get dat paper
fixed up, Cricket. Den we can catch de boat back
to town in de mornin. It ain' no use for you to
stay longer, not after Aun Missie talked like dat."
Man Jay came toward her.

"I had aimed to go to de graveyard to-morrow
an' see Uncle Wes's grave—an' Big Pa's—one
more time," she said slowly.

"I know dat, Cricket, but if we miss dis boat
we'll have to wait three more days. It's no tellin
what'll happen by den."

She made no answer and Man Jay turned to
Blue.

"We just come to get de testimony for Cricket's
deevoce. When de papers is fixed you'll be free
to marry to Cooch same like any single man."

Blue's mouth got dry as a chip. "Keep your

mouth out my business, Man Jay. If you want
Cooch to have husband, marry to em you'self.
Everybody knows Cooch had his first child for
you."

"Dat ain' de pint, Blue. Cricket's de one I'm
thinkin on. It ain' you, neither Cooch."

A spasm of rage seized Blue but he strove to
hold himself in. "You aim to marry my Cricket,
Man Jay, but I'll see you in torment first."

"No use to start any argument, Blue," Lawyer
Brown interrupted. "You can't deny living with
this other woman. That is all we need to know."
His steady eyes caught Blue's and held them fast.

"I ain' de first married man ever done dat."
Blue felt confused and nervish before the man's
cool gaze but he was determined to stand up for
his rights. "I never took up wid Cooch until after
Cricket left me. Now since Cricket is come home,
I'm glad to take em back."

"Oh, you is, is you?" Man Jay gave a scornful
laugh.

"You keep out o' dis, Man Jay."

Man Jay walked toward him with both hands in
his breeches pockets.

"What you think I come all dis way for? What
you think I paid Lawyer Brown to do?"

Blue felt like he had indigestus. A hard lump
in his breast made him labor for breath.

"So you thought you could treat Cricket like
de dirt under you feet an' get by, did you? Well,
let me tell you dis, son, you ain' fitten to look at

Cricket much less have any talk wid em. It makes
me have shame to know I'm kin to you."

"Hush, Man Jay," Cricket broke in.

"I'll hush when I finish tellin Blue what e is.
When I left here, Blue promised to look after you,
to stand between you an' trouble."

"E did too, Blue done de best e could for me."

"Till e got tired of a decent gal. Oh, I know
all Blue done, Cricket, an' you certainly make me
have surprise, takin up for Blue after de way
de scoundrel done you. Of course if you want him,
just say de word, me an' lawyer Brown ain' pushin
nothin on you."

"Listen, Man Jay, nobody alivin can talk to me
like dat." Cricket's eyes blazed, but Man Jay
shrugged his shoulders.

"Blue saved me from disgracement an' I'll love
em for it long as I live."

"Disgracement?"

"If you knew de full truth——"

"Hush, Cricket," Blue said hoarsely. "Better
let all dat rest between you an' me."

"So you an' Cricket is got a secret between
you."

"Yes, we is. It ain' none o' you business
neither. You crack you teeth about it again an'
I'll mash you face in."

"Whose face?" Man Jay laughed.

Blue's clenched fist struck him full on the chin,
sent him reeling backward, but he quickly caught
his balance and leaped forward. Before Blue

could dodge, Man Jay seized his throat, with two powerful hands that squeezed tighter and tighter.

Cricket screamed and Lawyer Brown tried to break their hold, but they held on until the room began to darken before Blue's eyes.

Man Jay would have choked him to death if Cricket had not been there, but she grabbed the iron fire stick and laid such a stunning blow across his forehead, he went down flat on the floor.

Lawyer Brown got a pan of water and began washing blood out of his eyes.

"Oh, God, is e dead? Do you think I killed em?" She wept and prayed with her head on Man Jay's breast.

"You hit him a devil of a lick, Cricket, but I think you just cut de skin." Lawyer Brown felt Man Jay's wrist and said his pulse was good.

"I don' know what made me do it. If e dies it'll broke my heart."

"What's de matter, honey?" Man Jay asked.

"Oh, Man Jay, I'm so sorry ... so sorry ... I just couldn' stand for you to choke Blue to death."

"Choke Blue? What you talkin bout? My mouth is all full o' blood." He raised up and spat in the fire. "Looks like a front tooth is gone."

"Well, that ain' nothin so bad, you been sayin a good while you wanted to get you a gold one."

Lawyer Brown smiled behind his hand.

Cricket ran to Blue and whispered. "Please go, Blue. Don' tarry here or Man Jay'll kill you."

"I ain' scared of Man Jay if e'll fight me fair."

"Please, Blue, don' talk bout fightin no more.
I'm most crazy now."

"If you say I must go, den I'll go, Cricket."

"Yes, Blue, yes, an' don' come back until after
we go."

"So you's gwine too?"

"Yes, Blue, on de boat in de mornin."

"I won' see you, not no more?"

She shook her head no.

"Den, good-by, Cricket."

"Good-by, Blue."

He laid his lips on her hair and hurried out into
the night.

Cun Fred was coming, walking fast, too.

"Is dat you, Blue?" he called ahead of him.

"Yes-suh."

"I got some fine news for you, son. Cooch
birthed you a fine pair o' twins. David was comin
to tell you, but I sent em on back. All-two is boy-
chillen. You sho is blessed. I count on you namin
one o' em for me."

Cun Fred took his hand shook it warmly.

"You look troub-led, Blue. Is anything wrong?"

"No, suh, not wid me. I'm just sort o' took
back by de news." He started off toward the
Quarters but when he got to the fork in the road
he turned to look back. "Good-by, lil Cricket,"
he whispered softly. "Good-by, my lil star-lily."

THE END